The Sinful Suitors

Sabrina Jeffries's delightful Regency series featuring the St. George's Club, where watchful guardians conspire to keep their unattached sisters and wards out of the clutches of sinful suitors.

THE STUDY OF SEDUCTION

THE ART OF SINNING

Also from *New York Times*
and *USA Today* bestselling author

SABRINA JEFFRIES

The Duke's Men

*They are an investigative agency born out of
family pride and irresistible passion . . . and they
risk their lives and hearts to unravel any shocking
deception or scandalous transgression!*

IF THE VISCOUNT FALLS

"Jeffries's addictive series satisfies." —*Library Journal*

HOW THE SCOUNDREL SEDUCES

"Scorching. . . . From cover to cover, it sizzles."
—*Reader to Reader*

"Marvelous storytelling. . . . Memorable."
—*RT Book Reviews* (4½ stars, Top Pick, K.I.S.S. Award)

WHEN THE ROGUE RETURNS

"Blends the pace of a thriller with the romance of the
Regency era." —*Woman's Day*

"Enthralling . . . rich in passion and danger."
—*Booklist* (starred review)

WHAT THE DUKE DESIRES

"A totally engaging, adventurous love story with an
oh-so-wonderful ending." —*RT Book Reviews*

"Full of all the intriguing characters, brisk plotting,
and witty dialogue that Jeffries's readers have come to
expect." —*Publishers Weekly* (starred review)

The *New York Times* bestselling "must-read series"
(*Romance Reviews Today*)

The Hellions of Halstead Hall

A LADY NEVER SURRENDERS

"Jeffries pulls out all the stops. . . . Not to be missed."
—*RT Book Reviews* (4½ stars, Top Pick)

"Sizzling, emotionally satisfying. . . . Another must-read." —*Library Journal* (starred review)

"*A Lady Never Surrenders* wraps up the series nothing short of brilliantly." —*Booklist*

TO WED A WILD LORD

"Wonderfully witty, deliciously seductive, graced with humor and charm." —*Library Journal* (starred review)

"A beguiling blend of captivating characters, clever plotting, and sizzling sensuality." —*Booklist*

HOW TO WOO A RELUCTANT LADY

"Delightful. . . . Charmingly original."
—*Publishers Weekly* (starred review)

"Steamy passion, dangerous intrigue, and just the right amount of tart wit." —*Booklist*

A HELLION IN HER BED

"Jeffries's sense of humor and delightfully delicious sensuality spice things up!"
—*RT Book Reviews* (4½ stars)

THE TRUTH ABOUT LORD STONEVILLE

"Jeffries combines her hallmark humor, poignancy, and sensuality to perfection."
—*RT Book Reviews* (4½ stars, Top Pick)

"Delectably witty dialogue . . . and scorching sexual chemistry." —*Booklist*

SABRINA JEFFRIES

The Danger of DESIRE

Pocket Books

New York   London   Toronto   Sydney   New Delhi

Pocket Books
An Imprint of Simon & Schuster, Inc.
1230 Avenue of the Americas
New York, NY 10020

This book is a work of fiction. Any references to historical events, real people, or real places are used fictitiously. Other names, characters, places, and events are products of the author's imagination, and any resemblance to actual events or places or persons, living or dead, is entirely coincidental.

First Pocket Books paperback edition December 2016

POCKET and colophon are registered trademarks of Simon & Schuster, Inc.

For information about special discounts for bulk purchases, please contact Simon & Schuster Special Sales at 1-866-506-1949 or business@simonandschuster.com.

The Simon & Schuster Speakers Bureau can bring authors to your live event. For more information or to book an event, contact the Simon & Schuster Speakers Bureau at 1-866-248-3049 or visit our website at www.simonspeakers.com.

Manufactured in the United States of America

10 9 8 7 6 5 4 3 2 1

ISBN 978-1-5011-4444-8
ISBN 978-1-5011-4445-5 (ebook)

Acknowledgments

Thanks to Lori Pacourek for naming Delia's cat, Flossie, as part of the charity effort of Authors for Cats. Your grandmother Florence (Flossie) would be so proud!

The Danger of
DESIRE

One

When Warren Corry, Marquess of Knightford, arrived at a Venetian breakfast thrown by the Duke and Duchess of Lyons, he regretted having stayed out until the wee hours of the morning. Last night he'd been so glad to be back among the distractions of town that he'd drunk enough brandy to pickle a barrel of herrings.

Bad idea, since the duke and duchess had decided to hold the damned party in the blazing sun on the lawn of their lavish London mansion. His mouth was dry, his stomach churned, and his head felt like a stampeding herd of elephants.

His best friend, Edwin, had better be grateful that Warren kept his promises.

"Warren!" cried a female voice painfully close. "What are you doing here?"

It was Clarissa, his cousin, who was also Edwin's wife—and the reason Warren had dragged himself from bed at the ungodly hour of noon.

He shaded his eyes to peer at her. As usual, she had the look of a delicate fairy creature. But he knew better than to fall for that cat-in-the-cream smile. "Must you shout like that?"

"I'm not shouting." She cocked her head. "And you look ill. So you must have had a grand time at St. George's Club last night. Either that, or in the stews early this morning."

"I always have a grand time." Or at least he kept the night at bay, which was the purpose of staying out until all hours.

"Which is precisely why it's unlike you to be here. Especially when Edwin isn't." She narrowed her eyes on him. "Wait a minute—Edwin sent you, didn't he? Because he couldn't be in town for it."

"What? No." He bent to kiss her cheek. "Can't a fellow come to a breakfast to see his favorite cousin?"

"He can. But he generally doesn't."

Warren snagged a glass of champagne off a passing tray. "Well, he did today. Wait, who are we talking about, again?"

"Very amusing." Taking the glass from him, she frowned. "You do not need this. You're clearly cropsick."

He snatched it back and downed it. "Which is precisely why I require some hair of the dog."

"You're avoiding the subject. Did Edwin send you here to spy on me?"

"Don't be absurd. He merely wanted me to make sure you're all right. You know your husband—he hates having to be at the estate with your brother while you're in town." He glanced at her thickening waist. "Especially when you're . . . well . . . like that."

"Oh, Lord, not you, too. Bad enough to have him and Niall hovering over me all the time, worried about my getting hurt somehow, but if he's sent you to start doing that—"

"No, I swear. He only asked that I come by if I were invited to this. I had to be in town anyway, so I figured why not pop in to Lyons's affair?" He waved his empty glass. "The duke always orders excellent champagne. But now that I've had some, I'll be on my way."

She took him by the arm. "No, indeed. I so rarely get to see you anymore. Stay awhile. They're about to start the dancing."

Uh-oh. Clarissa had been trying to find him a wife for years, and lately both she and Edwin's sister, Yvette Keane, had doubled their efforts. Probably because *they* were both now happily married and thought it just the thing for a bachelor.

He was in no mood for such machinations today. "Why would I dance with a lot of simpering misses who think a marquess the ideal prize? I'm too cropsick to deflect veiled questions about what I'm looking for in a wife."

Her frown revealed her intentions as fully as if she'd spoken them. "Fine. Be an old grump, if you must. But you could dance with *me*. I can still dance, you know."

No doubt. Except for during her disastrous debut, Clarissa had always been a lively sort, who wouldn't be slowed by something as inconsequential as bearing the heir to the reserved and eccentric Earl of Blakeborough.

Clarissa and Edwin were so different that Warren occasionally wondered what the two of them saw in each other. But whenever he witnessed their obvious affection, he realized there must be something deeper than personalities cementing their marriage. It made him envious.

He scowled. That was absurd. He didn't intend to marry for a very long while. At least not until he was much older. Even then, he would prefer a lusty widow who could endure his . . . idiosyncrasies. Certainly not some coy chit eager to use him as a ladder for climbing the ranks of high society.

Or worse yet, a sanctimonious female like his mother, chiding him for every attempt he made to enjoy himself. To forget.

Clarissa stared off into the crowd. "As long as you're here, I . . . um . . . do need a favor."

Damn. "What kind of favor?"

"Edwin would do it if he didn't have to be in Hertfordshire helping my brother settle the family estate, you know," she babbled. "And Niall—"

"*What's the favor?*" he persisted.

"Do you know Miss Delia Trevor?"

Miss Delia Trevor? God, would Clarissa *never*

stop trying to match him up? "Fortunately, I do not. I assume she's some young debutante you've taken under your wing."

"Not exactly. Although Delia was just brought out this past Season, she's nearly my age . . . and a friend. Her brother died last year in a horrible accident, and she and his wife, Brilliana Trevor, have been left without anything but a debt-ridden estate to support. So Delia's aunt, Lady Pensworth, brought the two of them to London for the Season."

"Agatha Pensworth, wife of the late Baron Pensworth? The woman who used to be great friends with my mother?"

"That's her. I suppose you've met?"

"Years ago, before Mother died. As I recall, she rarely minced words."

"She doesn't suffer fools easily. And she has a fondness for her niece, which is why they're all in town."

"So her ladyship can find husbands for the two young ladies."

"Yes, although I think Lady Pensworth is more concerned about Delia, since the late Mr. Trevor's wife has already borne him a child who will inherit the estate, such as it is. To make Delia more eligible, Lady Pensworth has bestowed a thousand-pound dowry on her, which ought to tempt some eligible gentlemen."

That put him on his guard. "Not me."

She rolled her eyes. "Of course not you. Things do not *always* concern you, for heaven's sake. She needs someone decidedly younger. She's only twenty-three, after all."

Decidedly younger? "Here now, I'm not that old. I'm the same age as your husband."

"True." Her eyes twinkled at him. "And given your nightly habits, you apparently possess the stamina of a much younger man. No one seeing you in dim light would ever guess you're thirty-three."

He eyed her askance. "I seem to recall your asking me for a favor, dear girl. You're not going about getting it very wisely."

"The thing is, I'm worried about Delia, who seems rather distracted these days. She keeps receiving notes that she slips furtively off to read, and she falls asleep in the middle of balls. Worst of all, she says she can't attend our house party, which I'd partly planned in hopes of introducing her to eligible gentlemen." She cast him a pointed look. "Eligible *young* gentlemen."

Thirty-three wasn't old, no matter what his sharp-tongued cousin thought. "Perhaps your friend had another engagement."

Clarissa lifted an eyebrow at him.

"Right. She needs a husband, and you're nicely trying to provide her with a selection of potential ones." He smirked at her. "How ungrateful of her not to fall in with your plans."

"Do be serious. When was the last time you

saw any unmarried woman with limited prospects refuse a chance to attend a house party at the home of an earl and a countess with our connections?"

He hated to admit it, but she had a point. "So what do you want *me* to do about it?"

"Ask around at St. George's. See if the gentlemen have heard any gossip about her. Find out if anyone knows some scoundrel who's been . . . well . . . sniffing around her for her dowry."

The light dawned. Perhaps this really *wasn't* about matching him up with her friend.

During her debut years ago, Clarissa had been the object of a scoundrel's attentions, and it had nearly destroyed the lives of her and her brother. So she tended to be sensitive about women who might fall prey to fortune hunters.

Indeed, having learned this summer what she'd gone through—and before that, what Edwin's sister had gone through to a lesser extent—he'd become far more aware of how easily men preyed on even the most respectable women. That was why Edwin had begun St. George's and Warren had joined—to make sure that men who cared about the women in their lives could look out for them more effectively in a society where fortune hunters and scoundrels abounded.

But it was still problematic for him to do what Clarissa asked. "You realize that if I start asking at the club about an eligible young lady's situation, our members will assume I'm interested in courting her."

"Nonsense. Everyone knows you prefer soiled doves to society loves."

"I like society women perfectly well . . . as long as they have inattentive or dead husbands. It makes matters infinitely less complicated." And there were plenty of those women about, which was one reason he wasn't keen to marry. He had a ready supply of bedmates without having to leg-shackle himself.

"My point is," she said testily, "everyone knows your preferences. And asking questions *is* the purpose of St. George's, is it not? To provide a place where gentlemen can determine the character of various suitors?"

"For their female relations," he said tersely. "Not for the *friends* of their female relations."

Clarissa stared up at him. "She has no man to protect her. And I very much fear all the signs lead to her having found someone unsuitable, which is why she's behaving oddly. I don't want to see her end up trapped in a disastrous marriage. Or worse."

They both knew what the "worse" was, since Clarissa had gone through it herself. Damn. He might not have been Clarissa's guardian for some time, but she still knew how to tug at his conscience. And it gnawed at him that he'd been unaware of what had been done to her before he'd become her guardian, that it had taken his best friend's perception to parse it out.

"It would be a very great favor to me," Clarissa went on. "I tell you what—she's here, so let me introduce you. You can spend a few moments talking to her and see if I'm right to be alarmed. If you think I'm overly concerned, you may leave here with my blessing and never bother with it again. But if you think I might be right . . ."

"Fine. But you owe me for this. And I promise I will call in my debt down the road." He forced a smile. "At the very least, you must introduce me to some buxom widow with loose morals and an eye for fun."

"Hmm," she said, rolling her eyes. "I'll have to speak to my brother-in-law about that. He has more connections among that sort than I do."

"No doubt." Her brother-in-law used to use a number of "that sort" as models in his paintings. "But I can talk to Keane without your help. So I suppose I'll settle for your promise not to be offended if I refuse your invitation to your house party."

"There was a possibility of your accepting? Shocking. Still, I did hope—"

"So where *is* this woman you wish me to meet?"

Clarissa sighed. "Last time I saw her she was right over there by the fountain." As she turned that direction she stiffened. "What on earth are those fellows doing with Delia?"

She stalked across the lawn and he followed, surveying the group she headed for: a woman surrounded by three young gentlemen who appeared to be fishing—fishing?—in the fountain.

He recognized the men. One was a drunk, one a well-known rakehell, and the third a notorious gambler by the name of Pitford. All three were fortune hunters.

No wonder Clarissa was worried about her friend.

He turned his attention to the chit, who had her back to him and was dressed in a blue-and-green plaid gown with a pink-and-yellow striped shawl and a multi-feathered coiffure that added at least a foot to her height.

For the first time, he wished their new king *hadn't* recently lifted the requirement for the populace to wear mourning for the late George IV. Even the dullness of black and gray gowns as far as the eye could see would be preferable to that nightmare of colors.

What's more, any woman who dressed that way was bound to be a heedless twit. He sighed. She would be a nuisance at best, a dead bore at worst. There was nothing he disliked more than a cork-brained female, unless she was sitting on his lap in a brothel, in which case intelligence hardly mattered.

As they approached, Clarissa asked, "What's going on here?"

The jovial chap with cheeks already reddened

from too much champagne said, "The clasp broke on Miss Trevor's bracelet and it dropped into the fountain, so we're trying to get it out to keep her from ruining her sleeves."

"I'd prefer to ruin my entire gown than see you further damage my bracelet with your poking about," the chit said, her voice surprisingly low and throaty. "If you gentlemen would just let me pass, I'd fish it out myself."

"Nonsense, we can do it," the other two said as they fought over the stick wielded by the drunk. In the process, they managed to jab Miss Trevor in the arm.

"Ow!" She attempted to snatch the stick. "For pity's sake, gentlemen . . ."

Warren had seen enough. "Stand aside, lads." He pushed through the arses. Shoving his coat sleeve up as far as it would go, he thrust his hand into the fountain and grabbed the bracelet. Then he turned to offer it to the young lady. "I assume this is yours, miss."

When her startled gaze shot to him, he froze. She had the loveliest blue eyes he'd ever seen.

Though her gown was even more outrageous from the front, the rest of her was unremarkable. Tall and slender, with no breasts to speak of, she had decent skin, a sharp nose, and a rather impudent-looking mouth. She was a pretty enough brunette, but by no means a beauty. And not his sort. At all.

Yet those eyes . . .

Fringed with long black lashes, they glittered like stars against an early-evening sky, making desire tighten low in his belly. Utterly absurd.

Until her lips curved into a sparkling smile that matched the incandescence of her eyes. "Thank you, sir. The bracelet was a gift from my late brother. Though I fear you may have ruined your shirt retrieving it."

"Nonsense." He held out the bracelet. "My valet is very good at his job."

As she took the jewelry from him, an odd expression crossed her face. "You're left-handed."

He arched one brow. "How clever of you to notice."

"How clever of you to *be* so. And it's hard not to notice, since I'm left-handed, too. There aren't that many of us around."

"Or none that will lay claim to the affliction, anyway." He'd never before met a lady who would.

"True." She slipped the bracelet into her reticule with a twinkle in her eye. "I've always heard it's gauche to be left-handed."

Well, well, she was definitely not a twit, if she knew that *gauche* was the French word for *left*. "I've always heard it's a sign of subservience to the devil."

"That, too. Though the last time I paid a visit to Lucifer, he pretended not to know me. What about you?"

"I know him only to speak to at parties. He's

quite busy these days. He has trouble fitting me into his schedule."

"I can well imagine." Pointedly ignoring the three men watching them in bewilderment, she added, "He has all those innocents to tempt and gamblers to ruin and drinkers to intoxicate. However would he find time to waste on a fellow like you, who comes to the aid of a lady so readily? You're clearly not wicked enough to merit his interest."

"You'd be surprised," he said dryly. "Besides, Lucifer gains more pleasure from corrupting decent gentlemen than wicked ones." This had to be the strangest conversation he'd ever had with a debutante.

"Excellent point. Well, then, next time you see him, give him my regards." Her voice hardened as she cast a side glance at their companions. "He seems to have been overzealous in his activities of late."

When the gentlemen looked offended, Clarissa put in hastily, "Don't be silly. The devil is only as busy as people allow him to be, and we shall not allow him to loiter around here, shall we, Warren?" She slid her hand into the crook of his elbow.

"No, indeed. That would be a sin."

"And so are my poor manners." Clarissa smiled at her friend. "I've neglected to introduce you. Delia, may I present my cousin, the Marquess of Knightford and rescuer of bracelets. Warren, this

is my good friend, Miss Delia Trevor, the clever-
est woman I know, despite her gauche left hand."

Cynically, he waited for Miss Trevor's smile to
brighten as she realized what a prime catch he
was. So he was surprised when it faded to polite-
ness instead. "It's a pleasure to meet you, sir. Clarissa has told me much about you."

He narrowed his gaze on her. "I'm sure she
has. My cousin loves gossip."

"No more than you love to provide fodder for
it, from what I've heard."

"I do enjoy giving gossips something to talk
about."

"No doubt they appreciate it. Otherwise,
they'd be limited to poking fun at spinsters and
then I would never get any rest."

He snorted. "I'd hardly consider you a spin-
ster, madam. My cousin tells me this is your first
Season."

"And hopefully my last." As the other fellows
protested that, she said, "Now, now, gentlemen.
You know I'm not the society sort." She fixed Warren with a cool look. "I do better with less lofty
companions. You, my lord, are far too worldly and
sophisticated for me."

"I somehow doubt that," he said.

"I hear the dancing starting up," Clarissa cut in.
"Perhaps you two can puzzle it out if you stand
up together for this set."

He had to stifle his laugh. Clarissa wasn't usually so clumsy in her social machinations. She

must really like this chit. He was beginning to understand why. Miss Trevor was rather entertaining. At least when she wasn't looking down her nose at him for his moral lapses.

Which was odd for a woman sneaking around to meet with an unsuitable suitor, wasn't it?

"Excellent idea." He held out his hand to the young lady. "Shall we?"

"Now see here," Pitford interrupted. "Miss Trevor has already promised the first dance to me."

"It's true," she told Warren, a hint of challenge in her tone. "I'm promised for all the dances this afternoon."

Hmm. Warren turned to Pitford. "Fulkham was looking for you earlier, old chap. He's in the card room, I believe. I'll just head there and tell him he can find you dancing with Miss Trevor."

Pitford blanched. "I . . . er . . . cannot . . . that is . . ." He bowed to Miss Trevor. "Forgive me, madam, but I shall have to relinquish this dance to his lordship. I forgot a prior engagement."

The fellow scurried off for the gates as fast as his tight pantaloons would carry him. Probably because he owed Fulkham a cartload of money.

And Pitford's withdrawal was all it took for the other two gentlemen to excuse themselves, leaving Warren alone with his cousin and Miss Trevor.

Smiling, he offered his arm again to Clarissa's friend. "It appears that you are now free to dance. Shall we?"

To his shock, the impudent female hesitated. But she obviously knew better than to refuse a marquess and took the arm he offered, though she wouldn't look at him, staring grimly ahead.

As they headed toward the lawn where the dancing was taking place, she said in clipped tones, "Do you always get your way in everything, Lord Knightford?"

"I certainly try. What good is being a marquess if I can't make use of the privilege from time to time?"

"Even if it means bullying some poor fellow into fleeing a perfectly good party?"

He shot her a long glance. "Pitford is deeply in debt and looking for a rich wife. You ought to thank me."

"I know what Pitford is. I know what they all are. It matters naught to me. I have no romantic interest in any of them."

Pulling her into the swirl of dancers, he said, "Because you prefer a fellow you left behind at home? Or because you've set your sights elsewhere in town?"

Her expression grew guarded. "For a man of such lofty consequence, you are surprisingly interested in my affairs. Why is that?"

"I'm merely dancing with the friend of my cousin," he said smoothly. "And for a woman who has 'no interest' in the three fortune hunters you were just with, you certainly found a good way to get them vying for your attention."

She stared at him. "I have no idea what you mean."

"The clasp on that bracelet wasn't broken, Miss Trevor." When she blinked, he knew he'd hit his mark. "So I can only think that you had some other purpose for dropping it into the fountain."

As they came together in the dance, he lowered his voice. "And if it wasn't to engage those men's interest in you personally, I have to wonder what other reason you might have to risk such a sentimental heirloom. Care to enlighten me?"

Two

Thank heaven the dance parted them just then, giving Delia a chance to debate her answer as she went through the moves. Bad enough that his lordship had run Lord Pitford off; must he also insist upon sticking his nose in her business?

Men like him did nothing without reason. They simply didn't let anyone else know what it was.

Like her brother, Reynold.

Grief knotted in her belly, and she gritted her teeth. She refused to think of that just now—how he'd selfishly abandoned them. How dared he leave her to clean up his mess, to make sure that Brilliana and little Silas were secure?

He'd probably assumed she would simply marry some fellow who'd take care of them. But aside from the practical difficulties of that, after Papa and Reynold, the last thing she needed was another selfish man in her life.

So, although she wanted to enjoy this glittering world of dances and music and witty lords, to be young and carefree, she could not. She had a family to care for.

And now she had Lord Knightford, a well-known rakehell, suspiciously asking her to dance. Surely he could tell when his cousin was up to her usual matchmaking, so why would he put up with that? Unless he had some other reason for going along.

Could he truly be interested in her? Delia glanced across the circle that she and Lord Knightford formed with another couple. Highly unlikely. A wealthy marquess like him could have any woman he wanted. Especially when he was possessed of fathomless dark eyes, a jaw chiseled enough to cut glass, and perfectly combed raven hair that made a woman want to reach up and tousle it.

What would he do if she did?

Lord, she must be daft. He could very well be the enemy. Never mind that he was supposed to be one of those St. George's fellows, a self-proclaimed protector of women's virtue, who shared information about fortune hunters to determine who was dangerous and warn their female relations. His rakish smile proved he was anything but a protector.

Unless . . .

Oh, fudge. Clarissa must have bullied Lord Knightford into cautioning Delia about those three fortune hunters. Bother it all. Clarissa was a lovely friend, one of the few in the *ton* that Delia trusted, but she couldn't afford the countess's interference. Not in this.

Delia and Lord Knightford came together in the dance again.

"Well?" he prodded. "Why did you drop your bracelet?"

"The truth, sir?" she said, stalling.

"It's generally more entertaining than a lie, so yes."

Oh, he had no idea. But in this case, the truth was just outrageous enough that it might spark an honest response. She doubted he was the man she'd been hunting for all these months—it made no sense for a wealthy marquess to be a card cheat—but it couldn't hurt to witness his reaction. "I wanted to see if the gentlemen had tattoos."

Gaping at her, he actually missed a step, which she found rather satisfying, since the man danced far too well for any woman's sanity. It also convinced her that she'd been right in her assumption about him. A guilty man would have sought to hide his shock.

Besides, at least one of his lower arms was unblemished—she'd seen it clearly through the translucent fabric of his wet shirt. Though it didn't necessarily eliminate him from being connected to the man she sought.

He quickly recovered his composure. "I assume

you're talking about those vile things sailors put on their skin?"

"I wouldn't describe them as vile. I have a fascination for them, you see."

"Because you want to acquire one?"

She couldn't help her burst of laughter. "Of course not. If being left-handed is gauche, only imagine what the gossips would make of my having a tattoo. It's simply not done."

"Yet you thought that those fellows—gentlemen of rank, no less—might have them."

"I hoped they might. How else am I to get a close look at one?"

Lord Knightford had just enough time to stare at her incredulously before the dance parted them once more.

But the music couldn't drown out the memory of her brother's rant on the night before his death: *I should have known that the scoundrel was a card cheat when I saw the sun tattoo above his wrist. What lord of any character would defile his body with such a thing?*

What lord, indeed?

A lord who would ruin a man for his own profit and drive him to throw himself into—

Delia choked down her futile rage. She'd believed Reynold when he'd sworn never to pick up Papa's habits. When he'd claimed to prefer caring for their estate, Camden Hall. But he'd proved just as reckless as Papa. Not only had he gambled, but someone had cheated him out of everything.

She would find out who it was. She would trap the scoundrel into cheating again and then threaten to expose him if he didn't pay back the money he'd stolen from Reynold.

Unfortunately, Reynold had refused to name the card cheat, no matter how much she'd begged him to. All Delia had to go on was the mention of his being a lord with a sun tattoo. She'd been searching for such a man the whole time she'd been in London for her debut, but it hadn't been easy. No gentleman would bare his arms to a lady except under unavoidable situations—which she'd been trying to create when Lord Knightford had ruined everything and run off her most recent suspects.

Now she'd have to find her information another way. Perhaps from his lordship, assuming he was as much a gossip as his cousin.

He approached her in the dance again. "So you want to see a tattoo in the flesh."

"*On* the flesh, to be more precise." She forced a light smile to her lips. It grew harder by the day to hide her desperation for the truth. "Do you know anybody who has one?"

"No one respectable enough to introduce to *you*."

"So, no gentlemen." Bother it all.

"Gentlemen do not have tattoos," he said firmly, which didn't help her at all. "And why on earth would you have a fascination with them, anyway? It's not exactly a ladylike pursuit."

"Nightly visits to the stews aren't a gentlemanly pursuit, either, yet that doesn't stop you."

He lifted an eyebrow. "I see my cousin has told you quite a bit about me."

"Enough for me to be aware of your . . . proclivities."

"How unfair, since I know nothing about *your* proclivities, beyond your fondness for tattoos. Do you tipple sherry? Write lurid novels?" He leaned nearer to whisper, "Embroider secret naughty messages on fire screens?"

A laugh sputtered out of her. He was trying to distract her from his own vices by being charming, blast him. And it was working. "I'm afraid I don't embroider much of anything. I'm horrible with a needle." She stared him down. "Besides, secret naughty messages seem more your type of proclivity."

"Trust me, when I spend my nights in the stews, I don't need secret messages. I say exactly what I mean."

"So you admit to spending your nights in the stews."

"Why wouldn't I admit it? It's the truth." He swung her about in a turn, making her feel lightheaded. "I take it that you disapprove."

"I have no feelings about it either way." She actually preferred honest rogues to lying gentlemen. Not that this rogue was interested in her. He was decidedly not. "Why should I care if you visit brothels?"

Judging from his searching glance, her remark surprised him. "Because you're a woman in search of a husband and I'm an eligible man?"

She lobbed that nonsense right back at him. "Are you, really? I was under the impression that you weren't remotely eligible, being in no haste to marry. And in truth, sir, neither am I."

"I can see why," he drawled, "if you're hoping for a tattooed gentleman."

"Don't be ridiculous. I want to look at one, not marry one."

"Well, if I ever hear of one, I'll be sure to tell you." The dance ended and he led her rather slowly to the edge of the lawn. "So who is standing up with you for the next dance?"

"You ran him off, too," she said, "so I suppose I'm sitting this one out."

"No need for that. Since it's my fault you're without a partner, I would be happy to dance with you again."

She eyed him suspiciously. "The waltz? You do know that if you dance a waltz with me after just dancing a set with me, people will talk."

"If you don't care, I don't."

"Why not?"

"The truth?"

"Certainly, since we're being so confessional."

He chuckled. "If Clarissa thinks I'm showing you interest, she'll stop matchmaking for a while and I can get some peace. I'm sure she hopes that you and I will become besotted with each other and end up married. That's why she was so eager to have me stand up with you."

"Ah. And you figure since I'm not interested in marriage, then it would be safe to be seen regularly with me."

"Something like that."

She considered his idea. It had certain advantages. She could move about society more easily.

But she would have a lord dogging her steps. "I like your plan, but I doubt it would work. Clarissa knows you're not the sort to become besotted. Or, for that matter, to easily end up married. And I'm definitely not the sort to inspire besottedness."

"*Besottedness* isn't a word."

"Besottedment? The point is, you're notorious for *not* having any interest in marriage, and she couldn't possibly believe you would change your ways simply because you laid eyes on *me*."

"Why not?" His gaze flicked down her. "You're a very pretty girl."

Skeptical of the easily given compliment, she lifted her eyebrow. "My figure isn't exactly stellar: My curves are in all the wrong places and I have none where I need them. I have too large a mouth and no sense of fashion, not to mention a deplorable tendency to say precisely what I mean. I'm sure I'm not remotely your preference."

Even if she *was* dressing badly on purpose to protect herself from inspiring too much enthusiasm in a suitor.

Other couples moved onto the lawn. He held out his hand. "I tell you what—why don't we discuss that fascinating assumption of yours while we waltz?"

She hesitated. But honestly, a waltz with him sounded enormously tempting. Not because he was handsome and eligible and possessed of the most stalwart pair of shoulders she'd ever seen on a lord. No. It was simply because he might give her information she could use.

"Very well," she said, and took his hand.

This time their dance was more intimate. The two of them swirled across the lawn as a couple, his hand resting familiarly on her waist and hers resting familiarly on his hip. Their other two hands were clasped—sealed together, really—and for some reason it made her positively breathless.

A pang of guilt gripped her. The only reason she'd agreed to a debut was so she could find who'd cheated her brother. She wasn't supposed to be enjoying it. Enjoying dancing with *him*.

What was wrong with her? She'd never been the sort to be made breathless by a man, and certainly not by a marquess with a penchant for bad behavior. Why was he having this effect on her, drat it? Her knees were wobbly, for pity's sake! She would give them a stern talking-to later.

He bent closer and she picked up the faintest scent of spicy cologne. "So why do you think you're not my preference?" he asked in a rough rasp that made every muscle in her belly melt.

If she wasn't careful, she'd soon be blushing and babbling like some schoolgirl. "Because most rakehells prefer flashy women with large bosoms and swaying hips. I am not that."

"You know nothing about rakehells if you believe we all have the same preferences. Go to any brothel, and you'll find women of every size and shape." He brought his mouth close to her ear to murmur, "And a man in each of their beds."

Jerking back, she caught the gleam in his eye and realized he was trying to shock her. Which he was very nearly doing. "Tell me, Lord Knightford, do you often discuss brothels with respectable young ladies?"

"No, but then, I rarely discuss tattoos with them, either."

She glanced away and spotted her brother's footman, the hulking Owen, one of the few servants they had left. He stood on the edge of the crowd, watching her. Oh, dear, it looked as if he'd read her message about tonight and needed to discuss it with her. Somehow she must get herself free of this horribly intriguing marquess.

"Which is all the more reason for us to join forces," he said, drawing her attention back to him.

"Join forces?"

"Let Clarissa think that we're interested in each other. Then she'll leave us be. And we can discuss tattoos and brothels to our hearts' content."

"I can't."

"You just were."

Curse the man for being deliberately obtuse. "No, I mean I can't join forces with you."

"Why not?"

"Because I just can't." Much as she would like to curtail not only Clarissa's matchmaking but that of Aunt Agatha, an association with his lordship was too risky. She couldn't keep up her nightly activities if he were sniffing around, no matter what the reason.

"You mean you have someone waiting in the wings, and you don't want me to scare him off," he said.

His blasted lordship was going to keep prying until she convinced him that she didn't want or need his interference. Leave it to a man not to believe a woman when she said she wasn't interested in marriage. So she might as well tell him what he wanted to hear.

"That's right." She stared him down. "I have a suitor at home in Cheshire. One I vastly prefer to all the rich and titled gentlemen in London. Which is why I'm not interested in being courted by this lot."

He looked unconvinced. "I see. And what is the fellow's name, if I may ask?"

Frantically she cast about for one. "Owen- . . . ouse." Oh, Lord. "Mr. Phineas Owenouse."

"Owenouse?" With a laugh he swung her

through the waltz. "What kind of surname is that?"

"Why, it's Welsh, of course." Delia couldn't help it—with Owen on the brain, it had been the first to leap into her mind. She was generally better at dissembling than this, but his lordship had thrown her off her game. "He's a farmer. We have a number of Owenouses in our town."

Oh, why had she hit upon that name? Clearly Lord Knightford didn't believe her.

"Hmm. And how long have you had a tendre for this Phineas Owenoose?"

"Owenouse. Like 'Owen's house,' except without the *h*."

"Ah. And does this Owenouser have a tendre for you, too?" His eyes twinkled suspiciously.

"O-w-e-n-o-u-s-e, not Owenous*er*. And I should hope so, or why would I pin my hopes on him?" she said blithely, ignoring his other question.

He tightened his grip on her waist. "Ah, but if you already have a suitor, why is Lady Pensworth bringing you out?"

Good question. "Well . . . er . . . my aunt doesn't approve of Phineas, of course. She wants me to marry well, and a Welsh farmer isn't good enough for her." Delia couldn't tell whether he believed her. She pressed on, knowing that embellishing a tale with details often made it more believable. "But he's a wonderful man, who raises chickens, pigs, and cows."

His eyes narrowed on her. "He raises all that, does he? And crops, too, I suppose."

"Of course. There's barley and rye and corn and—"

"My, my, what an enterprising farmer," he said dryly. "I didn't know that one could grow corn in Cheshire."

Uh-oh. Too *many* details could also ruin a tale. "Well, of course one can." She hoped one could, anyway. Reynold had only grown flax on his land, for the local linen mills.

"In Shropshire," he said, "only one county over from Cheshire, corn doesn't grow well at all."

Reynold and Papa had taught her that the best way to win at cards was to go on the attack. Surely that would prove true for dealing with overbearing lords, too. "How would you know? Clarissa says your estate is in Wiltshire."

An odd light gleamed in his eyes. "One of them. But I've owned a hunting box in nearby Shropshire for years."

"So you grow crops at your hunting box, do you?"

Irritation flashed over his face. "Of course I don't grow— What has that got to do with anything?"

"I'm merely saying that if you don't grow crops and you likely don't meet many farmers, you can't know too much about the local agriculture."

She cast a furtive glance at Owen. She had to

get rid of his lordship. It was clear from Owen's expression that he needed to speak to her. And he didn't dare stay out here very long or Aunt Agatha would wonder why he wasn't with the other servants.

Fortunately, the waltz was ending. As soon as the music stopped and they bowed to each other, she said, "Thank you for the dance, Lord Knightford. It was most intriguing. I wish you luck with Lady Clarissa."

But as she turned to walk off, he caught her by the arm. "I'm supposed to lead you from the floor," he said firmly.

She forced a laugh. "This is a lawn, sir. And I can find my own way, thank you."

His eyes narrowed on her. "Are you sure you won't consider joining forces with me to keep Clarissa from plaguing us with her matchmaking? Your Phineas Owenhammer would never have to know."

She started to correct him on the name again, then gave up. "Oh, but my dear Phineas could hear of it in the papers. You're a very popular subject in the gossip rags, you know. And given the difficulties he and I already face in being together, I don't want to take any chances."

This time when she pulled away, he let her go, but she could feel his eyes on her the whole way. Somehow she'd managed to snag his attention, and that was not good.

She could only hope that his interest in her was as fleeting as his interest in every other woman she'd heard associated with him. Because one way or another, she would find the man who'd cheated Reynold. And neither Clarissa nor the disturbingly handsome marquess was going to stand in the way of that.

Three

As Miss Trevor was darting away, Warren leaned forward and snagged a feather from her coiffure. She had so many of the damned things that she wouldn't miss one, and he'd need an excuse to approach her again.

Which he fully intended to do. Because Clarissa was right—something was up with Miss Trevor.

He wasn't sure what, but he knew that her tale about her "suitor" was created from whole cloth. She was good at lying—he'd give her that—but Phineas Owenouse? He'd wager there wasn't a man on earth with such a ridiculous name, Welsh or no. Not to mention that she'd had trouble describing what he did for a living.

Farmer, hah! No farmer did *all* of what she described. The fellow would have to be filthy rich, and there were few farmers who were *that* rich.

Besides, he'd noticed her furtive glances at the servant standing on the edge of the crowd. Something was up. Whose servant was he, and why would she communicate with him so furtively? Was she arranging an assignation? Accepting one of those notes she supposedly read at balls?

And why did *he* care, anyway? The woman had deplorable taste in clothes, she was a pain in the arse, and she was almost certainly not worth Clarissa's worry.

She also had a forthright manner that intrigued him, a lively enjoyment of dancing, and a fresh, lemony scent that made him think of tarts—not only the pastry kind, but the other kind. And unlike most debutantes, she didn't seem to care what he thought of her.

It was maddening. Women of her station usually cozied up to him; they didn't try to escape his advances. He was a bloody marquess, for God's sake, practically the holy grail of husbands in society.

And she talked about things no debutante would ever discuss. She had a quick wit and a ready smile, and her throaty laugh would make any man imagine making love to her.

Often. Thoroughly.

He groaned and clamped down on a surprising burst of lust. He was supposed to be protecting her from ravishment by some fortune hunter, not plotting how to ravish her himself.

Clarissa wanted him to save Miss Trevor from trouble, and that's what he meant to do. In years past, he should have pressed Clarissa harder about why *she'd* resisted marriage. If he'd known the truth, perhaps he could have prevented some of what she'd had to endure later. Doing this favor might go a long way toward assuaging his guilty conscience about that.

Besides, after all his ward had suffered, she deserved not to be fretting about her friend falling prey to a scoundrel. Clarissa, in her delicate condition, didn't need any more worry weighing her down.

Right. *That* was why he was now stealthily edging toward a woman who didn't want his attentions. Because of some need to protect his former ward.

The truth was, lately his life had become a monotony of smoky rooms and brandy-soaked nights spent in the arms of women he couldn't even remember. He needed a challenge.

Unknotting the mystery of Miss Trevor would certainly be that. And since she claimed to have no romantic interest in him, he wouldn't have to worry about her breaking out the leg shackles as soon as he so much as pressed her hand.

The object of his attentions reached the burly servant she seemed to be heading toward and then turned to look behind her. Quickly Warren pretended to be paying attention to another woman on the opposite end of the lawn. But as soon as Miss Trevor's back was to him, he watched as she and the fellow in livery ducked down a thinly traveled path through the garden. Hmm. This grew more curious by the moment.

Twirling her feather in his hand, he followed them. Surely Miss Trevor wasn't so foolish as to involve herself with a servant. She seemed too sensible for that, even if she *was* making up that ridiculous Phineas Owen-whatever.

Which meant that the servant must be connected to her secret admirer or to whomever she was running off to meet.

He approached the pair, keeping to the trees so he could sneak up on them unaware. As he got close, he overheard Miss Trevor speaking in an angry tone.

"But it *must* be tonight!" she said. "I have precious few nights left that I can go. Aunt Agatha is already annoyed at having to remain in town throughout the summer. If not for the king being dead and everyone having to come back to London for the opening of Parliament next week, she would have had us packed off to Cheshire already until next year."

Interesting. The chit didn't sound particularly eager to return home and reunite with her paragon farmer.

He slid behind a tree to listen.

"But, miss, it's too dangerous!" the servant said. "Only today your sister-in-law asked me who I was with last night. She saw me out the window during the wee hours of the morning accompanied by, as she put it, 'a fellow she didn't recognize,' and thought it odd. If she goes to your aunt about it—"

"We'll just have to be more careful. Leave by another entrance—one that doesn't lie beneath her window."

So Miss Trevor *was* meeting some fellow at night, apparently escorted by this servant. Her aunt's servant? It must be.

"I don't know, miss—" he began, showing that he wasn't a complete idiot.

"You owe it to me. You owe it to *him*, Owen."

Owen? He stifled a laugh. Owenouse. Of course. But who was the *him*? Probably her hapless suitor.

The man huffed out an exasperated breath. "To be sure, miss, I know my duty. But we have to be careful."

"We will be, trust me. I have no more desire to be caught out than you. Too much is at stake."

Damned reckless woman. She probably fancied herself in love with whatever scoundrel she was meeting.

Warren frowned. He considered himself a relatively good judge of character, and had truly thought her too intelligent to be taken in by some fortune hunter. What a disappointment to discover that even a clever woman could be stupid when it came to men.

She drew her shawl more tightly about her shoulders. "I'd better return to the breakfast before someone notices I'm gone. Don't forget—

we meet at one a.m." Then, turning on her heel, she came back up the path.

That was his cue. He wasn't leaving here without at least reminding her that she was playing with fire.

He slid out from behind the tree to approach them. "Ah, Miss Trevor, I found you."

She practically jumped out of her skin. Excellent. Perhaps it would put the fear of God into her, since she clearly didn't have the sense of a goat.

"Lord Knightford! I . . . um . . ."

"You dropped this when you left the dance." He held out the feather. "I wished to return it."

"How kind of you." She took the feather. "But how do you know it's mine?"

"I saw it fall as you walked away. I looked about for you, but you'd disappeared. I took this path in hopes that I might run into you, since it was the only one nearby."

That seemed to make her suspicious, but he didn't care. He *wanted* her to be on her guard.

Not to be meeting a wretched fortune hunter in the dead of night. Clarissa's experience was too fresh and painful for him to forget. It still disturbed him that his cousin had suffered so, even if it hadn't been on his watch.

Miss Trevor took the feather from him. "Thank you. I appreciate your kindness."

He'd never heard such a grudging thank-you in his life. Bloody ungrateful female.

When he stared hard at the servant, she apparently realized that she should explain. "This is one of my late brother's footmen. He had a message for me from my aunt, so we moved aside to discuss it privately."

"I see. That must have been some message."

"Oh, my aunt is full of demands," she said with a wave of her hand, "all of which require deciphering."

"Well, then, if you're done, I should be happy to escort you back to the breakfast."

She paled. "Actually, Aunt Agatha is not . . . er . . . feeling particularly well, so I believe we're going home. That was what Ow— That was what *we* were discussing." With a quick nod, she added, "Again, thank you for your kindness, and I hope you enjoy the rest of the breakfast."

Then she headed up the path, accompanied by the servant.

Warren followed at a leisurely pace, enjoying the swing of her full hips, which must be the "curves in the wrong places" she'd been referring to. But he appreciated a fine, plump bottom, so he enjoyed watching hers. Plus, his walking behind her seemed to agitate her, since she kept casting furtive glances back at him and increasing her pace.

Good. Whatever she was up to seemed decidedly unwise, and he hoped he'd made her think twice about it.

They reached the party once more, and she

headed off at great speed toward her aunt. Meanwhile, Clarissa headed at great speed toward *him*.

"Well?" she asked in a terse whisper as she reached him. "What do you think? Isn't she behaving oddly?"

To put it mildly.

But he wasn't about to say that to Clarissa. For one thing, Edwin would shoot him if he allowed Clarissa to become involved in midnight meetings and roguish doings. For another, he could handle this on his own. He would simply wait outside Lady Pensworth's town house tonight, confront the lovers as they met clandestinely, and make sure the fortune hunter stopped playing with Miss Trevor's heart and reputation.

"She's behaving no more oddly than other young women in love," he told Clarissa.

A frown creased her brow. "That's not saying much."

"True. But she seems a rather sensible sort." Or she had when he'd first met her, anyway.

"She is, most of the time. But apparently she took her brother's death very hard, and her aunt says she hasn't quite recovered from it, even though it's been almost a year since it happened."

"Do you know if she has any suitors at home in Cheshire?"

"She's never mentioned any. Why?"

"I wanted to rule out the possibility that some unworthy fellow followed her to London."

"If he has, I've seen no evidence of it."

"And does she speak fondly of her home?"

"Not at all. In truth, she seems eager to remain in London as long as possible."

So she could meet with her secret suitor. That made sense.

Clarissa let out a breath. "I just don't want her to . . . to . . ."

"I understand. I'll do some asking around at the club and see what I can find out, if that will make you feel better."

"It will, thank you."

He chucked her under the chin. "Now stop worrying and come dance with me. If you're up for it." It would take her mind off Miss Trevor.

She brightened. "I'm always up for a bit of dancing."

They headed for the lawn, and by the time they had taken their places, Miss Trevor seemed to have vanished. That was all right. Let her enjoy her last hours believing that she was the mistress of her own fate.

Because tonight he meant to discover who was after the pretty Miss Trevor's fortune. And he would make sure the man never preyed on an innocent again.

⁓

Shortly after 11:00 p.m., once the maid had left, Delia opened the window-box seat in her bedchamber. She removed several books before lifting the lid of the false bottom. She'd been lucky to stumble upon the hidey-hole her first week here, and she'd made good use of it since then.

Just as she was about to take out the hidden contents, a knock came at the door, and a muffled voice asked, "Delia? Are you still awake?"

Brilliana. Blast.

Swiftly, Delia closed the false bottom and began piling books atop it. "Come in," she called out.

Her sister-in-law slipped inside, looking like a wraith in her nightdress and filmy wrapper. "I hope I'm not disturbing you. Aunt Agatha said you'd gone to bed with a headache, but I thought I heard you about."

Thank heaven Delia was still dressed for bed. "Yes, my head is feeling much better. So I got up to look for something to read." She grabbed a book and closed the window-seat top. "I couldn't sleep."

"Me either." Brilliana seemed lost, like a princess who'd stumbled out of a fairy tale. She'd always been gorgeous—a full-figured beauty whose hair was *not* a mess of corkscrew curls like Delia's—yet Delia couldn't envy her.

Hard to envy anyone who'd been dealt the hand that life had dealt Brilliana.

Brilliana sat down on the bed, and Delia's Persian cat, who'd been dozing on the pillow, woke up to hiss a warning.

"That cat hates me," Brilliana said ruefully.

Delia chuckled. "Flossie hates everyone."

"Except you."

"And Reynold."

A sigh escaped Delia's sister-in-law. "Is that why you hold on to the cantankerous little devil? Because she was Reynold's?"

Delia tamped down her grief-ridden anger. "I suppose. I don't have many things to remember him by."

Brilliana stared at her hands. "You have a nephew."

"Of course. I didn't mean—"

"I know. This has been hard for all of us."

Delia ventured a smile. "At least little Silas is unaware of his lack of a father. You take good care of him."

Brilliana's face lit up. "He's the most beautiful baby. I wish Reynold could see how he has grown." Pride crept into her voice. "He walks very well now."

"I noticed," Delia said. "Give that child a couple of years and he'll be leading us all a merry dance."

Her sister-in-law's brown eyes darkened to black. "If there's anywhere left for him to dance."

With a clutch in her heart, Delia sat down beside Brilliana. "Don't worry. I have matters well in hand. If I have anything to say about it, Silas will have a fully working, debt-free estate by the time he's old enough to manage it."

Brilliana stared off into space. "That's why I'm

here, actually. I fear I know how you mean to 'manage it.'"

Fighting to keep the alarm from her voice, Delia said, "What are you talking about?"

"Aunt Agatha mentioned that your friend Clarissa's cousin, Lord Knightford, was very interested in you at the breakfast."

Delia stifled her sigh of relief. She should have known Brilliana wouldn't have guessed the truth. There wasn't a suspicious bone in her sister-in-law's body. "I wouldn't say that, exactly."

Brilliana seized her hands, which provoked another hiss from Flossie, who was jealous of everyone who came near Delia. The cat had already lost Reynold, after all. "I don't want you to sell yourself for our sake."

"Sell myself?" She pasted on a smile. "Isn't offering a nice dowry more like buying myself a husband?"

"You know what I mean. You shouldn't have to . . . cozy up to some ugly old marquess in hopes that he will marry you and solve all our problems."

A laugh bubbled out of her. "Trust me, Lord Knightford is neither old nor ugly." More's the pity. "And he isn't in the least interested in marrying me." Also a pity.

No, she didn't mean that.

"Are you sure? You're prettier than you give yourself credit for."

"Quite sure," Delia said dryly. "Though I'll

admit Lord Knightford might be interested in pretending to court me to get his cousin out of his hair."

"Oh. That makes sense. I'm told that Lady Clarissa can be very forceful."

"You have no idea." Delia cast her a hard stare. "But you would, if you didn't hide every time she came to visit."

Brilliana released Delia's hands, and Flossie crept into Delia's lap as if to better protect her. "I don't hide. I'm in mourning, remember?"

"You don't hide from anyone else."

Rising to pace the room, Brilliana wouldn't look at Delia. "She's a fine countess, that's all. I get nervous around such ladies." Brilliana shook her head, sending lush waves of chestnut hair spilling over her shoulders. "Besides, we weren't talking about your friend. We were talking about her cousin. Aunt Agatha says Lord Knightford has a reputation with women."

"I'm well aware." Delia scratched her cat behind one ear. And the marquess's reputation was richly deserved, judging from how easily he could unsettle a woman and make her pulse leap. A fact which Delia dared not let on to Brilliana.

So she went on the offensive. "Anyway, why would it be wrong for *me* to marry in an attempt to save Camden Hall when you're proposing to do the same thing?"

Brilliana shrugged. "First of all, your marrying isn't likely to help us, while my marrying will. I've already been married, so I know how it works, and it wouldn't be that difficult."

"It wouldn't be that easy, either. How will you find a husband in enough time to prevent the foreclosure? You're certainly beautiful enough to attract a man, but burdened with a debt-ridden estate and having a small child will complicate matters. Besides, you're still in mourning; you can't even go into society."

"It ends soon. As long as we can convince your aunt to remain in London a bit longer, while Parliament is in session, we might have some nice social engagements where I can meet gentlemen. She has said she would give me a small dowry, too. And besides, Silas needs a father, particularly someone wealthy enough to bail out the estate and oversee his education as heir."

"In exchange for having *you* under his control." The very idea of her sister-in-law being forced to marry yet again under such circumstances made her stomach roil. "It's not fair. You shouldn't have to sacrifice yourself because of *my* brother, who went off to London to gamble and then abandoned you and Silas. It wasn't right of him to do what he did to you."

Dear Delia, I've lost everything. There's no more reason to live. Take care of Brilliana and Silas for me. I can't bear it anymore. Forgive me.

"He was drunk. It was an accident," Brilliana said.

Blast. Delia had forgotten that her sister-in-law didn't know the truth about how Reynold had died. No one but Delia did. "An accident. Yes." She hated lying, but there was no point in heaping another burden on Brilliana, who already staggered beneath a host of them.

Much as Delia had loved her brother, the way he'd gone about gaining Brilliana as a wife had left much to be desired, and the woman had deserved better than to be abandoned in the end.

The raw anger swelling in Delia's throat threatened to choke her. "I should have seen how upset Reynold was and kept him from going out that night."

"If I couldn't, how could you? Your brother always did as he pleased."

How well she knew. He was as selfish as every other man in that respect. "And no more so than when he came to London to gamble. Did he never say why he felt compelled to do that, when he claimed to dislike it as much as I?"

Brilliana shook her head. "All he told me was that he wanted to call on a friend." A shadow crossed her face. "Imagine my shock when I learned he'd gone to some gaming hell, where he'd lost so much money he had to mortgage Camden Hall to pay his debt."

That was the crux of it. Reynold had gambled with strangers for no reason that they could discover, and the only way Delia could save the estate from foreclosure—and either her or Brilliana from having to marry for money or become governesses or something like that—was to catch the card cheat in the act.

No lord of any reputation dared to be exposed as a cheater, so the wretch would pay back what he'd taken from her brother—even if she had to blackmail him into it. Because there was no way on God's green earth that Reynold had lost all that money simply by playing badly.

Not the son of Captain Mace Trevor, card sharp extraordinaire, who'd taught her and Reynold everything they knew.

Which reminded her . . . Delia glanced at the clock. Nearly midnight. She only had an hour to make her preparations; she needed to get rid of Brilliana.

With a big yawn, Delia rose from the bed. "My, my, I must be more tired than I realized. All that dancing."

As she'd expected, Brilliana leapt up. "Oh, I'm so sorry. Here I am going on and on, and it's far too late for that." She headed for the door. "I'll see you in the morning. Try to get some sleep."

"You, too," Delia said as she walked her to the door. "And put your mind at ease about Lord Knightford. Even if I wanted to marry him—and I assure you, I do not—he would never choose as a wife the daughter of a gambler who once won a sizable estate from a hapless squire."

An estate on the verge of foreclosure.

But that was about to change. She would make sure that it did.

Four

Warren glanced at the clock at St. George's. He still had some time before 1:00 a.m., when he meant to be at Lady Pensworth's town house in Bedford Square. Fortunately it wasn't far from the club, since he'd have to walk there. The bright streetlamps, seclusion, and exclusivity of the neighborhood would make any carriage stand out like a beacon at midnight, especially a marquess's.

Besides, he could move about easier on foot. And conveniently, Bedford Square had a large private garden in the center where he could wait. He already had a key for it. He had keys for most of the private gardens in Mayfair. Aside from the fact that he lived in the vicinity, he found it convenient to have keys for when he wished to meet with certain bored wives for a bit of . . . enjoyment.

But first he wanted to finish his conversation with one of the club's members about Miss Trevor's situation. He'd already discovered that she was highly regarded by gentlemen in search of a wife. Some had even courted her. But the woman had dismissed their attentions as firmly as she'd dismissed his less serious ones.

It made no sense. A woman of her situation should be grabbing at any decent suitor who came along. So why wasn't she? Because she'd fallen for some fortune hunter? She didn't seem the type to be easily swayed by a smooth talker. And she seemed too practical not to acknowledge the advantages of having a suitor with more connections and more wealth.

Yet her suitors had all been rebuffed, even the important ones.

Including the fellow he was presently speaking with. "She's very polite about it," the man said, "but she's also very clear that she's taking her time to evaluate her choices."

On the surface of it, that sounded sensible. But if she were so sensible, why was she meeting some arse in the middle of the night? "Didn't you find that odd, given her late entry into society?" Warren asked.

"I would have, except I know what happened to her brother. I suspect she's still grieving him."

"The brother who died in an accident."

"If you can call it that."

That sparked Warren's interest. "What do you mean?"

The man shrugged. "Supposedly he stumbled

off a bridge and drowned while he was drunk. But there have been rumors that it was not an accident. That he jumped."

"Why would he do that?"

"I don't know for sure, but I imagine it would be for the usual reasons—gambling, financial difficulty of some other kind . . . a thwarted love affair."

"Ah." None of those would enhance a family's reputation, which would certainly suffer if it was bandied about that their beloved patriarch had killed himself. The scandal would be enormous.

Then again, gossip was often wrong. People were always trying to make more out of something than it might be.

After it became apparent he would learn little else of interest, he walked over to Bedford Square and let himself into the garden with his key.

Now all he had to do was wait.

He pulled out a flask and swigged some brandy. It was quiet here. And dark. Too dark. He didn't like quiet *or* dark places, hadn't liked them since he was—

Don't be a sniveling coward, boy. Lords aren't afraid of the dark. Buck up and be a man.

Fiercely, he thrust the hard words to the back of his mind. He mustn't think about those nights right now, or his mind would spiral down into the depths and he'd have to escape before he'd accomplished what he'd come here to do.

Instead, he concentrated on the sounds of the outdoors—the carriages in distant streets, the summer crickets chittering in the garden, a frog croaking in the tiny pond. If he had to endure the night alone, he much preferred it be outdoors. At least there he didn't feel hemmed in. That was crucial.

A new sound came to him—of a door opening—and he looked over the fence. He'd timed matters perfectly. There was that Owen fellow, emerging from the front servant entrance with a young gentleman.

Although *gentleman* might be stretching it a bit. Even from here, Warren could tell that the man's clothes were ill-fitting and not the least fashionable, that he walked hunched over, and that his beaver hat was too large for him. Indeed, the fellow looked more the height and build of a boy than a man.

But where was Miss Trevor? Had he somehow missed the assignation, and her secret suitor was the lad now being ushered out of the house?

No, that made no sense. Why would Miss Trevor meet with a lad beneath her aunt's very nose? It wasn't wise *or* clever.

Besides, why was Owen accompanying the fellow, and without wearing any livery, either? Had Miss Trevor lied about Owen's position? Was Owen her suitor's servant, rather than hers?

That made no sense, either. From what Warren

had overheard, Owen had been concerned about Lady Pensworth dismissing him. So the man had to be the baroness's servant. What the bloody hell was going on here?

The two fellows headed down the road, and Warren watched until he felt it safe to go into the street to follow them. This wasn't his usual sort of pastime. Unlike Lord Rathmoor at the club, he wasn't adept at trailing suspects and uncovering skullduggery.

As they turned toward a seedier part of town, he continued shadowing them, his curiosity roused. Was the younger gentleman another servant? Why was the footman accompanying him, and where? What were they up to?

All entertaining questions. Yes, perhaps he should look at this as his night's amusement. Because God knew he hadn't had much else to entertain him lately, what with his best friend settling into comfortable married life and his youngest brother doing the same, and the world passing him by—

The world was not passing him by. That was ridiculous.

Annoyed by the very notion, Warren stalked the two chaps for some time. He'd begun to wonder if it was worth his trouble when he realized they were going into Covent Garden, where the theaters lay, along with some choice brothels.

It was the area of London where he spent

most of his nights, so he was heading in the direction he would have come anyway, just a little later than usual.

Owen and his companion were likely here for the same reason he would have been. They certainly weren't attending the theater—those were all closed at this hour.

For their sake, he hoped the two fools had condoms or they could find themselves in deep trouble long after their entertaining jaunt. He always carried preventives, having learned long ago the risks of his way of keeping the night at bay. Not for him a bout of the clap, or supporting a slew of dubious by-blows.

In any case, this was proving to be a fool's errand. Perhaps Owen had convinced Miss Trevor not to meet her suitor; it looked as if the fellows were merely servants out on the town.

But their departure at precisely 1:00 a.m. was enough to keep him following them until they entered a gaming hell.

Damn. He hated these places. He preferred to play cards at a club where he trusted his fellow players. He'd learned the dangers of gaming hells in his youth, while trying to keep busy and awake until dawn. This particular hell, a hazy den called Dickson's, was frequented by both respectable and not-so-respectable gentlemen.

Which category did Miss Trevor's suitor fall into, if indeed the youth *was* her suitor? And if he was, why on earth was Owen accompanying the man? Perhaps the two had become friendly during their setting up of assignations with Miss Trevor.

Warren paused outside as if to light his cigar and surveyed the two chaps through the door. They didn't stop in the taproom, but headed right through it to the card room in the back.

Sauntering into the taproom, Warren debated how to act. Pretending to be someone else would be pointless. Aside from the fact that Owen had seen him today, many of the other gentlemen would know him from his numerous visits to the stews.

He supposed he could leave and just warn Miss Trevor next time he saw her that her suitor was a gamester. But he still wasn't even sure the youth in the too-large hat *was* her suitor. Besides, he wanted to at least get the fellow's name and find out his intentions. Not blunder in without understanding the situation.

Very well. Best to join the card play as himself. But first, he'd see what he could glean about the gentleman he could hear being greeted jovially by the other players.

As Warren walked up to the bar and ordered a brandy, the owner of the hell approached. "Knightford!" Dickson cried. "It's been an age."

"Indeed, it has. I've been too busy up the street at Mrs. Beard's to come wallow with you fellows much," Warren said. "More congenial company there."

"I'll wager you're right about that," Dickson said with a chuckle. "Her girls know how to keep a man happy."

They certainly did. And how to keep his mind off the night.

Sipping his brandy, Warren watched through the doorway as the chap with Owen took a seat at a piquet table. That was a game primarily of skill. It made sense that a fortune hunter would prefer it.

"Who is that young devil there in the oversize hat, who just came in?" he asked Dickson. "I don't recognize him." In truth, he still hadn't even had a good look at the youth's face.

"That's Jack Jones. He's a Welsh cousin of that other fellow Owen, although Owen never plays, just watches."

A cousin, hmm. Perhaps Owen was trying to broker a marriage between his mistress and his cousin? Or perhaps his mistress didn't know that the arse *was* Owen's cousin.

Warren took a drag on his cigar. "Where in Wales is he from?"

"He's never said. All I know is he don't talk much, don't drink much, just plays his cards. Always leaves well before dawn. Don't seem to like people. And in the month since he's been coming here, he's brought in more business than I've had in the previous three."

"How the bloody hell has he done that?"

Dickson shrugged. "He doesn't lose. Jack's

damned good at cards, although he can't be more than twenty, at the most. He prefers games of skill like piquet, and he plays them well. So word has got round that Jack Jones is the man to beat, and all the players in town have been trying to prove they can top him. But nobody ever does."

"Which means he's probably cheating."

"I've never once caught him at it."

Stubbing out his cigar, Warren downed the rest of his brandy. "Perhaps I can."

"You can try, but I'm pretty good at ferreting out the sharpers. And I would swear that young Jack is as good as he seems. Hell, I'm not even sure I care if he's cheating, as long as he's not found out. If he brings me more people, I can make money on what they lose at hazard alone."

"Tell you what," Warren said. "I'll see what I can discover myself. It just so happens my brother Hart and my cousin Niall used to bet me that I couldn't catch them cheating at cards, and I always did. Took a lot of money off them. They were young, and I figured it would teach them to behave themselves."

"And did it?"

"They don't cheat. Although they're both still rascals of the first order." He grinned. "And yes, so am I. Which is why I shall see if I can't beat your Jack Jones."

As Dickson chuckled, Warren strode into the room and joined a group of watchers that had formed about the table where the piquet game

was going on. He was careful to stay behind
Owen—it wouldn't do for the servant to notice
him yet.

While observing the play, he looked for anyone standing behind Jones's opponent who might
be signaling Jones concerning what his opponent's cards held. Warren knew all the tricks
from spending so much time gambling in the
evening. A slightly open mouth generally signified hearts, a glance at the stack of cards between
the men signified a knave, and the combination
meant the opponent had a knave of hearts.

There were many such signals, and while he
didn't know them all, he knew enough of them
to recognize when someone was using them.

But after a half hour of playing, he could see
no signaling being done. The only thing he *could*
tell was that Dickson hadn't lied about Jack
Jones being a damned fine piquet player. The
man never took a step wrong. He had a strategy
for every combination of cards, and he knew precisely how to work it to his advantage.

Dickson was right about the fellow's disposi-
tion, too: He was as quiet as an executioner. He
sat hunched over the table, muttering his declarations just loudly enough to be heard. The
observers might chatter around him, but he
didn't participate in any conversation.

When he did speak, his voice had the odd tim-
bre of a youth trying to sound older. From time
to time, he would wipe his nose on his sleeve—

not exactly the behavior of a gentleman. But though his hands looked a trifle dirty, they were nimble and his plays quick. It didn't take long for him to trounce his opponent.

As Jones raked in the money, Warren stepped forward. "Evening, sir. The name's Knightford. Might I try my hand at a game with you next?"

Apparently taken off guard, Jones jerked his head up to meet Warren's gaze. And as Warren caught sight of arresting blue eyes, he realized that everything he'd thought about Owen's friend was wrong.

The forced husky voice, the lack of gentlemanly behavior, the ill-fitting clothes, all made sense now.

Because the card player taking the gaming world by storm was none other than Miss Delia Trevor.

Bloody, bloody hell.

Five

The bottom dropped out of Delia's stomach. What wretched luck! Why must it be *him*? Why here? Why now?

She ducked her head, praying he hadn't recognized her.

Oh, what was she thinking? Of course he hadn't recognized her. No one ever associated the outrageously attired miss who liked to tease with the mumbling, nondescript young chap who played cards like a sharper, had dirty hands and dirty habits, and kept his hat low over his face. She'd actually met some of her suitors in this place, and they hadn't noticed anything.

But most of them were fools. Lord Knightford was decidedly *not* a fool. And Owen's nudge of her knee—their signal for danger—reminded her that Lord Knightford had seen Owen with her. That alone would register with the man.

That is, if he'd noticed the servant. Most lords did not.

"Mr. Jones?" the marquess prodded. "May I play you in piquet . . . sir?"

That hesitation before "sir" gave her pause. *Please, Lord, let him not have figured me out. He could ruin me with a word, and then all my plans would be for naught.*

But she dared not refuse to play him. She had never refused anyone else, and the others would wonder about that change in behavior.

"Certainly, my lord." She opened a new pack of cards and began to shuffle.

He took a seat. "How did you know to call me 'my lord'?"

Bother it all. He was already rattling her. "Everyone knows the Marquess of Knightford around here."

"So we've met before."

Was she imagining the sarcasm in his words? No one else seemed to notice. And if he *had* figured her out, wouldn't he have said something right away? "Of course not. But your reputation precedes you."

"It generally does. Though I didn't imagine it stretched to Wales. That's where you're from, isn't it?"

Oh, Lord, he'd been asking around about Jack Jones before he'd even sat down to play. "Yes, but I came to London a while ago. A man's got to work, you know. And are we playing cards or not?"

They settled the terms, then drew to see who got to choose who dealt. She won the cut, so she chose to deal and be Youngest, while he would be Eldest. Although Eldest had the advantage in every *partie* of the six, the alternating deals meant that she would end up Eldest for the last *partie*—so it was a strategic move to let him have the advantage for the first one.

They began the game. He actually allowed her a whole five minutes before he began chattering away again. "Who taught you to play cards so well, young Jones?"

Oh, for heaven's sake. Was he seeking to distract "Jones" in an attempt to make him lose? Or had his lordship figured out who she really was and was toying with her, like a cat batting at a mouse?

She couldn't tell from his faintly amused expression. "My father taught me to play. He enjoyed a game of whist or piquet now and then."

"So he was a gamester."

She grunted, her usual response when people got too inquisitive. She was telling the truth, after all. She and Reynold had inherited Papa's talent for cards, which Papa had cultivated. And that was why she knew Reynold couldn't have lost so much without being cheated by someone very adept.

Unfortunately, in all the nights she'd been playing here, no one had shown up who fit that description. There *had* been the occasional cheater—it was almost impossible to avoid that in the hells—but they'd been clumsy ones she could easily get around.

She'd considered trying other hells in her search, but it seemed better to stick with the one where the sharper had played her brother. If the man had come here once, he'd come again. Besides, only certain hells specialized in piquet, and this was one.

She and the marquess played a few cards, the silence only broken by their declarations of points.

Then Lord Knightford started his inquisition again. "Where in Wales are you from?"

She swallowed her panic. It certainly *seemed* as if he were trying to find her out. "Corwen." It was Owen's home village. He'd schooled her in everything she needed to know about it.

"Ah, I've been there. The town famous for its well."

Owen nudged her knee. *Danger.*

"Don't know about a well, sir. But there's sheep and cows."

"And corn?"

Her heart stuttered. Oh, Lord, could he be referring to their conversation earlier? "Beg your pardon?"

"Nothing." He eyed her intently over his cards. "What did you do in Corwen, before you came to London?"

Time to put an end to this. "None of your damned business."

"You should be more courteous to your betters, brat," he said mildly.

"And you should pay more attention to your cards, old man," she countered as she played her last card and won the *partie*.

Though she knew she shouldn't have beaten his lordship, since it was unwise to make him angry when she wasn't sure if he recognized her, it gave her a secret satisfaction when the faintest frown marred that perfect brow of his.

Take that, Lord Inquisitive. Perhaps now you'll stop hounding me and start paying attention to the game.

He gathered up the cards and shuffled slower than anyone she'd ever seen. "So, brat, have you sampled any of the other pleasures in Covent Garden?"

"Naw, I only like the pleasures that make me money. Like trouncing *you*, which is quite a pleasure, m'lord, I'll admit."

She loved that aspect of pretending to be Mr. Jones. She could say what she liked, which was enormously freeing, since she normally had to govern her words.

And why was it that women had to stifle themselves while men got to say whatever they pleased? It simply wasn't fair. Sometimes she thought she wouldn't mind becoming Jack Jones for life, being able to live on her own terms.

Except that then she'd be just like Papa and Reynold, risking her future on the turn of a card. That was no way to live. Bad enough that she had to do it to find the unknown card cheat; she couldn't continue forever. Someone was bound to catch her.

Like the pesky Lord Knightford—who even as he dealt the cards was watching her with that brooding gaze that made her stomach quiver.

In alarm. *Only* alarm.

Catching the attention of the taproom maid named Mary, Lord Knightford ordered a bottle of port and a glass. With a wink and a flirtatious smile, Mary flounced off to the bar to fetch it.

After a long moment of watching the swing of Mary's derriere with obvious approval, Lord Knightford picked up his cards.

For some reason, his private little smirk annoyed Delia. "From what I hear, my lord, you sample enough of the pleasures of Covent Garden for the both of us."

He eyed her over his hand, a hint of calculation in his expression. "You're telling me that a randy young lad like you, here every night in the stews, doesn't ever take a tumble with a whore?"

A chill swept down her spine. What had she been thinking, to bait him? She hunched over her cards and prayed she wasn't blushing. "I ain't throwing my money away on a whore when I need it for keeping a roof over my head and getting my supper."

"From what I hear," Lord Knightford said as he arranged his cards, "you take in more than enough to cover that. So, perhaps you have another reason. Perhaps you simply don't like women."

The room fell silent, and the very air froze. Even the smoke from Lord Knightford's cigar seemed to pause in its writhing. Was he accusing Jack of what she thought he was?

She'd learned all sorts of unusual things during her month in the stews, including what it meant when a man preferred to have other men as bed partners. If the fellows in the gaming hell thought she was a molly, they would turn on her, and that would be the end of her career as Jack Jones.

"I like women well enough," she muttered. Just then, Mary returned with his lordship's port, so as she passed, Delia slapped her on the derriere the way she'd seen some of the men do. "But why should I spend my winnings on whores when there's good loving to be found for free?"

As the tension broke and the men laughed, the maid scowled at her. "Mr. Jones!" She tried to mop up some of the port that had spilled out of the glass onto her tray. "And here I thought you was a gentleman!"

"Never claimed to be that, Mary," Delia said

gruffly. She laid a coin on the tray. "But here's for the spilled wine, if it'll make you quit your complaining."

Taking the coin with a sniff, Mary waltzed over to his lordship. "Well, there *are* gentlemen here who know how to treat a lady right." She set the bottle and the glass down in front of Lord Knightford, then bent low enough that he could probably see clear to her navel inside that loose blouse. "Can I get you somethin' else, m'lord?" she cooed.

He smiled at Mary. "Not at present, luv," he said, and tucked a sovereign in her cleavage. "But I'll be sure to take advantage of the offer another time."

Delia couldn't resist a snort, which drew his attention back to her. The gleam in his eye gave her pause. Was he just having a bit of fun at Jack Jones's expense? Or trying to annoy Miss Delia Trevor? Because if it was the latter, he was succeeding.

"Something wrong, Jones?" the marquess asked lazily as he sipped his port.

"Nothing that getting on with this game wouldn't take care of."

"You really are a surly sort. It's a wonder anyone ever agrees to play with you."

Ignoring that remark, Delia laid down her card, and the next *partie* was on. For a while, he was blessedly quiet except for his declarations.

Since it was her turn to be Eldest, she had the advantage and she used it ruthlessly. The cloud spreading over his brow showed that he knew she was trouncing him. Again.

But she couldn't glory in it for fretting over whether he'd guessed who she was. Even winning the second *partie* and having her score leap ahead of his by twenty-two points couldn't banish her worry.

Grimly, she gathered up the cards and began to deal.

"I see you're left-handed," he said.

She paused half a second before forcing herself to go on. The fact that he was bringing up the subject they'd discussed at the breakfast earlier didn't have to mean anything. Perhaps the conversation had merely stuck in his head, so that now he noticed left-handers everywhere.

And if wishes were horses, beggars would win the Derby. "Actually, I'm ambidextrous. Use both hands the same." Which was a lie, but she had to tell him *something* to get him off the track.

"*Ambidextrous*, is it?" Lord Knightford said. "You have an awfully big vocabulary for a country lad."

"You have an awfully big mouth for a card player. Do you ever shut up?"

The marquess chuckled. "When it suits me."

"Could it suit you now, if you please? Because I'd like to finish this game before the morn."

"Very well," he said, but his smirk told her he wasn't done with her.

Was he building up to exposing her? Or was she just so nervous around him that she was reading too much into his remarks?

Whatever the case, she'd best find a way out of here before he either revealed who she was or plagued her until she slipped up and revealed who she was herself. Leaving before the game was over would rob her of the chance to beat him at cards, which she sorely regretted, but it wasn't worth risking exposure.

When they started the third *partie*, she could feel Lord Knightford's gaze on her, as if he were attempting to see beyond the layers of her disguise. Lord. She had to escape—and without his being able to follow, in case he *had* figured out who she was.

When Mary came through again, carrying a tankard to another table and glaring at "Jack" as she passed by, an idea leapt into Delia's head.

Delia leaned forward to lay down her card, calling, "Could you bring *me* one of those ales, lass?"

Pretending to be distracted by her ordering, she brought her hand back just enough to knock over the port bottle so it fell and spewed port into Lord Knightford's lap.

"Bloody hell!" he cried as he jumped up to blot the wine staining his perfect white shirt. Mary hurried over to help, as did others.

And while all was chaos, Delia slipped out the front.

Owen followed her quickly. "Are you mad, miss?" he muttered under his breath as she hurried away from Dickson's. "I daresay you would have won the game and a tidy pot as well."

"Winning has never been my only aim, as you well know. And tonight I had other concerns."

She called to a hackney. If they escaped fast enough, Lord Knightford wouldn't be able to follow them, and once they were out of sight, he wouldn't be able to track them to her aunt's house. He might have his suspicions about her true identity, but without proof, he wouldn't dare expose her.

Though she'd have to avoid Dickson's for a while. It was too risky to be caught by his lordship.

As soon as she and Owen were ensconced in the hackney and it was racing away from the gaming hell with no one following them, she relaxed.

She was safe now. Or mostly, anyway.

"Lord Knightford may have recognized me," she told Owen.

"Are you sure?"

"We danced together earlier today. Then tonight he kept mentioning things we talked about and watching to gauge my reaction. I had to leave. I couldn't risk his challenging me about my identity. And with my fleeing, he'll never be able to confirm it. It prevents him from unmasking me before witnesses, and he's not reckless enough to accuse a woman of good family without proof."

"I see. Then I suppose your wine ploy was clever. We'll have to take more care in the future."

"Yes."

Owen sighed. "I'm sorry I can't gamble in your stead. But you'd be broke in a week if I did. I don't know a thing about cards."

"I realize that. And I wouldn't want to force you to act against your beliefs, even if you *could* play piquet. You have enough trouble participating in this subterfuge as it is."

Owen was a strict Wesleyan and didn't drink or play cards. He wasn't keen on lying, either, but so far they'd managed it so she was the only one doing that.

"I hate that I haven't been able to learn anything about the tattooed man since we've been in London," he persisted. "But there hasn't been a single person in the hells who's ever heard of him. Or if they had, they weren't saying."

That was the trouble. A man of rank was rarely gossiped about to outsiders by those who ran the hells. They knew that they owed their bread and butter to such men, and they weren't about to risk that.

"You did your best. That's all I can ask."

"Have you considered that your brother might have lied about the man who beat him? That

Mr. Trevor might have overstated the case because he couldn't bear losing?"

She stiffened. "Certainly not. While I wouldn't be surprised anymore to hear that Reynold lied, he was as good a player as Papa, if not better. He wouldn't have lost unless someone cheated him."

"I suppose you know your brother better than anyone." Owen looked skeptical, which annoyed her.

"I bloody well do."

"Miss! You're picking up all sorts of bad language from these jaunts to Covent Garden. If you're not careful, you'll start using it in society, and then you'll never find a husband."

She glanced away. "I don't want a husband. Men only care about themselves." When he bristled, she added hastily, "Present company excepted, of course. But you're a Wesleyan—you've been raised to care about people. Most men do whatever they want, without considering what's good for their families."

Papa had dragged the family from pillar to post during the war and afterward, looking for better chances to make money at the tables. If he hadn't won Camden Hall in a stroke of amazing luck, who knew how long they would have wandered the world?

Then there was Reynold. She'd never forgive him for abandoning his family. For gambling away her and Brilliana's futures. And sweet little Silas's.

Tears stung her eyes. Silas *would* have a future, even if she had to gamble herself into the grave.

Lord Knightford could probe all he liked into her life, but he wouldn't stop her from finding the man who'd cheated Reynold.

And he damned well wouldn't stop her from getting back what Silas deserved to inherit. Woe be unto him if he tried.

Six

The day after Miss Trevor disappeared from the gaming hell, Warren waited in the foyer of Lady Pensworth's town house for his card to be accepted.

He'd dragged himself out of bed early to make certain he caught the ladies before they went shopping or some such feminine foolery. After Miss Trevor had left him dripping with port and his clothes ruined, only to disappear, he wasn't about to let that happen again.

Last night he could have roused her household and told her aunt what she was up to. But he hadn't wanted to make trouble for her—just put an end to her dangerous game.

He needed to speak to her privately, and he wasn't leaving until he did. Fortunately, Lady Pensworth was sure to have him admitted, since she wanted a husband for her niece.

The footman came back. "Her ladyship is in, my lord, if you will follow me."

With a nod, he allowed the servant to escort him back to the drawing room. Before the man could announce him, Warren heard Lady Pensworth say, "Out, you beast! I'm not putting up with your shenanigans today!"

The footman showed Warren in, where they found Lady Pensworth shooing a Persian cat. Or trying to, since the feline merely scurried beneath the furniture.

Either the baroness had not heard them enter or she was too intent on dealing with the puss to notice, for she stamped her foot in front of the settee.

That would have sent any other feline fleeing; this one hissed at her from beneath the settee.

"Lord Knightford, milady," the footman announced.

The tall, bespectacled woman whirled around. "Knightford! So glad you've come to call. Perhaps you can coax that horrible creature out from under the settee. The damned thing never heeds what I say."

He chuckled as he bowed. "I don't think there's a cat alive who will. If you want a pet who will obey you absolutely, madam, you should probably get a dog. They're more easily trained."

"Oh, the beast is not mine, but my niece's. She hates me."

"I doubt seriously that Miss Trevor is so foolish as to hate—"

"Not *her*." Lady Pensworth rolled her eyes. "The cat. I've no idea why it despises me. It's not as if I've done anything to her."

"Some cats are cantankerous."

Rather like Lady Pensworth, who had a reputation for being forthright, irritable, and a little eccentric. But he'd known her as a boy, when she'd visited his mother, and he always remembered her giving him lemon drops.

That had been before Mother had converted to Methodism and lost some friends in the process, including Lady Pensworth.

With a rustle of skirts, the baroness took a seat and eyed him closely. "How kind of you to call," she said, as if recalling her manners. "Though I assume my niece is the person you actually came to see."

So she knew of his attentions to Miss Trevor? Apparently the gossips were already pairing them.

That was just as well. It would make it easier for him to learn what was going on. "I assure you I came to see you both. And you're looking very well today. That color becomes you."

"Hmm." When he strolled over to take her hand and kiss it, the corners of her lips twitched. "Delia is still abed, I'm afraid. The poor girl had such a headache after dancing in the heat yesterday that she came home early, retired straightaway, and has not yet risen."

"Ah." He would swear the baroness believed what she was saying, which meant she didn't know about Miss Trevor's activities. A useful bit of information, though not a great surprise. "You must tell her I'm sorry to have missed her."

But he meant to take full advantage of having the aunt to himself to learn whatever he could about Miss Trevor's true situation. He began to think it was quite different from what either Miss Trevor or Clarissa had described.

"I have told Delia many a time not to overexert herself at these things, but she simply will not listen."

"Rather like her cat," he said.

"Precisely."

As if it knew they were talking about it, the puss crept from under the settee and strolled over to wind itself about his trousers.

"Flossie, stop that this minute!" Lady Pensworth snapped her fingers. "I swear I will have you banished to the garden, neighbor dogs or no!"

"No need for that." He picked up Flossie, then took a seat on the settee and began to scratch her behind the ears. She purred and nuzzled his fingers. "My mother had three tabbies and a tortoiseshell, so I don't mind cats in the least. They generally seek me out, as a matter of fact."

Perhaps they recognized that he was as nocturnal as they. His mother's old tomcat had often kept him company at the estate. Thank God, because he detested nights in the country if there were no houseguests. Lindenwood Castle was too dark, too quiet. Too full of troubling memories.

"Especially the female ones, I'm sure," she said archly. "From what I understand, females of all species generally seek you out."

"My reputation precedes me, I see," he said with a thin smile. Obviously he would not be leaving here with any lemon drops.

"Oh yes. Let's just say that your mother wouldn't have approved of your late-evening jaunts."

"I doubt many mothers approve of their son's 'late-evening jaunts' in town, but mine most certainly would not have."

She must have noticed the strain in his voice, for she sighed. "Yes, well, she did change quite a bit after those Methodists got hold of her. It was impossible to speak to her anymore without getting an earful of religion."

The last person he wanted to discuss was his intensely devout mother. "Indeed. You were saying, about your niece and how she does not listen to your advice . . ."

"May I be frank, sir?"

"I was under the impression that you already were," he said dryly. "But go ahead and see if you can exceed your efforts so far."

She looked as if she fought a smile. "Very well, then. I noticed how much time you spent with my niece at the breakfast. It was more than she generally allows most gentlemen. She's rather impatient with them, I'm afraid."

He acted on a hunch. "Because of her suitor back home, you mean."

"What suitor?" She paled. "She has no suitors back home."

"She mentioned a rich farmer by the name of Phineas Owenouse."

A frown beetled her brow. "I have no idea who that is. And I've never heard of any Owenouses in the village. Sounds suspiciously foreign to me."

"He's Welsh."

"As I said, foreign. And entirely unacceptable as a suitor to a woman with her connections and fortune." She cocked her head. "You do know she has a small fortune, don't you?"

That put him on his guard. "I'm not sure what that has to do with me."

"I assume that you're here because you're looking for a wife. You do not, as a general rule, pay calls on eligible young ladies." Her voice turned steely. "Unless, of course, your intentions aren't honorable."

He stifled an oath. "I assure you, madam, that if I *were* to pursue your niece, it would only be for the most honorable of reasons. And since we're being frank, you should know that her fortune, small or otherwise, is immaterial to me. I have no need of it."

"Don't be silly. Fortunes are always useful,

even to a man like you. But does this mean you *are* interested in my niece?"

"I'm interested in being her friend."

"I do hope 'friend' is not a salacious euphemism you bucks are using these days to mean women you hope to entice into your bed."

Time for his marquess stare. "I am a gentleman, madam. And your niece is a lady." When she wasn't pretending to be a lad named Jack Jones. "And this is beginning to feel oddly like an inquisition."

"I merely want to determine why a man who has shown absolutely no interest in marrying heretofore has suddenly decided that my niece—"

"Lord Knightford!" cried a voice from the door.

Miss Trevor had apparently left her bed after all.

As he rose with the cat in his arms, she rushed into the room. She looked utterly different from when he'd danced with her yesterday. Her gown was a soft yellow that made her eyes shine pure azure, and her hair was very messily done, as if she'd put it up herself—or hurried a maid along to do it.

Someone must have told her he was here, for panic flickered in her eyes before she regained her composure. If he hadn't caught that glimpse, he would never have known she was rattled. Aside from the messy hair, that is.

He'd thrown her off her game, which gave him an odd pleasure. Because Miss Trevor at home was another creature entirely from the two versions that he'd met. Thrown out of kilter by his visit and clearly fresh from her bed, she was flushed and unguarded and the loveliest thing he'd seen in a long time.

Not that it mattered. He wasn't looking for a wife, and definitely not one who played a different character every time he saw her.

Then her gaze dropped to his arm, and her pretty mouth hardened. "What are you doing to my cat?"

Now *that* was the impudent Miss Trevor he'd met yesterday. He could practically see the walls going up around her. Which intrigued him even more, damn it.

"Petting it. Why? Is that not allowed?"

"It's just that . . . well . . . Flossie hates everyone but me."

"Clearly not everyone," he drawled.

Lady Pensworth stepped in. "Delia, do come sit down. His lordship has done us the honor of paying us a visit, so the least you can do is be courteous."

She flashed him a tight smile. "Of course. Forgive me, my lord, I'm not used to seeing Flossie cozy up to anyone."

"Cats are unpredictable," he said. "Much like their owners."

Casting him a wary glance, she took a seat on the chair across from him. "It's either be unpredictable or be boring."

He sat down on the settee and let the cat leap off to go to her mistress. "We certainly wouldn't want the latter. But then, I doubt there's any chance of that."

Lady Pensworth leaned forward. "I believe there's a lovely compliment buried in there, Delia."

"Buried quite deep, I'm sure," she mumbled as Flossie jumped onto her lap. Delia cast a furtive glance at her aunt, as if to gauge what he might have said to the woman before her arrival. "What brings you to Bedford Square, sir?"

"I'm paying you a call. That should be obvious."

"What's not obvious is why."

"Funny, but your aunt was just asking me the same thing. And I told her—as I'll tell you—I'm hoping we could be friends."

"Friends? I somehow suspect you have more than enough of those."

"But none as intriguing as you. Although I did make an acquaintance last night in the gaming hells—a fellow by the name of Jack Jones—"

She rose abruptly. "My lord, perhaps you would like to take a turn about the garden across the street. It's lovely at this time of year."

Suppressing a smirk, he stood. "What an excellent suggestion. Assuming it's all right with your aunt, that is."

Lady Pensworth blinked at them both, clearly thrown off by the odd conversation. "I'm sure a turn about the garden would be fine, sir."

"Thank you. I promise I won't keep your niece long." He offered his arm to Miss Trevor. "Shall we?"

Taking it, she practically dragged him from the room. How amusing that he could rattle her so easily. The chit was obviously suffering from a guilty conscience.

As soon as they were outside, she released his arm and stalked ahead to the garden. He followed at a leisurely pace. With five brothers, he'd learned early on how to draw out the suspense, make them nervously await his pronouncements. Miss Trevor might be a woman, but the same tactics applied.

Which was evident when they entered the garden and she rounded on him. "Why are you here, my lord?"

Time to put his cards on the table. "To ask you about Jack Jones, of course."

Though she blanched, she held his gaze. "I don't know who that is."

"Don't play games with me, Miss Trevor. I recognized you the moment I saw your pretty blue eyes at Dickson's last night. And you had Owen with you, which helped. I gather that his name was the inspiration for Mr. Owenouse, your supposed Welsh farmer suitor."

She glared at him. "You're quite mad, do you know that?"

"Not as mad as you, to be risking certain ruin by dressing as a man and gambling in the hells."

Whirling on her heel, she marched off down the path through the garden. "I have no earthly idea what you mean."

He strode after her. "Don't try to play me for a fool, Miss Trevor. You and I both know you've been masquerading as Jack Jones. My question is, why?"

"What a fascinating tale you spin," she said sweetly. "I can't imagine how you would think that I'm some dirty gambler."

Ah, he had her now. He halted her with a hand on her arm. "I never said that Jack Jones was a gambler, much less a dirty one. I said I met him in the gaming hells."

She blinked, then said in a hollow voice, "Isn't everyone in a gaming hell a gambler?"

"Hardly. There are hangers-on, servants like your Owen, and those who come to take advantage of the free ale and wine. As you well know."

"I don't understand why you persist in thinking—"

"I wonder, if I ask your aunt about your ability to play cards, will she enlighten me? I'm sure she knows how good you are."

Miss Trevor turned on him with panic in her gaze. "You can't speak of these ridiculous theories to my aunt."

"I don't want to, but I will if I must."

She huffed out a breath. "*Why*, for heaven's sake? It's none of your concern!"

"I hate to see a young lady of good family with

respectable connections risk her entire future for . . . what? The thrill of the game?"

"Don't be absurd." She snorted. "The game is what ripped our family apart. I wouldn't be playing at all if not for Reynold."

"So you admit that you've been playing cards at Dickson's as Jack Jones."

Her gaze shot to him. "Fine." She tipped up her chin. "I admit it. I am Jack Jones." Laying her hand on his arm, she looked up at him with a plea in her eyes that fairly slayed him. "And if you reveal my activities to my aunt, you will ruin everything. So please tell me what I must do to keep you from making an utter wreck of my life."

Seven

Delia could actually see Lord Knightford's temper flare—the frozen look in his eyes, the thinning of his lips. Odd, how she'd begun to notice those signs. Probably because he'd been meddling so much in her affairs in the past day.

"I am trying to *keep* you from making a wreck of your life," he bit out. "Do you have any idea how dangerous it is for a woman to go into the stews alone—"

"I'm going as Jack Jones, not a woman. And not alone, either. Owen is there to protect me if anyone gets too close. He does an excellent job of it."

"Someone will recognize you eventually. *I* recognized you."

"Because you danced with me yesterday! That's all."

"That's *not* all. Aside from the fact that you're too pretty to pass as a gentleman if anyone looked closely, you don't have the derriere of a man. It's far too shapely, and those trousers are rather tight for you."

That took her aback. He thought her pretty? Really? And he'd been observing her backside in trousers? Oh, Lord.

Wait, that was highly unlikely. "You couldn't possibly have seen my derriere. I was seated the whole time you were there."

"Not the whole time, trust me. And all it would take is your bending over once to pick something up—"

"I don't bend over. Women never do."

"Exactly. So don't you think someone would notice if you performed the usual ladylike dip to pick something up? Or any number of other feminine actions you take for granted?"

She swallowed. "No one's noticed heretofore."

"It's only a matter of time. It took me little enough effort to follow you and Owen on foot to the gaming hell—"

"Follow us! You *followed* us?" Her heart pounded. So *that's* when he'd seen her derriere in tight trousers.

And she'd thought she was being so clever by escaping last night. But he'd known exactly where she was going. He could have found her then, if he'd chosen. "If you knew where I lived, why didn't you demand to see my aunt last night and expose me?"

"Before I did anything drastic, I wanted to give

you a chance to stop your dangerous activities. I have no desire to get you into trouble with your relations." His gaze hardened. "But I will, if that is what's necessary to make you stop taking these risks."

Ooh, he could be so infuriating, him and his marquess high-handedness! "I am managing the risks perfectly well." She tipped up her chin. "I've been going nearly every night for a month and not a soul has guessed I'm a woman. Men only see what they want, and they assume that no woman could ever be as good at cards as I am."

She wasn't boasting about her abilities. It was a fact that even Reynold had acknowledged.

"You *are* good—I'll give you that. But you're not managing the risks as well as you assume. Don't you think people have noticed your ducking out to confer with Owen at balls, the private notes shared between you, your tiredness—"

"Oh, Lord, I knew it!" she said as awareness dawned. "Lady Clarissa put you up to this, didn't she? She keeps prying. But this takes the cake—setting her cousin to spy on me!"

He thrust his jaw out defensively. "Not spy. Observe." When she snorted, he added, "And everything I've seen tells me she was right to be concerned. This masquerade of yours is mad."

"Why? Because I'm winning money from lords who think they're better than everyone else?"

His dark gaze narrowed on her. "Is that what this is about? Money?"

She caught her breath. She didn't dare tell him the truth, since she still had no idea who her quarry was. For all she knew, the tattooed nobleman could be Lord Knightford's close friend or relation.

So she would have to give him the answer he expected. "Of course it's about money. I need enough to forestall the foreclosure of Camden Hall before we're all tossed out. I've put away quite a bit of blunt already."

"I can't imagine you've put away enough to forestall foreclosure of an estate of any size."

He was right, but she couldn't say that, since her hopes were set on a different source of funds entirely. "It's not enough yet, but if I can have a couple more weeks in London—"

"What about your suitor, the rich farmer, Owenouse?" he said sarcastically. "Can't he take care of all of you once you marry?"

His knowing look scraped her nerves. "All right, I admit that was a rather . . . clumsy lie." Turning on her heel, she stalked down the path.

He fell into step beside her with an easy stride that reminded her of a fine Thoroughbred's. Or a tiger on the prowl. Honestly, he was too unnerving to bear. Men rarely unsettled her, so how did he always manage to do it? It galled her.

So she lashed out. "You can be terribly annoying sometimes, you know, meddling in other people's business."

"And you can be terribly stupid." When she

shot him a black look, he caught her arm to halt her. "I have it on good authority that you've turned down some perfectly eligible, respectable suitors. Why on earth would you do that when marriage is the easiest way to settle your future for good?"

She tugged her arm from his. "My future isn't the only one at stake. Since *I* do not inherit Camden Hall, any man I marry would have no incentive to save it, or to support my sister-in-law and her child. So while marriage might save *me*, it won't save the rest of my family or their proper inheritance."

"Fine. If your sister-in-law is the one whose son will inherit the property, then help *her* find a rich husband. I hear she's pretty enough to land one."

"That's precisely what I'm trying to avoid! As soon as Brilliana is out of mourning, she means to marry the first wealthy man who offers for her, the first one willing to pay off the debt and save the estate. And I can't let her do that."

"Why, for God's sake? That would solve everything."

"Only if she can find one soon enough. How probable is that for a destitute widow with a son? So my only choice is to go on as I have."

"Really?" He stepped closer. "And what do you think will happen if you're discovered playing Jack Jones in the gaming hells? Scandal isn't the best way to ensure anyone's future."

"On the contrary, it wouldn't affect my life in

the least, since I don't intend to marry." At least not until she found the man who'd ruined her brother and made him pay the money back.

"You really mean it. You don't want to marry," he said, with the usual male skepticism that always grated. "Ever."

"You of all people shouldn't find that odd. You've shown no evidence that *you* wish to marry."

"Ah, but I can satisfy my desires without marrying. *You* cannot."

Desires—hah! "I don't care about that," she said, and meant it. "It's not the same for women as for men, you know. We don't feel . . . things like that."

The few times she had, she'd been alone with her daydreams about daring soldiers and noble knights of old. But in real life, she'd never felt anything for the gentlemen she encountered. Even the few who'd initially attracted her had proved disappointingly ordinary.

Except Lord Knightford.

She scowled. Well, of course she would find the witty and devastatingly handsome Lord Knightford compelling, but that didn't matter. He would never consider marrying her; he'd made that quite clear. Nor did she want to marry a man who would probably go on whoring and deceive his wife about it.

"You actually believe that women don't feel desire," he snapped, as if he found that some sort of personal affront.

"Absolutely." When she realized Lord Knightford was eyeing her as if she'd just grown a third arm, she added defensively, "Brilliana says that the 'pleasures of the marital bed' are pleasurable only for the men. A wife just has to put up with relations."

"Oh, for God's sake. That may say more about your brother and sister-in-law's marriage than about the 'pleasures of the marital bed.'" When she blinked at him, he leaned closer. "Tell me, Miss Trevor, have you ever even been kissed?"

That brought her up short. "I can't believe we're having this highly inappropriate conversation."

"Why not? We always have inappropriate conversations. It's why I find you so charming. Answer the question."

"Of course I've been kissed. But—"

"I should have said, kissed *properly*."

She slanted a wary glance at him. Her two kisses had both been distinctly unpleasant. Granted, one had been with a fortune hunter who'd taken her by surprise, but she'd rather fancied the other gentleman. Until he'd done some disgusting thing with his tongue and taught her that kisses sounded much better in stories than they were in reality.

Though she ought to lie and say she had been kissed properly, she suspected he wasn't referring to propriety. And the idea that kisses could be done wrong fascinated her. "What do you mean, *properly*?"

He glanced across the street to where her aunt stood in the window watching them. "I'm afraid there's only one way to explain that."

Before she could react, he tugged her into the midst of a circle of tall shrubs that hid them both from view. "I figure we have about ten minutes before your aunt sounds the alarm and we are interrupted." He flashed her a smile that hinted he could introduce her to secret, enticing temptations with the snap of a finger. "Fortunately, I'll only need a few."

He didn't snap his finger. He kissed her.

And it was nothing like those previous kisses. It wasn't too hard or too soft. His lips were warm enough to heat hers, his breath smelled like oranges, and his closeness made something stop in her heart. The way he possessed her mouth was almost . . .

Enjoyable. All right, *very* enjoyable.

She enjoyed how he toyed with her lips, how he gripped her waist with the confidence of a man used to taking charge. She enjoyed the heady feeling of doing something rather naughty, and the unfamiliar swirling in her belly that made her want to go up on tiptoe and kiss him back.

Lord, what was she doing, falling under his spell so easily?

She broke the kiss. "My lord, please—"

"My friends call me Warren." Catching her head in his hands, he ran a thumb over her lips.

She fought the sudden racing of her pulse. "I'm not your friend."

"But you'll call me Warren, won't you, Delia? At least in private."

"We are not going to be in private ag—"

He muffled the words with another kiss. Only this time he tried what that other fellow had done—he slipped his tongue between her lips.

And oh, what a difference. There was nothing disgusting about it, nothing messy and embarrassing. It thrilled her to no end. He tasted of marmalade and coffee, not at all what she'd expected, and his tongue delved lightly but insistently, rousing a response in her beyond anything she'd ever known.

She felt giddy, excited . . . aroused the way she did in her daydreams. Heavens. Desire *was* real for women, too. Who could have known?

He had. And now he was pressing her against his hard frame and feeding on her mouth with slow, silken strokes, and she couldn't think, couldn't breathe, couldn't do anything but feel the most incredible—

The creak of a gate made them both freeze. He released her, resuming the easy stance of a lord sure of his position. But his gaze smoldered, and the coals sparked fires in her blood. Just as his kiss had done.

"It appears I was wrong," he said raggedly. "Apparently a few minutes weren't nearly enough for me . . . Delia."

For her, either. She could have gone on and on . . .

But he was a rakehell. She must remember that. Such men were good at kissing; Lord only knew what other scandalous things he was good at.

Part of her dearly wanted to find out what those were. The other part was angry that he'd managed to get her so hot and bothered.

Just then, Owen came around the tall shrub shielding them from the path. He glanced warily from her to Lord Knightford and back. "Your aunt wants to know if his lordship would like to join you and Mrs. Trevor for luncheon."

Bother it all, she would never survive that. "I doubt that Lord Knightford has the time to—"

"I would be honored," the marquess said, his gaze still riveted to hers. "Miss Trevor and I have been having the most intriguing conversation, one I would dearly love to continue."

Panic rose up in her throat. "Owen, would you give us a moment more?"

"Her ladyship would not approve."

She glared at Owen. "A moment. That's all."

Owen retreated, but only to the other side of the shrubbery.

Delia neared the marquess and lowered her voice. "What do you intend to say to my aunt?"

"I don't know." He sounded truthful. And when he shoved a hand through his hair, looking suddenly off-balance, she realized that he was as uncertain about this situation as she.

"If you tell her about Jack Jones, I'll deny it. You'll simply look the fool."

He cast her an assessing glance. "Perhaps. But it would put your aunt on her guard, make her pay better attention to your activities at night."

"Or make her whisk me back to Cheshire. Then I'll never have a chance of marrying well. Which rather defeats your purpose of trying to convince me with your . . . your kisses that my best alternative is to find a decent husband."

"True." He stared her down.

"Miss Trevor!" Owen called out. "Your aunt is coming this way."

Lord Knightford—Warren—offered her his arm. "Shall we, my dear?"

Peeking through the shrubs, Delia saw that her aunt was indeed nearly to the garden. "Fine." She took his arm. "But I am not your *dear*. And you are *not* staying for luncheon."

He broke into a devious grin. "We'll just see about that."

Eight

Warren realized he was skating on thin ice with Delia, but he couldn't help it—she fascinated him. Most of the time respectable women were open books; he could see their machinations as clear as day. He spent half his time deflecting their attempts to snag him as a husband or snag him for someone else as a husband.

Not with Delia. She didn't want him for that. She didn't want him for anything. Except perhaps his kisses, which she *had* seemed to welcome. Still, another woman would have used the sensual interlude to draw him in. She'd used it to push him out.

Normal women simply did not behave that way. Certainly not with *him*. One moment, he thought she was like his mother—girding herself in feminine outrage against the very idea of lovemaking done for pleasure. And in the next, he wondered if Delia might simply be inexperienced. Which fired his desire to give her a bit of experience.

That was the trouble: Delia was a conundrum. And he loved unraveling conundrums, especially the ones wrapped up in a fetching female with spirit.

So he of course stayed for luncheon, easily overriding Delia's objections. Her aunt ignored them, too. Lady Pensworth wasn't daft enough to let a wealthy marquess slip away, especially one who'd shown interest in her niece. And since Warren was standing there expressing his great pleasure in having the opportunity to spend more time with Miss Trevor and her family, Delia had no choice but to surrender.

He did so enjoy when she surrendered, soft as silk, willing and wanton. Those kisses . . . God, he hadn't had the like in years. Innocent yet eager, they made his mouth water.

A cautious man would stay away. But he'd never been that. He much preferred recklessly attempting to get her to surrender again.

When he reentered the drawing room of the town house, he was introduced to Mrs. Trevor, Delia's young sister-in-law, who was busy sketching, a very ladylike endeavor. She was a beauty with abundant brown curls, whose gray-and-black half-mourning gown somehow accentuated her fulsome curves and creamy skin. But she lacked a certain something he couldn't put his finger on.

Delia's brashness, no doubt. Mrs. Trevor didn't look the sort to ever dress in men's clothes and gad about a gaming hell. She was too reserved, too subdued.

He glanced at her intricate images of classical subjects. "These are very good," he said with some surprise.

Mrs. Trevor blushed. "They're designs for porcelain. I figured that if Wedgwood could use the designs of women like Diana Beauclerk and Lady Templetown, perhaps they might consider mine."

Apparently Delia wasn't the only one trying to find ways to make money for the family. Though sadly, he didn't imagine that selling a few designs to Wedgwood would ever save Camden Hall.

"Your time would be better spent elsewhere," Lady Pensworth said, "though I suppose *some* gentlemen might find such a talent attractive in a prospective wife. Now come, let us adjourn to the dining room."

Warren bit back an oath. Delia and Mrs. Trevor were clearly under quite a bit of pressure already to marry, and Delia, at least, was not taking that well. He wished her aunt wouldn't be *quite* so forceful about it, since it was driving Delia in a different direction entirely.

As soon as they were seated around the smallish dining room table, with Delia across from him and the other two women on either end, Mrs. Trevor turned to him with a polite smile.

"So, Lord Knightford, do you have any favorite pastimes?"

"His lordship's favorite pastime is to be annoying by day and wicked by night," Delia said less than cordially, obviously still chafing at the way he'd ingratiated himself into her household.

"I beg your pardon." Warren sipped his wine as he stared her down. "I try to be wicked by day as well. I'm wounded that you haven't noticed."

"*I* noticed." Lady Pensworth eyed him over her glass of wine. "And it's hardly something to brag about, sir."

"His lordship fancies himself above the rules of society," Delia said with a lift of her pretty raven brow.

"For a woman I only met yesterday," he drawled, "you have a great many ideas about my favorite pastimes and what I fancy. In any case, I find that the only firm rule in society is to not be boring."

"Perhaps that's the rule for marquesses." She held up her own glass. "The rest of us are required to behave."

He stifled a retort involving pots and kettles, but he wasn't ready to unveil Delia's nighttime activities to her family yet. She'd made some valid points in the garden about how it could ruin her life.

"Lord Knightford," Mrs. Trevor put in hastily, as if to smooth things over, "I do hope that gambling isn't one of your wicked pastimes."

Odd that she'd chosen that particular vice.

Could the woman be privy to Delia's secrets? "Surely gambling is everyone's wicked pastime. Why, do you disapprove of it?"

"I disapprove of what it does to families. My father and late husband were both gamblers." Mrs. Trevor's eyes darkened as she toyed with her lobster salad. "That didn't turn out well for any of us."

Belatedly he remembered the gossip at the club. "Does that mean none of you play cards?"

"Don't be silly," Lady Pensworth put in. "Everyone plays cards. We just don't gamble. Not even Delia, though she could if she wished. Piquet is her forte."

"Is it? I happen to like piquet myself." He cast Delia a veiled glance, noting the color brightening her cheeks. "She and I shall have to play sometime."

"Be careful," Mrs. Trevor warned. "She's quite good. The whole Trevor family is."

"Including you?" he asked.

"Oh no. I'm horrible."

"Only because you hate figures," Delia said.

"I do not hate figures," Mrs. Trevor protested. "I just want them to add up and be logical. How does it make sense for an ace to beat a king? Or sometimes not? If it's a one, it should always be a one. Honestly, I don't know who comes up with these lackadaisical rules."

"They're no more lackadaisical than the rules for playing the violin, I would imagine, and you love that." Delia leaned toward Warren. "Brilliana not only draws magnificently, but she plays the violin to perfection. I can't even play the pianoforte. I'm all thumbs when it comes to instruments."

That remark just begged for a double entendre, but he knew better than to shock the ladies.

"Still," Mrs. Trevor put in, "Reynold thought me a dunce because I couldn't keep the rules for vingt-un straight. And piquet! Might as well have asked me to perform astronomy calculations in my head. Now *that's* a convoluted card game."

"I doubt that he thought you a dunce," Lady Pensworth put in. "And if he did, he should have had his knuckles rapped for it." She leaned toward Warren. "My nephew and Delia played piquet practically every day from childhood on. They led us all a merry dance at the card tables when my husband was still alive. They learned it from their father, my sister's husband, you see."

Their father. Something niggled in the back of his mind. The name Trevor. Gambling.

Good God. He stared at Delia. "Your father was Captain Mace Trevor?"

She looked startled. "You've heard of him?"

"Everyone's heard of him. I was at the game where he won an estate from Sir Geoffrey eleven years ago." It had been a masterful bit of whist playing. "Your father wasn't seen in gaming hells or clubs from that night on."

"No," Delia said stiffly. "Mama insisted that he

stay put once they had obtained Camden Hall. And miraculously, he agreed."

"Why 'miraculously'?"

"Because until then," she said with a decided note of bitterness, "he'd dragged our family around the world while he was an army officer during the war and then while he gambled his way across Europe. I think Mama found it exciting at first, but it grew old. Eventually he heeded her request that he settle down. Unfortunately, she didn't get to enjoy it for long." The quick flash of sorrow over Delia's face spoke volumes.

"Given your presence in London without her, I take it that she is no longer—"

"She passed away when I was sixteen," Delia said.

"I'm sorry to hear that." He truly was. He somehow suspected that her mother's death had been part of what had changed her into the wary woman sitting across from him now. "And your father?"

She drew into herself. "The following year."

"Ah. I remember reading about that in the papers." Warren still couldn't believe Delia was the daughter of Mace Trevor, though now that he thought about it, he could see the resemblance—especially in those keen eyes and the pugnacious chin.

"That's why Delia is just now having her debut," Mrs. Trevor explained. "My father-in-law died before she was old enough to be presented, and then my husband was always too busy at Camden Hall to bring us to London for any extended period."

Lady Pensworth sniffed. "Yet not too busy to come here and—"

"Aunt Agatha, please," Delia said in an undertone.

"Oh, very well. This topic of conversation has grown rather morbid, anyway," Lady Pensworth said. "Why don't we speak of something cheerier?"

"I know!" Mrs. Trevor exclaimed, her brown eyes twinkling. "We should plan when Delia and Lord Knightford are going to have their piquet match. I confess I'm eager to see if he can beat her."

"Of course he can. And will, I'm sure," Lady Pensworth said with a warning glance at Mrs. Trevor.

The young woman blinked at the baroness. "I'm not sure at all. Did you not hear me say how very good she is?"

Warren chuckled. "I believe Lady Pensworth is trying to spare my fragile male pride."

"I see." Mrs. Trevor arched an eyebrow at him. "I should hope that your pride isn't wounded by something as trivial as being beaten at cards."

"No, my male pride is quite capable of withstanding that," he said, ignoring the way Delia was trying—and failing—to smother a laugh.

"Then the game should be soon," Mrs. Trevor said. "Perhaps sometime next week?"

Delia's amusement vanished. "I'm sure his lordship has better things to do than—"

"Would you stop answering for me about my schedule?" he said irritably. "I know what things I have to do. Besides, I have no firm—" He paused, a brilliant idea coming to him. He wanted to prevent Delia from taking these mad risks. And now, he had an excellent means for doing so. "My only firm commitment is Clarissa's house party. You *are* all going, aren't you? I know you were invited."

"I'm afraid—" Delia began.

"*You're* attending, Knightford?" her aunt hastened to say.

"Of course. It's being given by my best friend and my cousin. Why wouldn't I be there?"

"Because you never go to house parties?" Delia said.

"Not 'never.' Rarely. And in any case, how did you happen to know that?" He cast her a speculative look. "Have you been listening to gossip about me again?"

She didn't so much as blush, though she jerked her gaze from him. "It's hard not to listen when there's so much of it. And you don't go to house parties because you're too busy spending your nights in the stews."

"Delia!" Mrs. Trevor said.

"Well, it's true," she said sullenly.

He chuckled. "It is indeed. But I can do without wickedness for a few nights. The question is, can you?"

Though the other two women gaped at him, Delia said smoothly, "Of course I can. I do without wickedness every day."

"Do you?" He shouldn't toy with her. But there was something profoundly satisfying about skirting the edges of the truth and watching her squirm. "I thought everyone enjoyed a bit of wickedness now and then."

"Not respectable young ladies, I should hope," Lady Pensworth said, peering balefully at him over the top of her spectacles.

"Certainly not this young lady," Delia said. "We aren't all like you, sir. I prefer tamer entertainments. And I can find those anywhere."

Delia's mutinous expression fairly dared him to spill her secrets, and he was sorely tempted to do so. But as she'd said, it would merely convince her aunt to banish her to Cheshire, which wouldn't help her situation.

Though he had an idea of what would. "Tamer entertainments do exist everywhere. Especially at house parties. So I see no reason for you not to attend Clarissa's."

Her eyes sparked fires. "We're not talking about my attendance," she said irritably. "We're talking about yours. I suspect you will find it quite dull."

"Not if you're there," he said flat-out.

To his satisfaction, she blushed. And the other two women exchanged glances.

"You know perfectly well that you don't care if I go or not," she said.

"I know no such thing. Why, have you decided not to go?"

"Don't be absurd," Lady Pensworth broke in. "We wouldn't miss it for the world."

Delia blinked. "But . . . But Brilliana cannot go. She won't want to leave Silas. Besides, she's in mourning, so it wouldn't be at all proper. And I would feel awful going without her."

"First of all," Lady Pensworth said, "Silas can stay with the nurse for a few days. It won't hurt anything. Secondly, Brilliana has mourned a full year this week. It would do her good to be around some lively young people after a year in widow's weeds. And you, too."

"Still—" Delia began.

"I never was comfortable with refusing the invitation, niece," her aunt went on, "but you assured me that there would be no young persons there other than the Blakeboroughs."

"That's what Clarissa said," Delia protested, a lie if he'd ever heard one.

"You must have misunderstood my cousin," he interjected.

"Indeed," Lady Pensworth said.

"And I would *like* to attend," Mrs. Trevor said. "It sounds lovely."

"You see?" Lady Pensworth said. "Besides, if Lord Knightford is going, there will clearly be at least *one* young person in attendance, and more will follow once they hear that a man of his consequence will be there. So we are going. All of us." She nodded at him. "Especially since his lordship is taking such care to press the invitation. I shall send my response today, Knightford. If you think it's not too late."

"I know it's not too late." The urge to crow his triumph died when he saw the murderous look on Delia's face. "Don't worry, Miss Trevor. I'm sure it will be an entertaining week."

Not that it mattered. What mattered was keeping Delia out of trouble for a while. And she couldn't be gambling at Dickson's if she was at Stoke Towers in Hertfordshire.

Luncheon was nearly finished, and he'd done what he'd come to do. So after a few more moments of polite conversation, during which Delia glared at him rather fetchingly, he told them he regretted that he had more calls to make.

When he rose to leave, Delia stood, too. "I'll see his lordship out."

"Why, thank you, dear girl," her aunt said. "I'm sure he would get lost otherwise."

Ignoring her aunt's tart remark, Delia led him from the room. As soon as they were in the hall and out of earshot, she muttered, "That was a dirty trick."

"You mean like the dirty trick you played last night by dumping a bottle of wine into my lap? You ruined a perfectly good shirt, you know."

"Is that why you're tormenting me today? I can pay you for the shirt."

"I don't doubt you can. Given the rumors

I heard at Dickson's, you must have acquired a tidy sum by now. You ought to quit before you're caught." He shot her a quelling glance.

Judging from her scowl, she wasn't the least bit quelled. "Is that a threat? If I don't quit, you'll tell my aunt?"

"Don't tempt me."

She glanced about, saw no one near, and tugged him into the parlor they were passing. "What do I have to do to ensure that you allow me to continue my activities? I'm sure I have something you want."

He raked his gaze down her fetching form. "Oh, you have plenty I want, but nothing I can have."

Though she colored at the innuendo, she met his gaze evenly. "That's not true." There was a hint of desperation in her tone. "I know you probably don't find me that pretty, but you did seem to enjoy our kisses in the garden and . . . well . . . I would be willing . . . that is . . ."

God help him. "I do hope you're not implying what I think you are," he clipped out.

Her cheeks shone scarlet now. "I'm just pointing out that if you wanted to, as you put it, 'satisfy' your desires 'without marrying'—"

"I would go to a bloody brothel." Anger roared up in him that she would even consider *selling* herself to keep him quiet. Or think him the sort to gleefully accept such an offer. "You may not believe this, but I am a respectable gentleman. I do not blackmail young women into giving me their virtue. Good day, Miss Trevor."

When he turned for the door, she caught his arm. "It wouldn't be like that. I'd offer myself freely."

He glared down at her. "Would you, indeed?" She clearly actually believed that nonsense. Either that, or their dalliance in the garden had filled her head with moonbeams. Time to shatter that delusion.

Giving her no warning, he pushed her against the wall behind the open door and crushed her lips under his. This time he took her mouth with merciless disregard for her stunned response. And when, to his mingled shock and delight, she let him, he went a step further, allowing one hand to roam freely over her lush hips and the other to cover one breast.

Shamelessly he fondled the soft flesh through her gown and reveled, despite himself, in the hardening of her nipple. With his other hand, he pulled her against the growing thickness in his trousers.

Apparently *that* had an effect on her at last. She tore her lips from his and shoved against his chest, her eyes wide and wary. He broke away, his blood racing and his breath coming as hard as hers.

"You'd offer yourself freely," he growled. "Right." He bent toward her and she flinched, which annoyed him even though he'd deliberately tried to put her on her guard. "As freely as a sacrificial lamb to the altar. No thank you. I do not need a martyr in my bed. Especially one who would regret what she'd done as soon as it was over."

She swallowed. "I wouldn't."

"Well, I would. Because much as I would relish having you beneath me, writhing in the throes of passion, I'm not fool enough to succumb to such temptation when it can only lead straight to a parson's mousetrap."

"I am not trying to trap you into marriage," she protested.

"I know that. But I also know that seduction is a dangerous game, and sometimes the outcome is beyond one's control."

"I—I could be discreet."

"The way you've been discreet in the gaming hells?"

Their mouths were a breath apart, and he fought the urge to close that distance, to take her mouth more gently, explore it more thoroughly . . . throw caution to the winds.

He must have shown the mad urge in his gaze somehow, for her expression turned determined. "We might get along quite well together." As if to make certain he understood, she added, "In the bed, you know."

Bloody hell, those words brought all his need roaring to life again. God preserve him from females whose curiosity about desire was stirred up by a few kisses. Especially when they made him so hard, it hurt.

Uttering a harsh laugh, he braced his hands against the wall on either side of her head. "Trust me, if you and I were ever to share a bed, there would be no 'might' about it. We *would* do quite well together."

Skimming his lips down her cheek to her ear and then to her neck, he tongued the pulse at her throat before murmuring, "*Very* well, I suspect. Despite your assertions earlier, there's a craving for wickedness lurking inside that labyrinthine soul of yours."

He waited until her breath had quickened and her eyes had closed before shoving away from the wall. "But I won't be the one to satisfy it, I assure you."

Her eyes shot open, a strange mix of regret and wounded pride shining in them before they cooled to ice. "Then I guess there's no more to be said."

"Oh, there's one thing more." He put a hint of threat in his voice. "Don't go to Dickson's again. Because I fully intend to be there every night until the house party. And if you show up at the gaming hell, I will expose you."

It was a bluff, of course. Revealing her true identity in that place would drag not only *her* through a scandal but her aunt and her sister-in-law as well, and he wasn't cruel enough to do that. He was trying to help her, not ruin her.

She stiffened. "Then it will be your fault when Brilliana and my nephew and I find ourselves shunned by society."

Damn her for calling his bluff. "For God's sake, if it's money you need, I can loan you some."

That was the wrong thing to say. She drew herself up like a beleaguered queen. "We do not need your charity, sir. Besides, taking a loan from you would ruin us as effectively as your exposing my gaming."

She was right, unfortunately. Frustrated, he dragged one hand through his hair. "You are the most infuriating, annoying chit I've ever met."

Her eyebrows shot up. "I highly doubt that. And you're just angry that you can't blackmail or bully me into doing what you please."

"I am trying to keep you from putting yourself at risk! The thought of some man figuring out your sex and trying to take advantage of it in a dark alley chills me."

"That's why I have Owen."

"Owen might be stalwart, but he's only one man and probably unarmed. He can't fight off a fellow with a knife. Or a pistol."

"Then I will make sure he's armed. Good day, my lord." And before he could counter with another argument, she pushed past him to walk out of the parlor with her back clearly up.

He started to go after her, but what would be the point? Unless he was prepared to make good on his threats, which he wasn't, they couldn't

scare her. Especially as long as her precious Owen
was willing to aid and abet her.

She would "make sure" the damned man was
armed. Right. How the bloody hell did she mean
to do that? And how could she put so much faith
in a footman who didn't even have the courage
to refuse to help her? If not for Owen accompanying her . . .

Ahhh, yes. Owen was the key. She might not
listen to reason, but the footman certainly would.

Stalking out of the parlor and down to the
foyer, Warren asked to speak to Owen. The servant appeared a short while later.

"Walk with me a moment, Owen," he ordered.

With a wary nod, Owen followed him out of
the house.

As soon as they were strolling down the street,
Warren said, "You know that what your mistress
is doing is very dangerous."

The footman paled. "I'm not sure what you
mean, my lord."

Not this again. "Don't take me for a fool. I
know that she's been masquerading as Jack Jones
to gamble in Dickson's." At Owen's defeated
sigh, he added, "Though I don't yet know why.
Perhaps you would tell me."

He bristled at once. "Forgive me, my lord, but I
would never betray the miss's confidence."

Warren was torn between relief that Owen
was so determined to look after his mistress, and

annoyance that the man was so unwisely keeping her secrets.

"All the same," Warren snapped, "while I realize that no one has uncovered her masquerade heretofore, it's only a matter of time before—"

"I agree, my lord. But she won't listen to reason. And I can't let her go to Covent Garden alone."

"Certainly not. On the other hand, if you refuse to indulge her, she might see sense and stay at home."

Owen eyed him uneasily. "You don't know my mistress as well as I do."

"I know she's not stupid. And I should hope that you aren't, either."

"You don't understand—"

"Damn it, Owen, do you mean to stand by and watch her be ruined?"

"Of course not. But unfortunately, my lord, once the mistress gets the bit between her teeth, there's no stopping her."

"Nonsense." Halting to fix the servant with a hard look, he tried another tack. "Either you refuse to take her there from now on, or you will force me to go to Lady Pensworth and get you dismissed."

Delia had called Warren's bluff, but Owen surely wouldn't.

The footman paled. "B-but my lord, what if she won't heed my cautions? What if she goes alone anyway?"

"You'd better find a way to make sure she doesn't. Claim to be ill or in trouble with someone at Dickson's, or whatever you must do." He gave the man his best marquess scowl. "But keep her out of that place. Do you hear me?"

With his shoulders slumping, Owen nodded. "I'll do what I must, even if I have to lock her in her room."

"See that you do."

Confident that he'd taken sufficient steps to keep her safe for now, Warren headed toward Edwin and Clarissa's town house.

The wench would be the death of him yet, with her maddening obstinacy and her foolish risks with her reputation and . . .

Her sweet scent. Her soft sighs. Her satin-skinned throat with the pulse that leapt beneath his kisses. The ones she gave only to him.

His cock instantly came to attention. Damn her to hell. What was it about her that kept him from pushing her from his thoughts? Why did the taste of her still linger on his tongue?

And why did part of him wish he'd taken her up on her scandalous offer?

We might get along quite well together. In the bed, you know.

Yes. They would. That was precisely what terrified him.

Nine

Delia tried to get her wobbly legs to work properly as she headed toward the dining room. Bother the man for arousing both her anger and her desire. The way he'd kissed and fondled her had been the most exciting thing ever to happen to her.

Had she lost her mind? Probably.

Perhaps he was right. Perhaps she *did* crave wickedness. A little. A very little. And only because he'd made it seem so . . . well . . . crave-worthy. She wasn't likely to forget the shockingly amazing feeling of his hand on her breast for a very long time.

She halted outside the dining room. How could she face her aunt and Brilliana as if her whole world hadn't just tilted sideways? What was she to say?

A meow sounded from behind her, and she turned to find Flossie in the window overlooking the street, staring out with her nose to the glass.

Delia came up beside her and glanced out to see Warren striding away from the house.

Oh, Lord. "Not you, too," she chided, taking Flossie into her arms. As the cat strained toward the window, she said, "Stop that, he's gone. Do you think he gives one farthing for you? I swear, that man charms every female who comes into his orbit."

"He does, doesn't he?" said a voice behind her. She jumped, then whirled to find Brilliana watching her with a guarded expression. "He's a very charming fellow."

Delia schooled her features to nonchalance. "When he wishes to be." She slid past her sister-in-law and up the stairs toward the drawing room. The last person with whom she wished to discuss Warren was Brilliana.

That didn't stop her sister-in-law from following her. "You like him. Admit it."

"I do not like him." *Like* was too puny a word for what she felt. She *wanted* him. With a handful of kisses, he'd made her feel the most astonishing . . . hunger for something beyond her ken. It was ridiculous. Especially given his attitude toward marriage.

Because much as I would relish having you beneath me, writhing in the throes of passion, I'm not fool enough to succumb to such temptation when it can only lead straight to a parson's mousetrap.

She snorted. She didn't know whether to be flattered that he would relish having her beneath him, insulted that he nonetheless had no desire to marry her, or disappointed that he'd turned down her proposal for an illicit encounter.

Disappointed? She wasn't disappointed. Truly, she wasn't. "And he certainly doesn't like me."

"I'm not so sure about that," Brilliana said. "He seemed to like you quite a bit at luncheon."

Delia strolled into the drawing room. "Don't be fooled by him." Clearly, her sister-in-law had some notion that Warren was a normal man who behaved in normal ways. Best to disabuse her of that idea. "He likes to bedevil me, that's all."

Brilliana squared her shoulders. "He seemed very insistent upon your attending Lady Blakeborough's house party."

Only so he could keep me from gambling. "Because his cousin put him up to twisting my arm. Clarissa has been throwing me at eligible gentlemen since we first arrived, and no doubt she has invited a score of them to her affair."

"And would that be so awful?"

Delia caught her breath. She kept forgetting that Brilliana assumed that Delia was genuinely looking for a husband. "Awful? No. But I prefer to choose my own gentlemen, thank you very much. Not to be trapped at an estate with those of Clarissa's choosing."

"Or with Lord Knightford."

The words caught Delia by surprise. She'd been so focused on why he was trying to get her out of town that she'd forgotten how intimate a house party could be. How many times they'd be thrown into each other's company. How many chances there might be for kisses and caresses . . .

"You're blushing," Brilliana said.

Delia fought the urge to cover her cheeks with her hands. "I am not."

"Admit it. You wouldn't mind having Lord Knightford as a suitor."

"I told you, he has no interest in me that way. He's a marquess, for heaven's sake. He's not going to marry a mere miss."

Brilliana's eyes narrowed on her. "I saw how he looked at you. If he doesn't wish to marry you, then he certainly wishes something more wicked. But either way, he definitely has an interest in you."

Delia was tempted to tell her sister-in-law everything about her plans to hunt down Reynold's nemesis and make him pay back what he'd cheated them out of, but she kept silent. Brilliana could be rather stuffy about things like propriety, especially where Delia was concerned. At the very least, she would disapprove of Delia's masquerading as a boy and going to gaming hells.

And Brilliana would almost certainly disapprove of Warren's kissing and caressing her.

"You're wrong about Lord Knightford," Delia said. "He has plenty of other places he can go to satisfy his 'wicked' desires. And he's a gentleman, besides. He would never mistreat a respectable lady."

Oh, Lord, she was echoing his protests earlier. But if she were honest, he'd had good reason to be insulted when she'd implied that he might accept her virtue in exchange for his silence. Because despite all the gossip about his cavorting in the stews and in the beds of a few notoriously loose wives and widows, there'd never been a whiff of scandal about him misusing any woman—eligible or otherwise.

Though clearly he had no qualms about pinning *her* against a wall and kissing her senseless.

That was different. She'd wanted him to.

"For your sake, I hope you're right," Brilliana said. "I don't wish to see you end up with a broken heart. I know how that feels."

Delia shot Brilliana a sharp glance, fairly certain that the woman had never lost her heart to Reynold. So who had broken it? "Trust me, my heart is in no danger of being damaged."

Not by the likes of *Warren*, anyway. Only a fool would fall for his brand of charm. Or a woman who was woefully inexperienced at playing sensual games. But eager to try. Like her.

Delia groaned.

Brilliana observed her closely. "I'm merely saying you should be careful."

"And I will be." Oh yes, she would.

Though tonight, she intended to go to Dickson's. To the devil with Warren. Unless he planned to ruin her, he could not act.

But before then, she had to attend a musicale

with her aunt and Brilliana. She had little chance of finding her tattooed gentleman there, but she couldn't get out of it. Aunt Agatha was determined to offer her to gentlemen across London and wouldn't be talked out of the musicale.

At least it wouldn't interfere with her other activities.

Some hours later, they were preparing to set off for the musicale when her aunt's butler whispered something in her ear. When Aunt Agatha blithely announced that Owen was ill with a stomach complaint and would not be attending them, Delia's heart dropped. Owen couldn't be ill. He had to accompany her to Dickson's later.

For the next few hours at the utterly dull musicale, she fretted. She had only two nights left to find her card cheat before the impending house party, and Owen's inability to protect her would hamper her.

So when she, her aunt, and Brilliana returned home, she sneaked down the servants' stairs to Owen's room, as she'd done a number of times before on their nightly jaunts. But when she opened the door, Owen was decidedly *not* looking ill. Indeed, he was in bed, reading a book, fully clothed.

Clearly startled by her appearance, Owen fell to moaning.

Why, that rascal! "Stop that, Owen. You are not ill, and you know it."

He clutched his belly. "Oh no, miss, I think I

ate some bad meat, because my stomach aches something fearful."

She eyed him askance. "You're the worst actor I've ever seen. You couldn't convince a flea that you were sick."

With a tortured sigh, Owen slumped his shoulders. "I told him it wouldn't work. He just wouldn't listen to me."

Trepidation curled about her. "He?"

"His lordship. He was adamant that I was to keep you from returning to Dickson's."

"Was he really? And why did you go along?"

"He said he would have me dismissed if I didn't keep you away."

"That devil!" Ooh, Warren was infuriating! What right did he have to meddle in her life?

The footman cocked his head. "I think his lordship really cares for you, miss."

She snorted. "Lord Knightford doesn't care for anyone, especially not a woman who might catch him in 'a parson's mousetrap.'" That accusation still stung.

"All the same, I think he means what he says."

Perhaps. Men didn't like it when women got the better of them. And it wouldn't be fair to let Owen risk being dismissed. "Very well. For now, I will not go to Dickson's. I have no desire to see you end up destroyed by this battle between me and his lordship."

Relief flooded Owen's face. "Thank you, miss. I confess I didn't know what to do."

Guilt assailed her. She'd never meant to put Owen in such a difficult position. But she knew *precisely* what to do. Without telling Owen, she would go to Dickson's without him. Warren couldn't do a thing about *that*.

She'd be fine on her own. She would simply take one of her brother's pistols for protection. Reynold had shown her how to fire it a few times. As she recalled, it was a fairly simple procedure.

In any case, she probably wouldn't have to use it. Jack Jones roamed the stews often enough that everyone knew and respected him. She would play a few hands of piquet, win some money, see if anyone had a sun tattoo, and then slip out as usual if she found that no one did.

What could possibly go wrong?

～⁓～

Warren was at Mrs. Beard's long past midnight, trying to enjoy himself. Sadly, he wasn't succeeding. Because he couldn't banish Delia from his mind. Two different whores had already attempted to engage his interest and had been unable to do so. It was most uncharacteristic of him.

Now he found himself oddly alone in a sitting room, downing whiskey and wondering if he should go on to another brothel. Or a pub. Or to

St. George's in hopes that he might drum up a game of cards.

Cards made him think of Delia again, damn it. He laid his head back and closed his eyes, trying to picture how she'd looked in that cheery yellow gown. Why did she dress so nicely at home and so badly in society? To put suitors off? Probably.

If she dressed better, other men would almost certainly swarm about her for more than her fortune. He'd never seen her at an evening event. What did she wear then? Pomona green and puce? Fussy bows? Perhaps she draped her head in one of those awful turban hats he disliked . . . or . . .

Lulled by the whiskey and images of turbans, he slid effortlessly into sleep.

The dream began as it always did. *He was blind. No, it was just too dark to see. The lantern had gone out. But how? No wind here in the old cellar.*

A ghost had blown it out. "No such thing as ghosts, no such thing as ghosts," he chanted, squishing himself into the corner.

How his brothers would mock him if they heard.

But they wouldn't hear. They were at Grandmother's. He hadn't wanted to go.

He should have gone.

So now he was truly alone. Except for Pickering. His hateful tutor, Pickering.

Something skittered over his leg. He squealed and kicked out. Someone—something—other than him squealed. A rat. He shuddered. Rats were worse than ghosts.

Jumping up, he stomped about. "Die, die, die!"

Then something crashed, and pain shot through his leg—

"My lord?"

Warren jerked awake, his skin clammy and his heart racing. He wasn't in the cellar. Thank God he was at the brothel.

"Are you well?"

He straightened to find a pretty whore standing in the doorway, regarding him with wary alarm. Bloody hell, he hoped he hadn't said anything.

"I'm fine. I just . . . dozed off." He couldn't believe he'd fallen asleep *here*. That's what came of rising too early to go to Delia's, after staying out all night.

This was *her* fault, damn it. She was upsetting the rhythm of his days, and now the nightmares were catching up with him. God only knew how he'd survive a week in the country, with everyone retiring at some ridiculously early hour.

"Shall I go?" the woman asked, still watching him uneasily.

Don't be a sniveling coward, boy.

"Certainly not." He forced a rakish grin to his lips. He couldn't bear to be alone right now. "I didn't come here to sleep, I assure you."

Relaxing, the woman smiled coyly and sauntered over to him. She was exactly his sort, full-figured and blond and clearly willing to do whatever he would want.

Climbing onto his lap, she ran a soft hand over his cheek. "My lord, you seem very distracted this evening. Perhaps I can take your mind off your troubles."

He truly wished she could. But his troubles centered around a slim, full-hipped debutante with sparkling blue eyes and a sharp wit who made all other women seem rather . . . lackluster, even the buxom blonde who wriggled purposefully on his lap.

In a flash, he remembered Delia's shock when he'd pressed his hardening flesh against her. That shock had rapidly turned into a sweet yielding when he'd approached the second time to kiss and tongue her throat. Just thinking about it made him harden. If it were *Delia* wriggling atop his lap—

Damn it all. This was ludicrous. "How would you propose to take my mind off my troubles?" He would thrust the innocent little Delia from his mind if it killed him. She could keep him from sleeping late in the morning, but he wouldn't let her keep him from this.

The whore slid forward on his lap just enough so she could slip her hand down to cup his cock. It was already erect. But not for her. No, it was for some chit who didn't have the good sense to know when she was wrong.

"I can take care of this," the woman cooed. "If you wish."

He did wish. Except that he wished another woman entirely would take care of it. What idiocy.

"Fine," he said, though in truth he had no desire to engage with this woman when his head was filled with another. She started to position herself over his hard cock, and he said, "No. I want your mouth on me."

Because then he could pretend it was Delia. He could pretend her mouth was engulfing him and her lovely hands were gripping his thighs and . . .

"There you are, Knightford!" said the voice of some fellow he half knew, as the blonde knelt in front of Warren. "I expected you to be at Dickson's, gambling."

Irritated by the interruption, he growled, "Why would I be at Dickson's?"

The gentleman shrugged. "Because Jack Jones is there. And since the two of you didn't finish your game last night, I thought you'd be there demanding another go at it."

God help him! Warren rose, ignoring the whore who was already unbuttoning his trousers. Impatiently, he shoved her hands away and refastened his buttons, his cock already softening. "Are you sure?"

"Of course I'm sure. The lad is hard to miss. And his card playing is even more distinctive. I swear, I've never seen a fellow so adept at . . ."

As Warren headed for the door, he listened to the rest of the fellow's babbling with only half an ear. Delia had lost her bloody mind. And Owen, too, apparently.

He stalked out the door, ready to do whatever he must to take the chit in hand. Now that she and Owen had called his bluff, he had no choice but to make certain she stayed out of trouble. Or get her to leave Dickson's.

That would undoubtedly be a feat. And even as irritation surged through him, another feeling mingled with it. Anticipation at the thought of sparring with Delia.

Bloody hell.

~~~

As soon as he entered the place, Dickson greeted him jovially, but Warren brushed him off and strode straight to the card room. He spotted her at once, playing cards with some dandy. And Owen was nowhere to be seen.

God, she was here without any protection at all. Foolish woman.

He strode up to the dandy and said, "Get up. I have a game to finish with Jones."

The dandy blinked. "But my lord, I have already—"

"What are your stakes?"

"Twenty pounds."

He dug in his coat pocket and came out with a

fifty-pound note. "Here. That's more than double your stake. Get up."

The dandy goggled at the note, then snatched it and jumped to his feet. "You're welcome to him, sir."

Him? Oh, right. Delia was a *him*. Warren kept forgetting that. Probably because the way her eyes glittered at him as he took a seat was decidedly feminine. Only a woman could put that much anger into a mere glance.

"What if I don't wish to play you, m'lord?" she said in her gruff approximation of a male voice.

"You wished to play me last night," he countered. "And you ran off in the middle of the game, no doubt because you thought I was winning."

Her eyes flashed fire. She had to know that a reputation for abandoning a game to keep from losing would make others cautious about playing her. "I do not avoid fights, sir. I merely remembered I was supposed to be somewhere else. I'm sorry we weren't able to finish then, but—"

"We'll finish now." And then he would take her somewhere and put the fear of God into her, if it were the last thing he did. "Sadly, we can't reconstruct the hand from last night. So we'll have to begin that *partie* again. If that suits you."

She hesitated, clearly debating whether she could get away with choosing not to play him. But she had to know that would be frowned upon by the onlookers, who might assume she really *had* run off to avoid losing. "Of course it suits me. I was winning handily after the second *partie*, remember?"

"Hard to know who's winning when the game isn't even half finished." He picked up the deck of cards. "It was your deal last night, wasn't it?"

"It was." Smug satisfaction crept into her voice. "And I had twenty-two points more than you."

"Don't remind me." He shuffled the cards, then set the deck in front of her.

As she dealt, it occurred to him that although she rightfully wouldn't accept a loan from him, he could give her money by letting her win. Which wouldn't be hard, given her skill. Piquet wasn't his game, and he'd never been that fond of cards. It had always been just a way to pass the time in the evening.

So once the game began, he played with his usual haphazard nonchalance. It was only money, after all. God knew he had plenty enough of that.

Somewhere in the next *partie*, she seemed to realize he wasn't taking the game seriously and began to press her advantage. He let her.

Better than having her come here night after night, risking her reputation and forcing him to come here to keep her from trouble. There were still two days until the house party. Anything could happen in that time.

"So where is your friend Owen tonight?" he asked.

She stiffened. "He's ill. Stomach ailment."

"Ah." So she'd come without her guard rather than give up her plans. Reckless chit.

But a clever one. By the fifth *partie*, she was winning by a substantial margin.

"Are you sure you've played piquet before, my lord?" she asked blithely, clearly determined to goad him into giving her a challenge.

"Once in a while. Perhaps after this game, we should switch to vingt-un."

Her brow clouded over. "I don't like vingt-un."

"Because vingt-un has more of an element of chance?"

"Because vingt-un was my father's game," she admitted.

Interesting. "Ah yes, I remember your saying your father was a gambler."

"An avid one. My mother despaired over him."

In that one sentence she told him more about her upbringing than she could have done in hours of polite conversation. Of course Mace Trevor would have been hard to live with. Gamblers usually were.

Warren's brother Hart had been a heavy gambler in school. Fortunately, being an army officer had knocked that tendency out of him. He still played cards, but he'd found a profession that he enjoyed, so he felt less need to spend his time at the tables.

Besides, Warren had been very strict with him after their father had died. He'd not allowed his young brother any funds to pay his gambling debts, and Hart had soon learned not to gamble unless he was prepared to pay for it out of his own pocket.

Delia didn't seem enamored of gambling, just what it could bring her. That no doubt came from having a famous father who'd won an estate with his skill.

"So, Jones," Warren said, determined to make her realize the madness of her scheme, "what do you generally do with your winnings?"

She eyed him coldly. "I have a family, sir. I must take care of them."

"Of course. Though I do wonder if your family is aware of how you go about supporting them."

"It doesn't matter. A man has to do what he must to fulfill his obligations."

He couldn't help snorting. "Indeed, *a man* must. Still, gambling is an uncertain profession, even for someone as skilled as you."

"Then why do *you* engage in it, sir?"

"To entertain myself, of course."

"Only a rich lord would entertain himself by losing money," she muttered.

"I can afford it." He eyed her over his hand. "And I don't always lose."

The barmaid from the previous night sauntered over and leaned down, probably purposely to give him an eyeful of her ample bosom. Which *was* quite nice. A pity he had no interest in it.

"Can I get you anything, my lord?" she cooed.

"He's playing badly enough already, Mary," Delia snapped. "Don't distract him."

Warren glanced at Delia to find her staring daggers at Mary. How interesting. The chit was jealous. Though he generally found jealousy in a woman tedious, in this case he rather enjoyed it. Because it meant she was as susceptible to him as he was to her.

"Ignore my surly friend," Warren told Mary with a wink. "And fetch me a bottle of port. Only don't put it too close to Jones. I don't relish having another shirt ruined."

The onlookers laughed as Delia hunkered down with a scowl.

"And here's something for your trouble," he added, and tucked a sovereign between Mary's breasts, watching to see Delia's reaction.

"Thank you, my lord," Mary said silkily, and ran a hand up his thigh. "I'm happy to give you whatever pleases you. You need only ask."

"Looks to me like he doesn't even need to ask," Delia grumbled.

Warren bit back a smile. "Poor Jones, without a woman to please him. Here's another sovereign for you, Mary, if you go give Jones what you're giving me."

"Gladly, sir," she said, and walked over to Delia.

But as the taproom maid leaned toward "Jones," Delia growled, "Lay a hand on me, Mary, and I swear I'll break it off."

When Mary froze, Warren burst into laughter. Delia was very good at playing the grouchy Jack Jones. If he hadn't known who she was from the beginning, he would never have guessed.

"It's all right, Mary, leave Jones be. You don't want such a grumbler for a companion when there are more amiable gentlemen to be had."

With a sniff, Mary flounced off to fetch Warren's port.

Delia glowered at him from beneath her hat. "Are we going to play or not, sir? Because there are plenty of brothels down the street where you can take your pleasure without wasting my time."

"Sheathe your claws, Jones. I'm beginning to think you envy my prowess with women."

"I don't give a damn about your prowess with women, except when you try to use it to throw me off my game. Now, stop your chattering and play."

With a chuckle, Warren played his first card, and the game was on. Delia played like an exquisite machine, always aware of the perfect strategy and always determined to implement it. He found it fascinating. He'd never met a woman so adept at cards. She understood the game far better than he.

Tonight Dickson himself brought in the port. Hmm. What had the maid said to the fellow?

Whatever it was, he didn't appear disturbed. As he set out a glass and decanted the wine, he asked, "Anything else, my lord?"

"No. Thank you, Dickson."

Dickson nodded and started to leave, then paused near the table. "So, Jack, where is Owen?"

She shot Warren a black look. "He's ill."

Bloody hell. Clearly, she had figured out that he'd attempted to force Owen into staying away.

Dickson was of course oblivious to the undercurrents. "Well, will you tell him that I've been asking around about that lord with the sun tattoo above his wrist? So far I haven't heard anything or found anyone who has such a thing."

Tattoo? Like the ones she'd claimed to have an interest in at the breakfast?

When the color drained from her face and her gaze shot to Warren in alarm, everything shifted in his brain.

He'd completely misread the situation.

This scheme of hers wasn't about money or supporting her family at all. She was *searching* for someone at Dickson's. *That* was why she kept asking questions about tattoos. *That* was why she persisted in coming here, even when Owen wasn't available to protect her.

Bloody hell.

But whom did she seek? And why?

A sudden chill ran through him. Had she been attacked by a man with a tattoo, perhaps at some masquerade? Good God, could she have gone through something similar to what Clarissa experienced?

Then again, if she had, she certainly didn't act like it. Whenever he kissed her, she melted into his arms so sweetly that he—

Damn it, that didn't matter. Whomever she was looking for and whatever the tattooed man meant to her, he intended to find out the truth. Because that was clearly the key to Delia's secrets.

Ten

Delia tore her gaze from Warren. How should she handle this? He would surely find it odd that she'd been asking about some lord's tattoo after she'd expressed an interest in tattoos to *him*.

She needed to come up with a lie to cover her purpose. But first she needed to get rid of the pesky gaming hell owner, who was hovering about the table as if eager to talk about Owen's quest.

"Thank you for the information, Dickson," she said. "I'll be sure to let Owen know."

Dickson shoved his hands in his pockets. "He never said why he was looking for the man."

"I'm sure it's nothing," she said. "Probably idle curiosity about some chap he met here before. I'll pass on the message."

"I told him I didn't see how there could be *any* lords with tattoos, on account of its being such a vulgar practice, but he insisted—"

"*Thank you*, Dickson. I'll see that he's told."

The man blinked, but apparently realized he was being dismissed. With a shrug, he headed back to the taproom.

"Dickson has a point, you know," Warren drawled. "It's very unusual for a lord to have a tattoo of any kind."

A pox on the man. He was a dog with a bone, and *she* was the bone. And she had no desire to see him sink his teeth in her.

Although the thought of his mouth on her . . .

No, she mustn't let that image rattle about in her head or she would lose her ability to trounce him. And she fully intended to trounce him, if only to wipe the smirk off his lips.

An onlooker spoke up. "Sailors have sun tattoos, you know. To show they've crossed the equator. I suppose a lord who's a naval officer might have one."

That was what the sun stood for? Perhaps it would help her narrow her search.

Warren snorted. "Yes, but sailors are one thing. Lords are quite another. Gentlemen don't mark their bodies to announce such things."

"How do *you* know?" she asked. "It's not as if tattoos are easily visible."

"Yes, but I know a few naval officers—friends whom my army officer brother grew up with. I've seen most of them casually dressed but have never spotted a tattoo on them."

"Perhaps not on those particular men, but that

doesn't mean no one has them. Your brother's friends might even know some. I'm sure Owen would like to talk to your brother or his friends."

Warren lifted an eyebrow. "That will be rather difficult. Hart's friends spend most of their time at sea. For that matter, Hart has been posted with his regiment on James Island for a couple of years now. So *Owen* is out of luck. And he's probably looking for someone nonexistent, anyway."

She stared him down. "I'm sure Owen knows whom he's searching for."

"Whatever you say. Seems spurious to me."

Blast Warren. He was making everything difficult. On purpose? She didn't think so, but she honestly didn't know.

They were almost done with the game, anyway. Soon it would be over, and he would leave.

Please, Lord, let him leave.

Warren dealt the cards for the final *partie*. In a short while, she'd finished him off. Even knowing that he had probably let her win, she took a certain pleasure in it.

When they were done, she raked in her winnings. "Thank you, my lord. My family greatly appreciates your generosity."

"Then let's play once more. Give me a chance to recoup my losses."

"I don't think so, sir. You talk too much."

"Afraid to take me on again, are you?"

She bristled. "Just bored with your conversation."

His eyes gleamed at her. "Bored, eh? Well, how about we make it more interesting. We'll up the stakes to a thousand pounds."

Her heart dropped into her stomach. A thousand pounds would go a long way toward forestalling the foreclosure. It was more than she'd taken in during all these weeks of gambling.

Yet the longer she stayed here, the more chance he might expose her. For all she knew, *he* could be the man with the sun tattoo. She hadn't seen his right wrist, only his left. He could even be planning to cheat her.

She sighed. That seemed unlikely. It was probably his way of giving her money to help her out of her situation. Which she would consider lovely and sweet, *if* he had no ulterior motive. And she wasn't sure of that.

Well, if he was fool enough to throw funds at her, she should take them. A gambling debt wasn't the same as a loan, and she could easily trounce him. She'd better. She didn't *have* a thousand pounds.

"Very well," she said smoothly. "A thousand pounds it is. I'll even give you the choice of who deals first."

"Good," he said. "Because this time I mean to prevail."

He could try all he wished. No one ever beat her.

The next game was long, heated, and intense. There was no chatter. No baiting her. Warren seemed determined upon winning, which she preferred. She didn't like knowing that he had let her win the last game.

In the end, of course, she still won. It took an effort for her not to crow over it, but she had no time for that. The hour grew late. She had to be home.

She waited for Warren to hand her an IOU, but instead he said, "I tell you what. My rig is outside. Why don't you come with me, and I'll pay you at my town house? That way you don't have to wait for your funds."

"An IOU is acceptable, sir. I trust you to pay your debts."

She wouldn't let him trap her at his town house, although how she would claim the funds otherwise, she wasn't sure. It wasn't as if Miss Delia Trevor could ask for them. Although Owen could.

"Come now, Jones. It's not far. And afterward, I'll have my coachman take you to wherever you stay."

She hesitated. It didn't sound at all wise to be alone in a carriage with him, even for a short amount of time. "I shall call on you tomorrow, my lord, if you will give me your direction."

"Whatever you wish." He scribbled his address and handed it to her, though his shuttered gaze warned that if he ever got her alone at his town house, matters might go differently than she would like.

He might try to kiss her again. Or caress her. Or—

Stop thinking about that! It makes you go all squishy inside. Which can't possibly be healthy.

Exactly. So she would have to send Owen to claim the funds and hope that Warren wouldn't balk at that. "Thank you, my lord," she said again, and meant it.

With an enigmatic glance, he stood. "Enjoy the rest of your evening."

After he left, she released a pent-up breath. He hadn't exposed her. He hadn't stayed around to badger her. She'd bluffed her way through his threats and won. For now. At last she could go home.

She lingered only long enough to allow Warren a chance to have left the area entirely. Then she walked out the door of Dickson's and started for home.

But she didn't get far. Within moments, a carriage came up next to her, keeping an even pace with her. One look at the crest on the side told her who it must be. Blast the man.

Warren opened the door. "Get in, and I'll take you home."

"I will not, and you will not."

But she had to admit she was tempted. A number of men were on the street, all of them watching her. Or it seemed like it, anyway. She wasn't used to navigating the stews without Owen. She'd never felt so exposed.

Warren ordered the coachman to stop, then climbed out. Picking her up bodily, he tossed her into the carriage. It took her so by surprise that she just sat and gaped at him as he threw himself into the other seat and told the driver to go on.

"You had no right to do that!" she cried as she recovered her wits.

"I certainly didn't. Not that it matters. What can you do to stop me?" He brandished that cocky smirk that maddened her. "Scream for help like a woman? Pretend to be Jones and report me to the magistrate? Who, by the way, has gone drinking with me a time or two. He'd be fascinated to hear about your masquerade as a Welsh male card player."

She crossed her arms over her chest. "What about *your* masquerade as a gentleman? When really you're a bully?"

His smirk disappeared. "Yes, I'm the biggest bully in the world, forcing you not to walk the streets of London alone, keeping you from being attacked by footpads and scoundrels. I cannot believe you came here without Owen."

"You left me no choice. How dare you threaten to have my servant turned off? He nearly had heart failure over it."

"Yet he let you go out without him."

"He doesn't know I did that. I told him I would stay in tonight." She glared at Warren. "Otherwise, he would have felt compelled to go along, thus risking his position. So if you dare to go to my aunt about him when he did nothing wrong—"

"I won't." He leaned forward, eyes glittering. "*If* you answer my questions."

The leashed threat in his stance, the hot intensity of his gaze on her, gave her pause. And did funny things to her insides.

It was maddening. As her blood warmed, she jerked her gaze to the window. "Certainly. What do you want to know?"

"Who's the man with the sun tattoo?"

She sighed. Curse him. "If I knew who he was, why would I have Owen ask around about him?"

"Damn it, Delia, I mean, who is he to *you*?"

"Until I find him, he's no one."

"You are the most stubborn, irritating—" He halted to drag in a deep breath as if to calm himself. "Stop evading the question."

"I'm not evading anything. I'm simply not answering. Because I don't *have* to answer to you." She tipped up her chin. "You're not my relation or suitor or guardian, so it isn't your concern. *I'm* not your concern."

"I've chosen to make you my concern."

"Because Clarissa put you up to it."

He ignored that. "You do realize I can find out the truth with or without your cooperation. I can hire a Bow Street runner, or nose about at St. George's, or speak at length to your aunt and your sister-in-law. I can get to the bottom of it on my own perfectly well, if I so choose."

A knot twisted in her stomach. "Then go ahead," she bluffed. "See what you can learn."

"Very well. I will." He sat back against the squabs, seemingly unperturbed about spending gobs of money hiring investigators.

Oh, Lord, if he went so far, he would surely learn the truth. Then he might figure out the whole sordid story about Reynold, which she didn't want. Bad enough that Aunt Agatha knew. Delia refused to have the whole of polite society knowing about Reynold's suicide. What would a scandal like that do to poor little Silas's future?

She eyed him warily. "You wouldn't *really* hire a runner, would you?"

"If I had to."

"But *why*?" she asked. "Because you claim to be worried about me? You're not the sort of man who gives two farthings about women of good reputation."

He bristled. "You know nothing about the sort of man I am. I have my own reasons for concern. My point is, I don't *need* you to tell me the truth. It may take me a while to get to the bottom of it, but I will. Before I take that step, however, I'm giving you the benefit of the doubt by allowing you the opportunity to explain yourself. Because if you keep on like this, it will surely be the ruin of you."

She thrust out her chin. "I have a weapon on me."

He snorted. "What sort of weapon?"

"One of my brother's pistols."

"And do you know how to use it?"

"Of course. Reynold taught me."

Before she knew what he intended, he was across the carriage, restraining her while he searched her coat.

"Get off me, you big oaf!" she cried, shoving against him, but she was no match for his superior size and strength.

In seconds, he found and retrieved her pistol, then retreated to his side of the coach. Opening the panel to the driver's seat, he thrust it through the opening to his coachman. "Keep this safe, John." Then he shut the panel with a bang.

"You can't do that!" she cried.

"Obviously I can. And so could any other fellow with half a mind to it."

"Give it back. It doesn't belong to you!"

"You'll get it back as soon as you tell me why you're searching for the bloody fellow with the sun tattoo."

"That's none of your concern," she said with a sniff.

"Then I suppose I've just added a pistol to my collection."

Her throat tightened. "You can't keep it! It's one of the few things I have left of Reynold."

He narrowed his gaze on her. "Wait a minute—does all of this have something to do with your brother? Did he gamble at Dickson's, too?"

"Don't be absurd." Lord, he was veering closer

to the truth. And she couldn't have that. The world thought Reynold had died accidentally.

"Because if it does, I can help you. Just tell me what—"

She leaned forward and kissed him. She'd tried everything else to stop his questions, and none of it worked. And he did seem to like kissing her.

He froze, then jerked back. "What are you doing?"

"Kissing you. I know you're familiar with the practice. A woman places her lips against a man's—"

"You're trying to distract me from getting answers."

Placing her hands on his knees, she asked, "And what if I am?"

His gaze dropped to her hands, and his breath grew fractured. "It won't change anything."

Feeling reckless and wild and oddly light-headed, she rubbed his knees. "Are you sure?"

"Yes." Still, he hauled her across the carriage and onto his lap. "But you're welcome to have a go at it, anyway," he growled. Then he brought his mouth down on hers.

It should have alarmed her. It didn't. *This* was what she wanted. He'd made her crave him, and she couldn't help craving his kisses, too.

No, that wasn't it *at all*. She was doing this to get his mind off his questions. That was the only reason.

It was also the only reason she threw her arms about his neck, the only reason she let him clutch her close and drive his tongue into her mouth with quick, sensual strokes. The only reason she squirmed on his lap and turned to pudding in his arms.

He drew back to clasp her head between his large hands, and his eyes swallowed up the night as he stared into hers. "Just to be clear, this discussion isn't over."

As far as she was concerned, it was. "Shut up and kiss me."

Heat flared in his face. "With pleasure."

He seized her mouth once more, taking and conquering and intoxicating her. The odor of port and cigars overwhelmed his usual scent of spicy cologne, which should have put her off. Instead it made her ache for more kisses, more touching, more *everything*.

Honestly, how could she not have known that a man could make a woman feel so delicious? His whiskers scraped her chin and even *that* was a sensual delight. Her blood felt near to boiling over, and she wanted, *needed* more.

So when, after he'd feasted for a while, he slid his hands down to cover her breasts, she let him. Oh, Lord.

She'd never bound her breasts, trusting to her lack of a corset, her oversize coat and waistcoat, and her voluminous cascading cravat to hide her modest attractions. But that, of course, now meant it was far too easy for him to . . . touch them once he pushed her cravat aside and unbuttoned her waistcoat.

Thumbing her nipples through her shirt, he pressed his mouth to her ear. "These, my dear, deserve to be better displayed."

"Do they?" She couldn't breathe for fear he would stop. Her skin felt alive, her heart ready to explode, and her nipples, which he'd begun to pluck, tingled and grew taut beneath his caress. "You don't find my bosom too . . . too small?"

His eyes gleamed in the gaslights from the street. "Not particularly. But I can't be sure without examining them more . . . thoroughly." Opening her waistcoat, he bent to seize one breast in his mouth through her shirt.

"Oh. My. Word!"

With a chuckle, he flicked his tongue over her nipple, then sucked hard on it before drawing back to murmur, "I need to make an even closer inspection."

Unbuttoning her shirt, he pulled it open to bare one of her breasts entirely.

She should protest. She should get off his lap.

Instead, she reveled in the way his eyes slid closed as he laved her nipple with rough lashes of his tongue.

"I find your breasts delicious in every way," he rasped.

Gratified, she pressed her breast into his

mouth and clasped his head closer. "I find *this* so . . . ohh . . . so very . . ."

"I believe we've established that you *do* feel the same urges that a man feels. Thank God."

Thank God, indeed. Though now she didn't know what to do with all this . . . excitement. Her pulse ran amok, and her body ached to have him crawl inside her clothes and touch every inch of her.

"Damn, I just want to devour you," he muttered under his breath, and opened the shirt more so he could suck her other breast.

"Yes. Do."

"Careful, brat, or you'll . . . infect me with your recklessness." He dragged his mouth up to her neck to tongue the hollow of her throat.

"I think . . . I . . . already have."

"In that case . . ." He slid his hand between her legs to rub her at the jointure of her thighs, through the fabric.

Heavens, it felt good. So *good*. Much better than when she'd touched herself there. Or perhaps that was because *he* was doing it.

"Be glad you're wearing trousers," he said as he fondled her shamelessly through them. "Because if you were wearing skirts, it wouldn't be my hand there but my mouth."

His mouth? On her *privates*?

"That sounds . . . interesting." So interesting that something dampened her trousers, as if he already had his mouth on her.

He froze, and she wondered if he'd actually felt the dampness. "Delia," he said, "we must stop."

"Must we?" she choked out.

Even as he kept caressing her and nuzzling her neck and making her want to fly, he said hoarsely, "Yes. Before I embarrass myself."

"I don't . . . understand."

"When a man becomes aroused . . . Never mind, it isn't an appropriate conversation."

She wriggled against his hand, which was *still* fondling her. "I think we've . . . gone beyond appropriate. Besides, we always have inappropriate . . . conversations. That's why you . . . find me . . . charming, remember?"

"Too damned charming by half," he growled and took her mouth once more.

She could feel the bulge in his trousers pressing against her bottom, and she wondered how it would be to touch it, caress it the way he was caressing her—

The carriage shuddered to a halt, and both of them froze. She looked out to see that the coachman had pulled up in the mews behind the houses. Oh, Lord, what was she doing, letting him caress her like this?

She scrambled off his lap and buttoned her shirt up while he sat there panting, his hands curling into fists on his knees as if he fought the urge to grab her again.

Her body was on fire. And there was no way to douse the flames, even if she wanted to. Which she didn't. No one had *ever* made her feel like this. It thrilled and terrified her all at the same time.

He gave a shaky breath. "Delia, I didn't mean to—"

"I have to go." She had to escape him, to get to her room before she did something insane—like tear the rest of her clothes open and beg him to take her.

Before Warren could stop her, she opened the door and climbed out, then took off at a run through the gate.

"Delia!" he hissed behind her. "Damn you, come back here!"

Not a chance. She heard the carriage door open, heard him vault out after her, but she was quicker than he and she knew the backyard well. She'd already found the unlocked window and slipped inside the house before he'd even made it past the back gate.

Sure that the darkness had hidden her entry place from him, she stood by the window, heart pounding, listening for him to leave. What if he didn't? What if he roused her aunt and demanded answers of her?

The fear of that reminded Delia that her waistcoat still hung open. As she buttoned it up, her hand accidentally brushed the damp spot on her shirt where he'd sucked her nipple through the fabric. She stifled a groan. Thank heaven their mad interlude had been interrupted. It could never have led to anything but her ruin.

Oh, but part of her wouldn't mind being ruined. Indeed, she was surprised more women weren't ruined regularly.

She heard him mutter a curse just outside, and her pulse jumped.

"Come out for a moment, Delia," he said in a low voice, so near that she caught her breath. "I know you're in there, and we haven't finished our discussion."

Bother the man. Could he actually hear the beating of her heart, the heavy breaths she strove futilely to restrain? Of course he couldn't—that was silly.

And thank heaven Flossie had apparently abandoned her usual habit of waiting by the window for Delia's return, or the cat would surely have yowled at him. Or perhaps not, given his perverse effect on every female within his orbit.

His voice sounded again, husky and deep and so tempting, it made her ache. "We're not done, Delia Trevor. You *will* tell me your secrets one day soon. Or I will find them out on my own, I swear."

A shiver swept through her. A shiver of alarm, of course. Not of anticipation of their next battle, their next encounter. That would be daft.

He was making her daft.

She heard his footsteps recede, heard the carriage leave. Only then did she make her slow and stealthy way through the house, as she'd done many a night before.

This time she'd cut it rather close, and it was

all his fault. It had to be near dawn. If she weren't careful, she'd run into the servants coming to light the bedchamber fires. And Aunt Agatha always rose early, too, with Brilliana not far behind. They both thought Delia quite a layabed for her late rising.

Increasing her pace down the hall, she nearly wept with relief when she reached the door to her room. At last this interminable night was over.

A meow from the floor alerted her to Flossie's presence.

"Shh, puss," Delia whispered as she bent to pick up her pet. "Was I too late? You got tired of waiting?"

Cuddling the purring cat close, Delia slipped inside her room.

"Where on earth have you been?"

Delia jumped and nearly screamed before she caught herself.

Not that stifling her cry would save her from retribution. Because sitting on the bed was her sister-in-law, her eyes red, her nose swollen, and her mouth thinned with worry.

Brilliana rose and picked up the candle burning low on the bedside table. "And why in heaven's name are you wearing *that*?"

Blast. Delia had forgotten about her men's attire.

Apparently, her interminable night wasn't over after all.

Eleven

Slowly Warren returned to where his coach waited in the mews. He was still aroused from their utterly unwise intimacies. That had been too close, too reckless. She hadn't stopped him; he hadn't stopped. If they hadn't arrived at her aunt's house, who knew what might have happened?

"Home, my lord?" the coachman asked as Warren reached the coach.

"You go on. I'll walk to wherever I wish to go."

"Very good, my lord."

As the carriage pulled away, Warren turned back to look at the Pensworth town house. Truth was, he didn't know where he wished to go next. By the wee hours of the morning he usually *was* heading home, since his nightmares fled once the sun rose to flood his bedchamber with light.

But right now, the thought of entering his large and silent abode and climbing the stairs to his bedchamber with its cavernous, empty bed struck him as so lonely he could hardly bear it.

He scowled.

Ridiculous. He wasn't lonely. He could have a female companion any time he wanted.

So why the devil was he standing here, staring at a dark house in Bedford Square at four in the morning?

And why was the house dark, anyway? Were there no candles lit anywhere inside? If Delia had made it to her room—which surely she had by now—he doubted that she'd be moving about in the dark to prepare for bed.

Telling himself he just wanted to be certain she'd reached her room without being caught, he left the mews and circled around to the front of the house. Ah, on this side there was indeed a single candlelit room, up in the corner. It must be hers. And if she *had* been caught sneaking in, there would be far more candles showing in windows, so she must have managed not to rouse anyone.

He could leave now. She was safe.

Yet still he stood watching the damned window. About now, she'd be peeling off that shirt and those ridiculous trousers. The ones he'd rubbed her through. The ones that had dampened beneath his caresses.

He groaned. She had grown wet for him. Because once he'd foolishly introduced Delia to the pleasures of the flesh, she'd fully embraced them. And that was his fault. He shouldn't even have kissed her, much less sucked and fondled her.

Yet he would do it again if he had the chance. The feel of her beginning to come apart beneath his hand . . .

As his cock stiffened once more, he growled a curse. This was absurd. He should go to a brothel, take care of this pesky erection. Or go home, for God's sake.

Instead, he used his key to the Bedford Square Gardens and slipped inside. He found the private spot where they'd kissed yesterday, where she'd first made him so aroused he could hardly hide it. Opening his trousers and drawers, he seized his cock and allowed his imagination free rein.

Delia had been bare beneath the shirt. Had she been bare beneath her trousers, too? She must have been, for him to have felt her dampness through the fabric as he caressed her. God, she'd been so wet and willing. How he wished he could have taken advantage of that.

Pumping his cock in his hand, he imagined her in her room. Was she naked now or had she already donned some fussy nightdress? Had she taken down her hair? He didn't even know if it was naturally curly or forced into ringlets by a hot iron. But he could still imagine the black silk of it cascading over her shoulders, all the way down to that winsome bottom of hers that he would love to grab and squeeze—

He came with a vengeance, spurting into the bushes as he stifled his moans. Then he stood there shaking, his hand sticky and his skin clammy.

After a moment of savoring his release, he felt the reality of where he was and what he was doing creep over him. Good God. He rarely pleasured himself. There was no need, when he could find a willing wench at every turn.

And to have done it in a semi-public place like some drunken lout . . . clearly he'd lost his bloody mind. Thank God no one was about in Mayfair at this hour, even servants or tradesmen.

Using his handkerchief to clean off his hand, he restored his clothing to respectability, then left the garden and hurried away from Bedford Square. He still wasn't sure where he was going, but he knew it had better be somewhere well away from Delia Trevor.

Because the more he delved into her secrets, the more fascinated he became, and that would not do. She was an innocent; he couldn't have a torrid affair with *her*.

Nor was he looking for a wife—certainly not some chit who recklessly gambled in the hells dressed as a man. Who'd mysteriously taken on a mission involving a tattooed lord, of all things, and blithely refused to tell him why.

Who went after whatever she wanted with a single-minded purpose and a refusal to be cowed by the obstacles. Damned if he didn't admire her for that.

But that didn't change the fact that marrying her would mean the end of his life as it was now. It would mean settling down at Lindenwood Castle, where the nights were always long and filled with nightmares. He wasn't going to let any woman see him like that. And she wouldn't settle for a marriage spent in town so he could roam the stews until the wee hours of the morning. What woman would?

Not that he wanted to marry her. Good God. He merely lusted after her. No great surprise that he should desire her; he was a randy fellow. Though he'd never in his life stood outside some woman's bedchamber boxing the Jesuit as a result of that desire.

Still, it was just an annoying attraction that had to be squelched. If he had any sense at all, he would cut all ties with her. He would stay away from Dickson's and go back to his old habits. Hell, he shouldn't even go to that damned house party of Clarissa's. Clarissa wouldn't think twice about it if he didn't. He'd done what she'd asked of him. Mostly.

He sighed. The problem was that cutting ties with Delia wouldn't change her behavior one whit. She would probably go to Dickson's on her own tomorrow night and get into some trouble, without him or Owen to look after her. Then she would spend all her time at the house party trying to peek up men's sleeves, looking for her quarry. Someone would take umbrage or misunderstand, and next thing she knew, she'd have some fellow trying to accost her in a secluded garden.

Some fellow like you.

"Shut up," he told his conscience. It wasn't the same.

He snorted. The hell it wasn't.

Regardless, he couldn't just let her go off alone to either place. If something were to happen to her, Clarissa would never forgive him.

He would never forgive himself.

Bloody hell.

Fine. He would go to Dickson's tomorrow night and the house party the next day, and *then* he would wash his hands of her.

If he could.

⌇

As Delia finished removing her men's clothes and donning her nightdress, Brilliana paced the room in her wrapper.

"Let me get this straight. You've been gadding about London late at night in men's clothing to *gamble?*"

"To find the wretch who cheated Reynold," Delia said defensively.

Pity suffused Brilliana's face. "Oh, my dearest . . ."

"Don't give me that look! I know Reynold was telling the truth about the fellow, even if you don't believe it."

"I'm not saying I don't believe it. But we don't know *why* he was in London. How can we be sure he told the truth about the gambling? I mean, he wouldn't even reveal the name of the man who cheated him."

"Because the man was of too high a consequence to confront." Delia's blood ran cold. "Wait, what are you saying? That Reynold lost the money some other way?"

With a sigh, Brilliana sat down delicately on the edge of the bed. "Of course not. The sum was too great, and if he'd made some poor investment, he would have admitted that."

"And surely he wouldn't have invented a man with a tattoo. That was a very specific detail."

"I know. I've been over and over it in my head. None of it makes sense." Brilliana cast her a worried glance. "But that doesn't change the fact that you shouldn't be going about London alone to play cards! What if some fellow tries to fight you? Or . . . Or . . ."

"Owen goes with me."

Brilliana lifted an eyebrow. "Not tonight. He was ill. I went down to look in on him before I came to bed, and he was there."

"True. That's why I brought Reynold's pistol with me tonight."

"Delia!"

The shocked cry went right over Delia's head as it dawned on her that Warren's coachman still had Reynold's pistol. For that matter, the marquess still owed her a thousand pounds. Bother it all.

"I've been gambling for weeks," Delia said. "No one has caught me yet." Well, except his cursed lordship.

"Wait a minute." Brilliana shot up from the bed, startling a hiss from the dozing Flossie. "*That's* why you've pushed Aunt Agatha to stay here longer? So you can do this mad thing? Not so you can find a husband?"

Delia shrugged. "I don't want a husband."

"But Delia—"

"I don't want either of us forced to marry for money, curse it!"

"Oh, sweetheart." Brilliana came over to lay her arm about Delia's shoulders. "Everything will work out for us somehow."

"I don't see how." Tears started in her eyes, which she wiped away. "If you marry, your husband may allow me to stay at Camden Hall, but more likely he will not. And if you don't marry, we'll lose it entirely . . ."

All the worries of the past year overwhelmed her, and tears escaped to slide down her cheeks. It wasn't fair. Reynold shouldn't have gambled, shouldn't have been cheated out of everything.

Shouldn't have killed himself.

Clucking her tongue, Brilliana tugged her into her embrace. "There, there, my dear. It's not as bad as all that. We're not even sure I can find a husband. And even if I do, I'll try to make your staying at Camden Hall a condition of whatever marriage I agree to." She held her, soothing her for a few moments.

Once Delia had regained her composure, Brilliana added, "But I still say you deserve better than a life of servitude to the estate."

"Like a husband who will risk his entire family's future on the turn of a card?" Delia regretted the words the instant Brilliana paled. "I'm sorry. I shouldn't have said that."

After a quick squeeze, Brilliana released her. "Look, I know you've watched Reynold and me have a rather . . . cool marriage, but that's as much my fault as his. I couldn't love him, so—"

"I don't blame you for that," Delia said. "Your father essentially sold you to pay his gambling debts to Papa. Reynold should never have accepted that situation."

"It's not as if your brother hadn't wanted to marry me already, you know. He offered for me even before our fathers got involved."

"And you turned him down. He should have honored that, instead of letting Papa push your father into arranging the marriage, anyway."

Her sister-in-law glanced away. "I accepted Reynold's offer the second time."

"Because they gave you no choice."

"That's not true. I could have said no."

"And watched your parents go to debtor's prison. It wasn't right." Delia crossed her arms over her chest.

"True, but I don't blame Reynold for that. I blame my father."

"Is that why you don't speak to him anymore?"

Brilliana shrugged.

Delia patted her hand. "Surely you blame *my* father as much as you blame yours."

"I suppose." Brilliana forced a smile. "And yet, my marriage to your brother gave me Silas. So how can I regret it? Besides, things weren't all bad between Reynold and me. He was a good man. We had a rocky start, but we'd begun to find our way—"

"Until he went off to London to gamble." Delia shook her head. "I'll never forgive him for that."

"I've forgiven him. Why can't you?"

Delia didn't know how to explain it. She just knew that Reynold had thrown all her beliefs about his character into disarray, and she didn't know how to get back to where she'd been. "The point is, I don't blame you for not loving him. I truly don't."

Seeming to pull into herself, Brilliana went to stand by the window and look out at the rising sun. "There's more to it than that."

"What do you mean?"

"Nothing." She turned from the window to fix Delia with a stern look. "And you're trying to change the subject. You cannot keep dressing as a man and running about Covent Garden alone. It's too dangerous."

"Brilliana—"

"I mean it! I refuse to let you risk your future for the sake of Camden Hall."

"I've made fifteen hundred pounds so far." Assuming that Warren paid his debt to her.

"Good Lord." Brilliana dropped onto the window seat. "So much?"

"Yes. It will go a long way toward erasing the debt. At least it ought to delay the foreclosure." Though not nearly for long enough.

Brilliana digested that in silence for a moment, her expression showing her divided feelings. Then she squared her shoulders. "All the same, you should quit before you're caught and ruined."

"Not until I find that card cheat and make him pay back what he stole."

"How do you mean to do *that*?" When Delia explained her plan, her sister-in-law blanched. "That is madness! If you corner this lord and threaten him, he'll have nothing to lose, no reason not to murder you rather than risk being exposed as a cheater."

"It will be fine, trust me."

"I do trust you. It's the men surrounding you whom I don't trust." Rising to her feet, Brilliana stared her down. "And it will be fine, I agree. Because you're not doing it anymore."

Delia drew herself up. "You can't stop me."

"I can." Brilliana crossed her arms over her chest. "If the choice is having you end up dead in some street or our having to marry for money,

I'd rather the latter. So if you won't stop of your own accord, you'll force me to go to Aunt Agatha—and you know perfectly well that she will whisk you right back home, and that will be an end to your activities."

Delia sighed. Brilliana wasn't making idle threats. Once she made up her mind about something, she acted. And she'd clearly made up her mind about this. "Is there no way I can talk you into going along with my plans?"

"None."

With an unladylike oath, Delia dropped onto the bed.

Softening, Brilliana came to sit next to her. "Come now, dearest, there are better ways to handle this. With the money you've already amassed, we can whittle away at the debt. I've been reading up on estate management, and trying to figure out if I could make some changes— improve our situation."

"There's not enough time for you to learn everything that my fool of a brother refused to teach us," Delia said.

Brilliana stiffened. "Perhaps not. But still, you might find a nice gentleman to marry at your friend Clarissa's house party, you know. And then you'll be well out of this mess."

"Without seeing you and Silas happy and secure first? No thank you."

"Delia . . ."

"Look, you can make me go to parties and

balls and flit about society with you and Aunt
Agatha. You can even make me stop gambling
in the hells. But you can't make me marry some
fool and leave you and Silas to fend for your-
selves. I won't do it."

It was Brilliana's turn to sigh. "Then I suppose
we'll be struggling through this together."

Delia slanted a glance at her. "That's not such
a bad thing, is it?"

"Not for me, it isn't." Brilliana hugged her. "But
I think you're worrying for nothing. We might
each find a nice gentleman at the house party,
someone we can love, who will solve all our
money troubles."

"You're not bothered that it's being thrown by
Clarissa, whom you keep avoiding?"

"I'm not avoiding her. Honestly, I don't know
where you get these ideas. I don't even know her."

"You'll like her, I swear. Except her matchmaking can be annoying."

"Undoubtedly," Brilliana said distantly. Then
she apparently shook off her odd mood, for she
added, "And if you really want to gamble, I'm
sure there will be games there. They won't be for
great stakes, but—"

"Don't worry about it," Delia said. "I'm not
like Papa, or, apparently, Reynold. I don't gamble
for the fun of it. I could go my whole life without ever gambling again. I don't need any sort of
stakes to enjoy playing cards."

Then it dawned on her. Clarissa *had* hinted

that she was inviting a number of eligible bachelors to Stoke Towers. No doubt they would be men of rank.

Delia's eyes narrowed. And who was to say that the tattooed lord might not be among them? So she didn't have to give up her efforts to find him. Perhaps Clarissa's house party wouldn't be a waste, after all.

"All the same," Brilliana said, "you ought to relax and enjoy this party. Who knows when we'll have another chance to live so lavishly at someone else's expense?"

"True." And who knew when she'd get another chance to find Reynold's nemesis?

She would simply make sure she got a glimpse of the wrist of every fellow there. Not even Brilliana or Warren could stop her from doing *that*. And if she happened to play a few games of cards along the way to trap a card cheat, then so be it.

Twelve

Warren's carriage pulled up in front of Stoke Towers long past the dinner hour. That was sure to earn him a tongue-lashing from Clarissa, but he didn't care. He had only come to their house party to make certain all was well with the Trevor ladies. And to discreetly pay Delia the thousand pounds he owed her. He might not even stay once that was done. There was no need.

Because Delia hadn't shown up at Dickson's last night, which meant she'd come to her senses. Either he had frightened her off, or stealing her pistol had made her cautious, or . . .

His advances had alarmed her.

If they had, he ought to be happy about it. Yet he wasn't. He didn't like thinking that their kisses and caresses might have made her wary of him. That she might be avoiding Dickson's to avoid *him*. Because that smacked too much of what had happened to Clarissa.

Damn it, it wasn't the same. Delia had been willing. She had practically thrown herself at him. She had been wet for him, had wanted him.

And the feeling was so mutual that he'd barely stopped thinking about their encounter ever since it had happened. He kept wondering how it might have felt to have her mouth on his chest, her hand on his cock, her—

God, he had to stop this madness! As soon as he was sure that Delia had attended the party and was behaving herself, and as soon as he managed to give her the money he owed her, he could leave.

He *would* leave. To hell with the mystery of the tattooed lord. He was done trying to protect a woman who didn't even want his help.

A few moments later, a servant showed him into Edwin's large drawing room, which was a scene of absolute chaos. Eligible young ladies chattered as they pawed through large boxes, eligible young bachelors laughed and measured each other—measured each other?—while Edwin's brother-in-law, the artist Jeremy Keane, set up an easel.

Warren hunted the room for Delia and spotted her with her sister-in-law, the two of them holding up what looked like togas. No longer wearing mourning, Mrs. Trevor was more beautiful than ever, but it was Delia who drew his attention.

She wore another horror of a gown—something

that combined sprigged pink muslin with orange ribbons and enormous sleeves—yet all he could see was the animation in her lovely features as she laughed at something Mrs. Trevor had said.

His chest tightened. It must be dyspepsia from his dinner. What else could it be?

Determinedly, Warren turned his attention away from the two ladies to see Clarissa dictating instructions to a footman. He headed toward her.

"What's all this?" he asked as he approached.

Breaking into a smile, she sent the servant off and approached to greet him with a kiss on the cheek. "You came! I thought you weren't going to." She drew back to look him over. "I would chide you for missing dinner, but I'm just so glad you're here."

"And what exactly am I here *for*?" He surveyed the room. "Wait, don't tell me. You and your guests are running off to join the circus."

She cast him a mock frown. "Don't be ridiculous."

"Taking acting roles at the Olympic Theatre? Planning to overthrow the government and reinstitute Roman rule? Starting a toga shop to be operated out of Stoke Towers? Edwin won't like that one bit."

"Would you stop your nonsense and let me explain?"

"By all means, explain. If you can."

"It was actually Delia's idea."

Of *course* it was. "What has the chit done now?"

Clarissa sharpened her gaze on him, and he realized what he'd said. For all Clarissa knew, the last time he'd seen Delia was when he'd danced with her at the breakfast.

He hurried to cover his slip. "You *do* seem to think she's in some sort of trouble."

"Is that why you paid a call on her a few days ago and convinced her to attend my house party?" Clarissa's voice held a certain glee. "Yes, I heard all about it from Lady Pensworth. All the interesting little things you said to persuade my friend that you *wanted* her to go."

Damn. "You asked me to keep an eye on her."

"How very . . . diligent of you, considering that I had to twist your arm to do so in the first place. You said that you would only do it if I allowed you to beg off this party. And now you're here to look in on Delia?"

Uh-oh. "I'm here to see *you*, of course. I missed you in London."

"I've been gone two days," she said archly, clearly not the least convinced.

So he changed the subject. "Are you going to tell me what all this is about or not?"

"All right." Sparing him an assessing glance, she turned to gaze out over the room. "As soon as the Trevors and their aunt sent their acceptance, I invited them to come up earlier than the others today so we could visit a bit before the rest of the guests arrived. So while we were talking this morning, Delia suggested that it might be fun to have Jeremy do a sketch of the house party guests. She said we could even wear costumes for it, if we had them. I loved that idea, so we started chatting about it, and eventually we decided on a Roman theme."

He stifled his snort. "*We* decided? You and Miss Trevor?"

"And Mrs. Trevor, who is a perfectly lovely woman. Did you know that she wants to try her hand at china designs for Wedgwood? Jeremy thought that was a fine—"

"Clarissa!" he said sharply. "The costumes?"

She sniffed. "*Anyway*, that was part of the reason we girls decided on Roman attire, since, as Delia pointed out, it would give Mrs. Trevor a chance to sketch some scenes herself. And Jeremy thought the whole idea quite grand, too. Consequently, Edwin sent servants off to London to borrow costumes from his friend who runs the Olympic Theatre, and there you have it. Part of our entertainment for the house party."

"I see." Oh yes, he saw a great deal more than his oblivious cousin. Delia was manipulating the situation to her own advantage.

Suddenly Clarissa huffed out a breath. "Oh, dear, those fellows over there are going to destroy the sandals with their tomfoolery. I must go."

And like the whirlwind that she was, she hurried off to lecture some reckless bucks in the corner.

Warren took the opportunity to saunter over

to where Delia now stood alone, examining a box full of headpieces that looked vaguely Roman.

Moving up next to her, he said, in a low voice, "We missed you at Dickson's last night."

She froze, then cast a furtive glance around them. "Keep quiet, for pity's sake. Someone might hear."

"No one is paying attention to us. And I figured this might be my only chance to get you alone and tell you I brought the thousand pounds I owe you."

She arched an eyebrow at him. "And my pistol? Did you bring that, too?"

"I'll hold on to that for a bit. Perhaps it will encourage you to behave sensibly."

"By *your* estimation," she muttered. "I think I've been behaving sensibly all along."

"You've certainly found a sensible way to hunt for your tattooed lord at Clarissa's house party."

She flushed. "I don't know what you mean."

"Weren't you the one to suggest a sketch involving Roman attire? It's very clever. Every gentleman's forearms will be bared, and you can look for your sun tattoo to your heart's content."

She shot him a suspiciously sweet smile. "I suggested it because Roman masquerades are all the rage. Didn't you know?"

"Hmm. I'm afraid I missed that bit of gossip."

Dropping her gaze to the headpieces, she said, "So, do you mean to participate in our little endeavor, too?"

Her not-so-subtle reasons for asking roused his temper. "You would dearly love it if I said no, wouldn't you? It would give you another reason to keep up your guard around me, because you could safely assume *I* am the villain you seek."

Glancing at him in surprise, she asked, "What makes you think I seek a villain?"

He stared her down. "Because you wouldn't hide your search if you were looking for someone trustworthy."

With a sniff, she picked up a gold-colored laurel leaf wreath. "An interesting theory. But you have no proof of any of this."

He bent to whisper in her ear. "Not yet. But I will."

"I wouldn't count on it." With a frown, she moved away. "Impossible to have proof of something that doesn't exist."

"Uh-huh." Damn, but she was stubborn.

And for some reason, that renewed his determination to unveil her secrets. Just seeing her again roused his blood more than any woman he'd ever met. Because any female who could come up with such a creative solution to her situation was a rare creature worthy of study. Worthy of sparring with.

Worthy of marrying.

He scowled. *Don't even think it. You know it wouldn't work.*

Yet he couldn't seem to make himself do the rational thing and leave the place. Instead, he followed her as she went to examine another box. "So when does your 'little endeavor' begin?" he asked.

Relief that he'd dropped the subject of her secrets flashed over her face. "Tomorrow. Tonight we're just picking out our costumes and such. Then, in the morning, Mr. Keane will begin sketching us in small groups, so the others can entertain themselves while two or three are being sketched. He says he can put everyone together later in one big image."

"I'm sure he can." He picked up a helmet that was too warlike for his taste. "And what are you wearing for this grand sketch?"

"You'll just have to wait and see, won't you?"

Her coy smile threw him entirely off guard. He'd never seen her coy. He'd barely even seen her flirtatious.

He enjoyed it. A great deal. He would like to see more of it.

In that moment, he flashed on the woman she *could* be if she didn't have to spend every waking moment worrying about how to take care of her family. He imagined a woman in her youthful exuberance, capable of teasing a gentleman and simply having fun with friends. A woman whose clever mind could be put to better use than card games. A woman who, in her full glory, could take society by storm. If only she didn't have the weight of the world on her shoulders.

To shake off that unnerving thought, he asked,

"Tell me, Miss Trevor, what should *I* wear for this sketch?"

Her pretty eyes brightened. "Why, Lord Knightford, you would trust me to choose your costume?"

"Judging from the sudden glee on your face, perhaps not."

She tucked her hand in the crook of his elbow and drew him across the room. "I can think of a few things I'd enjoy seeing you wear. Sackcloth. Ashes. Perhaps something called humility."

He chuckled. "Those aren't very Roman."

"True. The caesars weren't remotely humble." She smiled up at him. "So I suppose we'll have to settle for a toga for you."

"I'm game. As long as it's not short."

She laughed. "Why? Do you have knobby knees?"

What he had was a scar that might rouse comment. "Something like that."

"It can't be *that* bad. I tell you what. If you let me choose *your* costume, I'll let you choose mine."

"I don't think that's wise." He leaned down to murmur, "Because my choice for you would be a costume too scandalous for polite company. Or better yet, no costume at all."

Sucking in a breath, she rewarded him with a vivid blush that set fire to his blood. Amazing that the woman could still blush after her weeks hanging about a gaming hell. He must provoke her into it more often—it turned her cheeks such a lovely pink.

She released his arm. "Well, then, I suppose we'd best stick to choosing our own attire, since we can't trust each other with even such a small endeavor."

"Not true. I trust you with many things, big and small." Warren locked his gaze with hers. "It's you who won't trust me with a damned thing."

Swallowing hard, she walked off to approach a box overflowing with tunics and togas. "Oh, look, this one might fit you," she said brightly as she held up some regal-looking approximation of Roman garb.

She was changing the subject, her usual response when he tried to get at the truth. Very well. He would let her hide from him a little longer. Because this house party would give him the chance to speak privately with her aunt and sister-in-law as much as he liked, while Delia was busy looking for tattoos on gentlemen's arms.

If *she* wouldn't reveal the truth, perhaps they would. Or at least they could give him some hints about how to proceed.

So he would stay and stick this out. In for a penny, in for a pound. He would find out what the tattooed man had done to gain her ire, and then he would make sure that wrong was redressed.

Then perhaps he could put this odd interlude

out of his mind with a clear conscience, knowing he'd done all he could for her, and go back to his life of fulfilling his duties by day and wenching and drinking by night. Never alone, yet somehow always lonely.

Funny how that didn't sound all that appealing anymore.

Thirteen

Late the next morning, Delia wandered among the costumed guests gathered in the breakfast room, helping themselves to steamy heaps of shirred eggs, piles of sausages, towers of toast, and slabs of butter so creamy they could only have come straight from the estate dairy.

But the food didn't interest her as much as the costumes. While the ladies had dressed demurely, wearing floor-length tunics over their usual petticoats, with gloves hiding their hands and wrists, the gentlemen were more reckless. Some even wore the short-skirted togas that bared their legs from the knees down to the tops of their Roman sandals.

And just as she'd hoped, their arms were all bared, since Roman clothing for men rarely had long sleeves. As she moved about the room, she paused to peek at a wrist here, a forearm there. Unfortunately, she hadn't yet seen a single tattoo.

She sighed. It had probably been too much to hope that the man she sought would be at the house party. Neither Clarissa nor her husband, Lord Blakeborough, who stood near the door as if debating how soon he could flee the melee, seemed the sort to associate with such a man.

"I see that I'm late to the party," said a loud voice.

Delia turned to find Warren standing next to his friend by the door, wearing a short-skirted toga. Her heart nearly failed her. Warren did not have knobby knees, not in the least. And though his Roman sandals were the strapped kind that fully covered his calves, she could still tell that they were the well-muscled calves of a man who rode often and well.

My oh my. Warren in Roman warrior costume was truly a sight to behold. The man would make Mars himself look like Prinny bursting out of a kilt. Roman gods would fight to look like Warren.

Not that she was surprised he would be so . . . amazing in a toga. Warren had a way of putting every other man's looks to shame.

Lord Blakeborough said, "You know, old boy, if you didn't always sleep until noon, even in the country, you wouldn't be late to everything. But given that you stayed up drinking with Jeremy until the wee hours of the morning, I shouldn't be surprised."

"Have you ever known me to go to bed before dawn?" Warren quipped.

"Can't say I have."

It occurred to Delia how odd that was. Plenty of gentlemen stayed out all hours during the Season in town, but in the country? At a house party? Wasn't it odd that Warren kept such late hours *here*?

She had no time to contemplate that anomaly before he spotted her and headed her way.

"Good morning, Miss Trevor," he said as he approached. "You're looking quite fetching in your costume."

Unlike some of the other women, she wore her sleek, floor-length tunic without petticoats. And she was rather glad she'd left them off when Warren skimmed her with a heated look that sent her pulse into triple time.

The man had certainly perfected the rake-hell stare. With any other man she would have laughed, but *his* stare sparked fires in the most intriguing parts of her body, which made it hard to resist swooning.

Lord save her. Swooning, indeed. "You look rather well yourself," she murmured, treating him to a similar assessment. "I see that you chose the short toga after all."

"I always live dangerously."

"You do indeed." She sighed. "And lately so do I."

"I know." He leaned close. "That's what I like about you."

She fought a blush. This . . . thing between

them was insane. Whenever she was near him, she lost all common sense. He had this odd effect on her that would surely prove unwise in the end.

"It's not by choice, you know," she said.

"Isn't it? You could marry, yet you've discarded that possibility for the dubious chance of paying off your estate with your winnings."

"If I must choose between servitude to a man or servitude to Camden Hall, I choose the latter. It's more predictable."

"As the owner of several properties, I can assure you that running an estate is not predictable. One bad harvest, and you'll realize that."

She made a face at him. "Why must you depress my spirits? And just when I was beginning to enjoy myself."

"Were you? Then I suppose I shouldn't show you this." He brandished his arms for her inspection. "No tattoos. Did you notice?"

"Of course," she said, though she hadn't. She'd never really thought him a possibility for her quarry.

"Which gives you one more reason to trust me."

She glanced around, spotted a door leading out to the conservatory, and tugged him through it. As soon as they were at least partly alone, she said, "It doesn't rule you out as the friend of the man I seek."

"I would tell you if I were."

"No, you wouldn't. A man like you, with life-long ties to men of high rank, wouldn't betray them to a woman like me."

He bent to whisper, "You'd be surprised what I would do for a pretty woman."

"Stop that," she whispered back. "I know quite well that you say such things to every female you meet."

To her surprise, vexation tightened the corners of his lips. "Not exactly," he said tersely.

"You can't blame me for thinking so. I'm not the one spending my nights in the stews."

"No. That's Jack Jones."

"That's different."

"Is it? Perhaps I'm searching for a woman with a moon tattoo."

"Very amusing." She glanced into the breakfast room, but no one new had arrived, and she'd already looked over the guests who were there. It wasn't as if there were hundreds of them. Stoke Towers was large, but not *that* large.

As if he'd read her mind, he asked, "Have you found your fellow with the sun tattoo among the guests?"

"Regrettably, no."

"Personally, I think you're looking for something akin to a unicorn. But if I ever meet a man fitting your requirements, I'll let you know."

"Will you?" she asked tartly.

He eyed her askance. "There you go again, refusing to trust me."

"It's not you I don't trust. It's all men."

"Because of your brother. And your father."

His insight startled her. "Perhaps."

Compassion showed in his face. "I'm not like either. I'm very forthright."

"Hmm." She ventured a shot in the dark. "Then perhaps you'll tell me why you never go to bed before dawn."

His face closed up. "I prefer the night, that's all."

So there *was* more to his nightly habits than he would admit. "In other words, you don't want to reveal your secrets any more than I do mine."

"You have secrets?" he said, with that smirk that said he'd caught her in an admission she hadn't meant to make.

"None that would interest you." She returned her attention to the other guests. "So, with whom do you hope to be paired for the sketch?"

"You, of course. Who else?"

A thrill coursed through her that she swiftly squelched. "Your cousin, perhaps?"

"Clarissa has Edwin. She doesn't need me."

The strangest feeling came over her then. Envy, of Clarissa and Edwin. Which was ridiculous. Marriage meant sacrifice, and she had no desire to sacrifice her soul for a man.

Unless it was Warren.

She scowled. How absurd. They might enjoy their little encounters, but Warren had no desire for a wife. And though eventually he would have to settle for one, if only to sire his heir, he would choose one with stellar connections, who came from wealth and rank. Not someone like her.

She wouldn't want to be forced to cater to the whims of such a lofty fellow, anyway. Or wait for him to stop sowing his wild oats.

Certainly not.

"I'm surprised you haven't yet drummed up a card game," he said. "Shall you play piquet tonight?"

"I might. If *you* will play me."

He lowered his voice. "Having already lost a thousand pounds to you, I think I've filled your coffers enough."

"I still haven't seen the blunt," she said, mostly to tweak his nose.

"What a greedy chit you are," he said mildly. "I'll give you your money whenever it's prudent to do so."

Determined to provoke him, she said, "So you say."

"Do you doubt me?"

"Always."

"In that case . . ." He drew up what looked like a Roman purse and began to open it.

"Stop that," she hissed. "You know I'm only teasing you."

He chuckled. "Perhaps I'm doing the same."

Glancing into the room to make sure no one was taking note of them, she said, "Do you truly enjoy living dangerously?"

"It's preferable to living predictably."

"I would call it living responsibly. Dependably."

"It's possible to be responsible in the things that matter, and reckless in the things that don't."

She stared him down. "It's knowing which is which that's tricky."

"True."

Just then, Clarissa stuck her head out the door. "Are you two going to join us? Jeremy is finally awake and ready to start our sketches."

"We'll be right there," Delia said lightly.

She started for the door, but Warren caught her by the arm. "Promise me that if you find your villain, you will tell me. I don't know what you're about, but I don't think you should be confronting some fellow alone."

The request threw her into confusion. Was he asking because he *did* know who the tattooed lord was? Or because he just wanted to help her?

It really didn't matter. Because once she found the man, nothing would stop her from getting what she wanted from the card cheat. "I promise. As long as you promise to tell me if you find him yourself."

"Of course." He spoke the words so matter-of-factly that she was reassured. "Though it would help if you told me why we're looking for him."

She snorted. "Nice try, my lord. But I don't yet trust you *that* much." Then she returned to the breakfast room.

Sadly, her words weren't quite true. Because the more she came to know him, the more she began to think he might be serious about wanting to protect her. And given that her own brother hadn't had any such impulse, that made it harder for her to keep her distance.

So, conscious of her susceptibility, she spent the rest of the morning avoiding him. She made sure she wasn't in his group for the sketch and was nowhere near him afterward. And when she saw him glance her way midafternoon, she convinced Brilliana and Aunt Agatha to go for a walk on the beautiful grounds before he could approach her.

Though as soon as they'd headed off, with Delia setting a brisk pace to make sure he didn't try to join them, she regretted her ruse. Because Aunt Agatha was decidedly cranky today. Delia vastly preferred Warren's penetrating questions to Aunt Agatha's complaints about her bed and the noise coming from the gentlemen downstairs last night and the very air that she breathed.

"Lady Blakeborough sets an excellent table, mind you," her aunt was saying as they approached the deer park. "But she should also set a better example for you young ladies."

"What do you mean?" Brilliana asked. "I think Lady Blakeborough is lovely. Of course, I barely know her, but still . . ."

"She shouldn't have allowed this scandalous Roman costume business." Her aunt fixed Delia with a hard look. "And I cannot believe *you* were the one to suggest it. Don't you want to marry?

Because it seems to me you're doing everything to prevent it."

Careful, Delia cautioned herself. *This is risky terrain, no matter what path I take.* "Gentlemen like daring women," she countered. Or at least Warren said *he* did.

Aunt Agatha snorted. "Not too daring. A man like Lord Knightford may have some . . . unwholesome habits, but he will want a wife who follows the rules of respectability."

"How very unfair of him," Delia couldn't resist saying.

"The world isn't fair," her aunt retorted.

Which was precisely why Delia didn't want a husband. But she couldn't say that, of course. "It doesn't matter, anyway. The marquess has no interest in marrying me."

"I'm not so sure," Brilliana put in.

"Why? Because he flirts with me?"

"He *flirts* with you?" her aunt said. "That is most irregular for him. As is paying calls to a respectable young lady. Or, for that matter, asking a lady's relations the sort of probing questions only appropriate for a suitor to ask, as he did today at lunch. But you will drive him off if you continue to do this mad—"

"What probing questions was he asking?" Delia broke in, her heart dropping into her stomach.

Brilliana exchanged a glance with her. "Oh, things like how long we've been in town and why we decided to stay the summer."

"His questions were more pointed than *that*," Aunt Agatha said. "He wanted to know the details surrounding Reynold's death, and I told him in no uncertain terms that it was rude to ask."

Delia swallowed her panic. "So you didn't tell him."

"Certainly not. None of his concern." Her aunt drew herself up with a sniff. "Much as I would love to see you married to a marquess, I shan't allow such intrusive questions until you have an understanding. Though I'm sure there's been speculation about Reynold. There always is."

Aunt Agatha lowered her voice to a confidential murmur. "Besides, Lord Knightford is a member of that St. George's Club, which is nothing more than a place for men to gossip. I'm sure if he knew the truth, he would spread the word among its members, and then who knows if you would ever find a husband?"

Relief coursed through her. "So you didn't tell him about Reynold losing all our money gambling."

"Well, of course I told him of *that*. Everyone already knows about it."

Despair swamped Delia. Everyone did *not* know, and she'd worked hard to keep it that way. Aunt Agatha had surely said enough to rouse Warren's interest.

Curse him, why was he meddling? How could she make him retreat? Couldn't he see that Aunt Agatha would consider his interest a different kind of interest entirely?

He was going to ruin *everything*. She must get him alone somehow and demand that he stop. This couldn't go on.

The afternoon bled into evening, and still she hadn't found a chance to speak to him alone. Mr. Keane sketched more guests, but Warren left to go riding with his friend Lord Blakeborough, apparently keeping himself aloof from the proceedings now that his own sketch had been done. He was, after all, a marquess. Such people needn't concern themselves with parlor games.

Even after he returned, they were all with other guests until dinner was finished. And once the ladies retired to the drawing room, leaving the gentlemen to play cards and drink the night away, she'd lost her chance to speak privately with him. When a man was in his cups, he was virtually useless.

The next morning, she rose before dawn because she couldn't sleep. Warren was bedeviling her dreams. If she didn't have it out with him today, she might go mad.

She headed downstairs in hopes that some breakfast items might have already been put out for early risers, but strange sounds coming from the drawing room drew her attention. Aunt Agatha tended to rise early, and, worried that she might be having difficulties, Delia diverted her course.

When she entered the drawing room Warren was sitting on the settee, still wearing his dinner attire from the night before. But he wasn't awake. Indeed, judging from the way he thrashed about, he was having bad dreams.

She halted, uncertain how to act. Should she wake him? Leave him alone? Let the nightmare run its course?

"Please, no! I'll be good, I swear!" He tossed his head from side to side. "Don't leave me! Too dark . . . too dark . . . Come back!"

His desperate tone sent a chill down her spine. Even knowing he wasn't speaking to her, she felt a tug at her heart. The poor man. What on earth was he dreaming?

This couldn't go on. He would make himself ill.

Approaching him warily, she placed a hand on his shoulder. "Warren, wake up." She shook him a little. "You're having a bad dream."

Without warning, he grabbed her and tugged her onto his lap. "Yes. Yes. Help me. Stay with me!"

She struggled against his embrace, the beginnings of alarm rising in her chest. "Let me go. Warren, wake up!"

"You mustn't go!" he cried, clutching her so tightly she feared he might actually hurt her. "Don't . . . *can't* go."

"I won't." How could she abandon him when he seemed so panicked? She laid her hand on his cheek. "It's all right. I'm here."

He groaned in his sleep. "Don't leave me, Delia. I don't want to go back in the dark. Please, no. Don't."

The words, cries of a child spoken in the deep voice of a man, made something twist in her heart. "I won't leave you, I swear." She clasped him to her. "Hush, dearest." She pressed a kiss into his hair. "Everything will be fine now."

His breathing grew less frantic, though he still gripped her so fiercely that she couldn't have left even if she wanted to. Which she didn't.

"So nice. Ah, Delia. Sweet, sweet Delia." He covered one breast with his hand, kneading the flesh through her gown, thumbing her nipple. "You slay me."

"Do I?" she whispered, though she doubted he knew what he was saying.

His answer was a kiss, a hot, heady, deep one that shook her to her toes. She should stop him; someone could come in any minute. Yet she couldn't help herself—even knowing he was unaware of what he did, she wanted to revel in the delicious feel of his mouth on hers, his tongue inside her, his scent engulfing her.

She threw her arms about his neck and gave herself up to the kiss.

"Yes, my sweet girl," he rasped. "Be mine. All mine."

Both his hands were on her breasts now, and the very daringness of it thrilled her. Next thing she knew, he was pulling her astride him and pushing against her down there in a most intriguing way, and her heart was pounding hard enough to be heard in London and—

"My lord!" a strange voice intruded. "Stop that right now! What do you think you are doing with my niece?"

Oh no—Aunt Agatha! Delia leapt from his lap. "You don't understand . . . It's not how it looks—"

"You mean his lordship did not have his hands on your breasts and your legs about his waist?" her aunt snapped. "I may be old, girl, but I am not blind."

"Miss Trevor?"

Delia glanced back to see Warren, his eyes opening and confusion showing on his face.

He stood slowly, then threaded his fingers through his hair. "What's going on? Was I asleep?"

"Yes," she said swiftly. "I was just explaining to Aunt Agatha—"

"Do not play me for a fool, Delia." Aunt Agatha glared at him. "As for you, my lord, shame on you for behaving so outrageously with my niece."

His expression cooled to hauteur. "I don't know what you mean."

"You were having a nightmare," Delia said hastily. "And when I tried to wake you, you . . . well . . . You didn't mean to do it. I know that, but—"

Aunt Agatha snorted. "Don't be a green goose. If you believed he was kissing and fondling you in his sleep, then *you* are the fool."

"Fondling her! I beg your pardon. I would never . . ." Abruptly, he halted and the blood drained from his face. "So it . . . wasn't a dream. Oh, God."

"If you try to pretend that you didn't know what you were doing, sir," Aunt Agatha said firmly, "I swear I will call you out myself."

A new voice entered the fray. "That sounds intriguing. What has my cousin done now?"

Lord, no. It was Clarissa. And her husband. And some fellow Delia barely knew.

Warren glanced to the people in the doorway, then to Aunt Agatha and finally to Delia. Regret and something else she couldn't read flickered in his gaze before he gathered his dignity and said stiffly, "I believe I have just made an offer for Miss Trevor's hand."

That softened Aunt Agatha only a little. "I should hope you have. Otherwise—"

"Aunt Agatha, please," Delia cut in. "I need a moment to speak to his lordship."

This was all moving too quickly. He would think she'd entrapped him. Or that she and Aunt Agatha had conspired together to entrap him. Surely she and Warren could find some way out of this that didn't involve him being leg-shackled to a woman he didn't want. Or her being tied to a rakehell who was only interested in her physical attractions.

Her aunt regarded her with the steely-eyed gaze that cowed even ladies of the highest rank. "It won't change anything."

"No, it won't," Warren said firmly. "But I, too,

need to speak with Miss Trevor in private. I promise not to do anything untoward."

"Do I have your word as a gentleman on that? If you even deserve that appellation."

"Lady Pensworth!" Lord Blakeborough said sharply. "I will thank you not to insult my friends and guests."

"It's all right, Edwin," Warren told the earl. "She has just cause to be angry." He inclined his head toward Delia's aunt. "You have my word . . . as a gentleman and the son of your good friend."

That seemed to register with Aunt Agatha, thankfully. "Very well," Aunt Agatha said. "But don't linger. You and I must go to London right away to consult with our solicitors and arrange the settlement, not to mention procure a license."

A license! "A few moments, Aunt," Delia said, as panic rose in her chest. "Please. Before you bind us for life."

With a terse nod, Aunt Agatha withdrew, taking all the others with her.

And Delia was left alone with Warren.

Fourteen

While waiting for her to speak, Warren tried to catch his bearings. This situation was beyond his realm of expertise. He'd never ruined an eligible female before. He hardly knew how to proceed.

Especially when he wasn't sure how far he'd gone. As usual, the dream had caught hold of him like a swamp, dragging him down into its muddy depths. What had he said? How much had he revealed? Not too much, he hoped. Because right now, with a marriage looming, he didn't want to dredge all that up.

Not when she looked so vulnerable, her cheeks a pale pink and her eyes haunted. Was she that afraid to marry him? Good God, what had he done or said to her in the throes of his nightmare?

He didn't think he'd hurt her, but he'd lashed out against people physically in his dreams before. That was why he'd started sleeping during the day, when he tended not to have the nightmares.

She dragged in a shaky breath. "I want you to know I had no idea you would pull me onto your lap and—"

"I realize that. But you didn't fight to leave, did you?" God, if she'd fought him, and he'd hurt her, he'd never forgive himself.

For some reason, the question made her bristle. "Not hard enough, apparently. I realize I should have, but—"

"Forgive me, you misunderstand me." No surprise, since he'd put it very badly. "I'm not blaming you for my actions. Merely making sure that I did not . . . force my attentions on you."

Relief flooded her winsome features. "No. Not really. You held me rather tightly, but I'm sure I could have roused you from your sleep if I had been more . . . forceful."

It was his turn to feel relieved. "But you chose not to."

She blushed. "Yes."

"Because you were afraid to jar me awake? Or because you enjoyed . . . whatever I was doing?"

A faint smile touched her lips. "You really don't remember, do you?"

Mortification flooded him, but he made sure not to show it. At least she was still fully dressed. That was something. Because in the dream, he'd undressed her. "I remember holding you. Kissing you and . . . other things." Pulling her astride him. Plunging deep inside her wet, soft— "I just don't know how much was the dream, and how much was real."

"Your panic at the beginning, before I touched you, was certainly real. You seemed so desperate and sad that I couldn't bear to leave you. I don't know what you were dreaming to make you so frantic, but—"

"I had a nightmare, that's all. Then you entered it and changed it into something more . . . bearable." He winced. "And I showed my appreciation by ruining you."

She shrugged. "You didn't know what you were doing. Given how I responded to your far more intimate caresses a few nights ago, I'm surprised that you didn't go further."

Those had been "far more intimate"? Then he couldn't have done too much to her, no matter what he'd done in the dream. "I might have gone further if not for your aunt." He forced a smile. "I do find you . . . hard to resist."

Thankfully, she flashed him a shy smile. At last, he'd found the right thing to say. "You're not alone in that, my lord."

He raised an eyebrow. "Oh, don't start 'my lord'ing me now, when we're about to be man and wife."

She swallowed. "No matter what my aunt says, you mustn't feel compelled to marry me."

"It's a bit late for that. We were caught in a compromising position by your aunt, a fact rapidly made apparent when other people joined us. If we don't wed, you'll be ruined, and—"

"I don't care if I'm ruined, I told you."

"I care. Because it means I'll gain a reputation as a scoundrel who debauches innocents and doesn't take responsibility for it." When she winced, he softened his tone. "And surely you care if your sister-in-law and nephew are tainted by the scandal."

A hint of desperation crossed her features. "Perhaps we can quash the rumors. Clarissa is my friend, and Lord Blakeborough is yours. Surely they wouldn't say anything. We can explain about the nightmare to my aunt—"

"You already tried that, and she didn't relent. Why should she? She's been trying to find you a husband. Now that one has fallen into her lap, she's not going to give that up without a fight."

He didn't notice the bitterness creeping into his voice until the color drained from Delia's features.

She thrust out her chin. "I know you probably think this has all been some devious scheme to snare you, but I swear I wasn't—"

"I never thought you were." Cursing his clumsy words, he grabbed her hand. "God knows you've avoided me all day, dearling. And I'm well aware of how I get during my nightmares."

She blinked. "You've had them before?"

Damn. "A time or two, yes. That's not the point. Surely you see that we have no choice but to marry."

An insultingly large sigh escaped her. "I sup-pose."

"Do contain your enthusiasm at the prospect," he said dryly.

"Oh! No, that's not . . ." She reddened again. "I'm sure that you . . . I just . . . well . . . What was it you said that day at my aunt's house? 'But I also know that seduction is a dangerous game, and sometimes the outcome is beyond one's control.' Little did you guess that the seduction would be unintended, and the outcome beyond *your* control. I fear you will resent me for ending your bachelor life."

"Trust me, my bachelor life isn't as much fun as it looks."

Even as she snorted her disbelief, he realized that the words were true. His bachelor life hadn't been much fun in a very long time.

"In any case," he went on, "it doesn't matter anymore. What matters is that we settle this to everyone's satisfaction."

"Except mine and Brilliana's," she said glumly, pulling her hand from his. "Now she'll have no choice but to attempt to marry to save the estate." She cast him a hopeful glance. "Unless you're willing to let Jack Jones keep going to Dickson's to gamble?"

"Not on your life. So you'll also have to give up looking for the tattooed man, at least at Dickson's. Though perhaps if you would tell me why you're looking for him—"

"It doesn't matter now," she said hastily.

Something in her eyes told him that it did indeed still matter, but he wouldn't press her on it just yet. It was going to be hard enough to reassure her that they could rub along well as man and wife.

But there was one anxiety of hers he could put to rest at least. "As for Camden Hall, as soon as we marry, I'll speak to the lender for your mortgage and set up payments to keep foreclosure at bay until the estate can get on its feet again."

Her eyes widened. "You would do that? Pay the mortgage?"

"For a while." His desire to reassure her warred with his urge to maintain his dignity and not look as if he were groveling for her hand. Which he wasn't. Not exactly.

"If the choice is between watching my wife's relations tossed out of their home and forced to live with me, or helping them to stand on their own, I would much rather do the latter."

"Oh, of course," she said disappointedly. "That makes sense."

Now he wished he hadn't sounded quite so brusque. But God help him, he didn't want to start the marriage with her thinking she could twist him about her finger and get him to do whatever she wanted. This wasn't a love match. Best that she know it from the beginning.

It would, however, be a lust match. Perhaps he should clarify that, too. "You once said that you thought we might do quite well together in bed. Do you still think so?"

Her cheeks flamed. "I . . . that is . . . you said there was no might about it, and that we certainly would. So I shall have to take your word for it." She arched her brows. "Though you also said that you wouldn't be the one to satisfy my supposed 'craving for wickedness.' You were quite firm on that."

He debated whether to be honest. But this would be hard enough without trying to wrap it up in a fancy—and utterly false—package. "I admit I wouldn't have chosen to marry just yet." He was still wary about joining himself to an innocent who would eventually expect something more than he could give.

Not to mention a persistent chit who might pry into his past until she unearthed his most humiliating secrets. He mustn't let that happen. Bad enough that she would soon know about his way of life—that he kept busy during the night, slept until midafternoon, and then conducted his business or went to Parliament in the afternoon and early evening, when the world was still full of activity. She would already wonder about that.

But he couldn't let her discover firsthand how difficult he could be, how the nightmares were getting more vivid over time. She would grow terrified of him.

Lords aren't afraid of the dark. Buck up and be a man.

Or worse, regard him with contempt for his damned inability to get over his fears. He couldn't stomach either response.

And she already distrusted men. He didn't want to make that worse.

"But I'm sure we can find a way to make it work," he went on. He hoped they could, anyway.

"You mean, as long as I toe the line and do as you say."

He eyed her askance. "Is there really any chance of that?"

A hesitant smile graced her lips. "Probably not. The 'obey' part of the vows always sticks in my craw."

"Personally, I prefer the part that says, 'with my body I thee worship.'"

She colored deeply. "Of course you do. I'll be doing the worshipping."

"Actually, no. That vow is only made by the man." He reached up to tuck a curl behind her ear, then let his hand trail down her cheek. "So I'll be doing the worshipping, and I daresay I shall enjoy every moment." That much was true.

A shaky breath stuttered out of her. Their gazes locked, and his mind leapt ahead to when he would have her in his bed. He could finally ease the lust that had seized him practically from the moment he'd met her.

He bent close. "As I said, dearling, I believe we can find a way to make it work."

Her eyes turned a luminous blue that made

his pulse thunder. He was on the verge of kissing her when the door banged open.

"It is time to leave, sir," said a stalwart female voice.

Damn. Lady Pensworth had reached the end of her patience. But she could go to hell if she thought he would be ordered about like some schoolboy. "Another moment alone, madam, if you please," he said coldly, keeping his gaze fixed on Delia's flushed features.

The baroness bristled. "Solicitors do not stay open until all hours, my lord, so if we wish to have the settlements done in time—"

He tore his gaze from Delia to stare down her aunt. "I will not be hurried. This is too important. So I suggest you allow me a few more moments to woo my future wife."

Lady Pensworth blinked, looking owl-eyed beneath her spectacles. Clearly, the harridan wasn't used to being spoken to in that tone. But she had the good sense to nod and back out, though he noticed that she left the door cracked open.

It mattered not. There was only one question left to ask. "Yes or no, Delia? Will you marry me?"

She stiffened. "Don't pretend I have a choice. You've made it quite clear that I do not."

"You always have a choice. And if you choose to be ruined, I will walk out right now, and to hell with the consequences. I suppose I can weather a few years of being considered a scoundrel." He narrowed his gaze. "But I daresay you're not quite so much a rebel that you'd trample over the reputations of me and your family just to avoid marrying."

She hesitated a long moment before uttering a defeated sigh. "Blast you for being right."

Oddly, that answer reassured him. He liked her spirit, and he hoped to see more of it. But a rebel with no sense would not make him a good marchioness. "Does that mean your answer is yes?"

"It does." She searched his face, and her expression grew calculating. "Assuming you grant me one request."

Uh-oh. "Depends on what the request might be."

Was that a twinkle he saw in her eyes? "I must be allowed to bring Flossie to my new home."

A relieved laugh escaped him. "Done. If all your requests are as easy as that one, we shall rub along quite nicely, I expect." He held out his arm. "Shall we?"

She took it with a smile that gratified him. "Lead on, my lord. It appears I have a wedding to plan."

Her aunt came in just then, her expression softening as she saw them arm in arm. "I do hope you're not aiming for a large wedding, niece. Because this must be done quickly, before the guests can return to London and start gossiping about what happened."

Clarissa entered behind her. "You can marry here!" She clapped her hands in delight. "Oh, that would be such a fabulous addition to my house party. People will be talking about it for ages."

"Wonderful," Edwin muttered behind her, though Warren would swear he saw his friend smile fleetingly.

"Wonderful, indeed," Lady Pensworth said. "Though it will require the acquisition of a special license."

"I'm sure I can manage that," Warren drawled. "The archbishop is a cousin of mine."

"Of course he is," Delia said under her breath. When he shot her a sharp glance, she added, "What? I'm just saying that you know everyone of note in society. I'm surprised you aren't demanding to have the wedding in Westminster Abbey."

"I'm afraid they reserve that for royal weddings and parishioners, my dear." But her comment reminded him that none of them had yet asked her what she wanted. "You don't mind having our wedding here, do you?"

Her quick look of gratitude told him that she appreciated his gesture. "Not in the least. I can't imagine anything more marvelous than to be married in a beautiful house like this, among all the friends and family I have in the world."

"Then it's settled," Lady Pensworth said. "Tomorrow morning we'll have the wedding."

All Delia's pleasure seemed to vanish. "Tomorrow! So soon? Can't I have another day or two to plan?"

"The sooner the better," her aunt said grimly.

"Before the gossip hits town. You should arrive there already wed, so that the worst they think is that you two got carried away by your romantic feelings and insisted upon marrying right away."

"But it may take more than one day to procure the license and settle matters with our solicitors," Warren said in a steely voice. If his future wife wanted a couple of days to plan, then she would have them, by God. "I don't think waiting until day after tomorrow will hurt anything."

"Oh, very well, if you insist," Lady Pensworth said. "And now, my lord, we really must go."

"Of course." Though he wasn't looking forward to an hour or more of being interrogated by the baroness in his carriage.

So he took one more moment to gaze down at his new fiancée and say, sotto voce, "Everything will be fine, dearling. I swear it."

"You cannot guarantee that, my lord," she said. "But if you're willing to try to make it so, then I am, too."

Then she surprised him by kissing his cheek. It touched him deeply. And made him wish they were alone.

He glanced around at the waiting company. To hell with that. In for a penny, in for a pound. Tugging her into his arms, he gave her a hearty buss on the lips.

"Now that, my dear, is more like it," he murmured. Leaving her standing wide-eyed, he strode out the door.

Moments later, after he and Lady Pensworth were ensconced in his coach and headed to London, she said, "Nicely done, Knightford."

He raised an eyebrow. "What part?"

"Getting past my niece's silly objections to marriage."

"Her objections? What about mine? You assume that I wished to marry. She wasn't lying, you know. She really did happen upon me having a nightmare. I really did grab her thinking she was—" *In my bed.* He paused, figuring he'd best not tell that much of the truth. "Let's just say I wasn't exactly in my right mind at the time. And she was just trying to help me."

"I know."

He gaped at her. "You know?"

The harridan's eyes twinkled. "It was hard not to notice the look of complete shock on your face when you realized what you'd done. Or the panic on hers."

His temper flared. "But you chose to ignore the evidence of your eyes and force us into an untenable position. That is scheming of the worst kind, madam."

"Is it?" Lady Pensworth didn't look the least cowed by his accusation. "She likes you. You like her. Anyone who has spent more than five minutes with you can tell that the two of you would make an excellent match. But you both would allow your foolish ideas about marriage to keep you from something that could be wonderful. So, yes, I interfered."

She smirked at him. "It didn't require much, given that you were entwined in each other's arms when I found you. You will thank me later, I promise. Now be honest: Are you that unhappy about the situation?"

The question threw him off guard. In truth, he was not. He was worried about what might happen to them as a couple and whether Delia would eventually become content with their union. But he was rather looking forward to a lifetime of sparring with her. Which, in itself, alarmed him.

"That's what I thought," she said.

"It's not me you should be worried about. It's your niece. Delia deserves better than to be forced into marriage."

"Forced?" She snorted. "That girl has never been forced into anything in her life. Don't let her spin that line with you. Delia does as she pleases, and I can assure you she is well pleased to be marrying you. She just hasn't acknowledged it to herself yet."

"I hope you're right. Because if you're not, then we have a miserable future ahead of us."

"I doubt that." She leaned back against the squabs. "How about this? If you wish to stop this marriage now, then do. I will try to halt the gossip before it begins, and she can go on as she pleases. I daresay between you and me, we might be able to keep matters quiet. Is that what you want?"

He glanced out the window at the countryside whizzing past. What a choice. He could go back to being a bachelor, to drinking and gambling and whoring at all hours to keep the night at bay.

Or he could attempt to live a normal life with a wife and children . . . or as much of a normal life as was possible, given his night terrors.

The second choice could prove disastrous. He simply had no way of being sure that his rebel of a fiancée could be the sort of wife he needed, let alone the sort of wife he wanted.

Yet the first choice—of returning to endless nights in the stews alone—seemed horribly bleak. Not to mention monotonous. And frankly, he was getting a bit old for that life.

Besides, given the chance—and good odds—he had always preferred taking risks. Even when it meant marrying a chit who was liable to run him a merry dance.

He shifted to meet Lady Pensworth's gaze. "Very well. Assuming you're right and we could manage to keep what happened quiet, I still don't wish to halt this. And God help me if I'm wrong, but I don't think that's what she wants, either."

Lady Pensworth's sharply released breath told him she hadn't been entirely sure of him. Good. He'd never liked being predictable.

A calculating glint appeared in her eyes. "Then we might as well begin discussing the settlement. No point in waiting until we get the lawyers involved."

With a rueful laugh, he nodded.

Delia was definitely cut from the same cloth as her aunt. And for some reason, that reassured him that his decision was sound. Because any woman who would grow into being a Lady Pensworth might suit him quite well.

Now he just had to make sure he brought Delia around to feeling the same way about having him for a husband.

Fifteen

"It really depends on whether you choose the lavender or the Clarence blue for your wedding gown," Clarissa said.

Delia blinked. Once more, she'd been woolgathering. That was all she'd been doing since Warren and Aunt Agatha had left yesterday. "What does?"

Clarissa shook her head. "The flowers, silly. I have all sorts in my gardens. It's a pity you don't have a white gown that would work—or that one of mine wouldn't fit you—but it can't be helped. My Lavandula will go nicely with the lavender gown, and my blue hydrangeas are almost exactly the shade of the other. So which do you want in your bouquet with the white roses?"

"She'll have the hydrangeas," Brilliana answered, then smiled at Delia. "You look best in the blue, dearest. The lavender gown is lovely, but the blue gown is stunning. And you want to be stunning for your wedding day."

A sad smile crossed Delia's lips. "I doubt any gown could make me stunning."

"Nonsense," Clarissa said. "Every woman can be stunning if she just believes she can. It's all in the way you present yourself. Behave as if you *are* stunning and voilà, you will be. There's more to beauty than looks, my dear."

At Brilliana's nod, Delia stifled a sigh. Easy for them to say. They were both real beauties, with curvaceous bodies and attractive faces. Whereas her only real asset was her eyes. And her hair, when she could manage to tame it. Which wasn't often.

Yet Warren was dreaming of you *when he pulled you onto his lap. When he fondled you and asked you to stay.*

It was the only thing that had kept her going through this mad rush to wed. The only thing that made her eager for her wedding night.

Oh, Lord, she mustn't think of that, or she would blush.

"Well?" Clarissa asked. "The blue, then?"

Delia nodded. "If Brilliana says I look my best in it, then I do. Fashion isn't my purview, I'm afraid." Although at least she no longer had to dress garishly. She might not be the best with clothes, but with Brilliana helping her—

Suddenly it hit her that Brilliana would no longer be helping her with anything. The only females in Delia's new abode would be servants she barely knew, for Clarissa had already told her that Warren's mother was dead and he had no sisters, and only one sister-in-law, who lived in America.

So Delia would be virtually alone in some cavernous manor house with a *man*.

Unexpected tears stung her eyes, and she dashed them away. Lord, why was she becoming such a watering pot?

"Dearest!" Brilliana cried. "What's wrong? Are you that unhappy to be marrying Lord Knightford?"

Instantly, Brilliana embraced her, attempting to soothe her, which, of course, only made the tears actually fall. "I'm not . . . crying over *that*," she managed to get out. "I'm crying over . . . leaving you and Silas!"

With a murmur of sympathy, Clarissa and Brilliana hugged her between them. "You aren't leaving us," Brilliana said stoutly. "You're merely setting up your own household. We'll visit each other often, I promise."

"Lindenwood Castle is only a day's drive from London," Clarissa said, with a squeeze of Delia's shoulders. "You can come stay with me anytime you like."

"And doesn't Lord Knightford have a property in Shropshire?" Brilliana said. "Why, that's only a short drive from Camden Hall."

"It's a hunting b-box," Delia blubbered. "He only goes there with *men*."

"Never fear," Clarissa said soothingly. "That is sure to change now that he's no longer a bachelor. He'll want to stay at home in the country, all cozy with his wife, while he entertains his friends. The way Edwin does."

Despair swamped Delia. Much as she liked Clarissa's husband, he and his friends weren't remotely similar to Warren in their habits. She couldn't even be sure that Warren wouldn't continue his whoring. After all, he'd made her no promises on that score. He'd merely said that his "bachelor life" wasn't "as much fun as it looks" and that it didn't "matter anymore."

That hardly sounded like he meant to halt it.

Oh, Lord, she'd been so intent on figuring out what would happen to Camden Hall that she hadn't even thought to ask if he meant to be faithful to her. What if he didn't? Could she bear sharing his bed knowing that he would blithely leave it to go to another's?

She had to find out what he intended, or she would go mad worrying about it. "Have either of you heard when my aunt and my . . . fiancé will be returning from London?"

Clarissa exchanged a glance with Brilliana. "Not yet. But I imagine it will be in the evening. They'll have lots to do before they return."

Delia nodded. And she had lots to think about before then, too. "Are we done deciding about the gown and flowers?"

"Yes," Brilliana said. "Why?"

"I should like to go for a walk, if you don't mind."

"Of course," Clarissa said. "We can all use a stroll. You two haven't yet seen our folly, have you? The one that Stoke Towers is named for? I simply must show it to you. It's a perfect little triangular Gothic tower with turrets at each point. Edwin's grandfather built it back in 1765 in tribute to his late wife. You'll adore it. Wait—what do you think of holding the wedding there?"

"What a grand idea," Brilliana exclaimed, "assuming it's large enough and the weather is fine. But that will make a great deal of trouble for your servants, don't you think?"

"We could keep the breakfast here in the manor, and just have the ceremony there. It could be quite fun if we—"

"Forgive me," Delia broke in. "I need to go for a walk *alone*. To clear my head."

The two women blinked at her as if she'd just proposed lopping off her arms. Then Clarissa nodded. "Whatever you wish. But you could still see the folly. Just take the path behind the house that leads past the knot garden."

"I will, thank you," Delia said, and turned to leave.

"Wait!" Brilliana called out. "Before you go, do you have any questions about . . . well . . . what to expect on your wedding night? I know you and I have discussed it in the past, but—"

"You explained it admirably, thank you." Delia couldn't bear to hear more depressing comments about how a woman must endure a man's attentions. Especially after Warren had shown her that kissing could be so much better than she'd expected or experienced. "I believe I'm ready for that, at least."

What a lie, she thought as she left the two women and headed outdoors. She wasn't remotely ready. Not because she feared it; Warren had made it clear that he was very good at satisfying a woman in *that* area of marriage.

It was her inability to satisfy *him* that worried her. He was used to seductive, beautiful courtesans who were paid to know just how to pleasure a man. Or randy wives with plenty of experience in the bedchamber.

A sense of hopelessness seized her as she walked down the path past the garden. What if she did everything wrong? What if he found her terribly stupid at it? Would that make him go running back to the brothel or to some loose-living widow with more talent at pleasuring him?

And would she care if he did? This wasn't a love match. They both knew it. From what she understood about gentlemen and ladies of rank, a fashionable marriage meant the gentleman went his own way while the lady went hers.

She swallowed. She didn't want a fashionable marriage. Not with him. They were unfashionable in everything else. Couldn't they be unfashionable in this, too?

The sound of footsteps behind her arrested her. Someone was following her, and she didn't want a companion just now.

She increased her speed only to have the person behind her increase theirs, too. Without warning, an arm snagged her about the waist and jerked her to a halt.

Then her mouth was being smothered with a kiss, and the familiar scent of spicy cologne allayed all her fears. Warren. As if her thoughts had called him to her from some distant land, he'd returned.

His drugging kiss made every part of her body sing. Oh, Lord, but the man knew how to excite her. She could stand here all day just drinking from his mouth the way he drank from hers.

Here. In full view of the house.

Coming to her senses, she broke the kiss. "Anyone might look out and see us!"

His eyes gleamed at her. "Do you care?"

"I . . . well . . . I mean, I *ought* to care."

"Nonsense. You've never cared much about the proprieties before. Why start now?" His hands still gripped her waist, holding her anchored against him. "If anyone did see us, what could they do? Make us marry?"

A smile tugged at her lips. "Good point."

"I thought so." He bent his head to her ear. "Did you miss me, brat?"

"Not one whit." Then she belied the claim by looping her arms about his neck so she could kiss *him*.

That had him crushing her against him once more so he could plunder her mouth hot and long and hard, until her blood raced and her heart faltered. He made her feel as if she could fly. Or die . . . utterly happy, right here in his arms.

It was madness. It was joy. She wasn't used to joy. She didn't know how to handle it.

After several moments of devouring her lips, he released her. "I missed you, too."

Smiling shyly at that, she edged away to continue down the path. "How did you know I was out here?"

He fell into step beside her. "Clarissa told me you'd gone to see the folly alone, to clear your head. After witnessing the chaos in the manor, I figured you might want some company."

"You just wanted to escape all their questions about the wedding."

"That, too." He shot her a knowing glance. "And I daresay I wasn't the only one. You don't strike me as the sort to exult in wedding plans."

She cast him a rueful smile. "You're not far wrong. I swear, if Brilliana had asked me one more time which shade of ribbon I wanted for some particular frippery, I might have strangled her with it."

He chuckled, then skimmed his gaze down her relatively plain wrapped gown of pink gros de

Naples. "You're looking fetching today. Did you tire of plaids and stripes in warring colors?"

Heat rose in her cheeks. "I . . . um . . ."

"You don't have to explain. I long ago figured out that your manner of dress was one more way of keeping suitors at arm's length. When you aren't attempting that, you dress quite nicely."

"Don't be fooled by this gown," she warned. "Brilliana helped me choose it. On my own, I am by no means an arbiter of fashion."

"Neither am I."

"Nonsense." She looked him over. "Only you can make a gray coat, white waistcoat, and white trousers look the height of fashion."

"It's all due to my valet. He keeps me looking lordly enough for my exalted rank." He winked at her. "And despairs over whatever activities have me ruining my clothes at every turn."

"In the future, I shall try to refrain from pouring wine on your shirts," she said lightly as they entered the woods beyond the garden. "As long as you refrain from getting in my way."

"I can't make any promises." He shifted to block her path. "Getting in your way sometimes leads to intriguing interludes."

He reached for her, but she darted past him. "Oh no, you don't. Enough of that, or I'll never get to see this famous folly."

With a snort, he caught up with her and let her continue on. "Are the wedding plans complete?"

"As complete as we can make them, given the

limitations of time." She eyed him askance. "And speaking of the wedding, you're breaking the rules, you know. It's bad luck for the groom to see the bride on the eve of their wedding."

"It's not 'eve' yet. Besides, you and I never follow rules. I don't see why we should start now." He folded his arms behind his back. "I'm actually rather surprised you didn't insist on going to London with me and your aunt to participate in negotiating the wedding settlement."

Her laugh wafted on the wind. "There was no need. I knew Aunt Agatha would never let you get anything past her. She's far more knowledgeable about matters like this than I."

"She does know a thing or two," he said wryly. "She made my poor solicitor gasp with her demands. You now have what is probably the most generous jointure ever, given the size of your dowry, not to mention more pin money than even my mother had from Father."

She grinned up at him. "She got the best of you, did she?"

"She did. But I didn't mind. Given that I landed us in this situation, it was no more than I deserved."

"Don't be ridiculous. You didn't intend any of it. You were asleep and hardly knew what was going on. I don't for a moment blame you for what happened." She glanced away. "I blame myself."

"You mustn't." Taking her hand, he tucked it in the crook of his elbow. "I am well pleased with the result."

She darted a look up at him. "So am I."

They continued in silence another long while, content to enjoy the waning sun and chirping birds in the trees. Then they rounded a bend in the path and came suddenly upon the folly.

She gasped. She'd expected some somber tower of weathered granite. Instead, it was a fanciful edifice of white-painted stone, with arched Gothic Venetian windows and grand crenellated turrets. Three stories high, it looked rather like a medieval wedding cake.

"That is more than a folly," she said in awe. "It's magnificent."

"It is, isn't it? Clarissa, Niall, and Yvette used to play in it when they were young."

"Niall?"

"Clarissa's brother, the Earl of Margrave, who owns the neighboring estate. That's how Edwin and I came to be friends—from all my visits to see my cousins at Margrave Manor."

"Lord Margrave is the one who's been abroad for years, right?"

"Not anymore. He returned to England a couple of weeks ago, though he went straight to Margrave Manor, where he and Edwin have been trying to put the place to rights. You'll probably meet him tomorrow at the wedding." He took her hand. "Come, you must see the inside. The view from the rooftop is spectacular."

They entered through an elaborately carved

door into a scene of serene beauty. With ornate plasterwork, mahogany floors, and other elegant flourishes, the tower reminded her of the tale of Rapunzel.

Except that Rapunzel's only means of exit was her hair. In the center of this tower was a lovely spiral staircase leading to the upper floors. The windows faced the woods on two sides and the fields on the third, and though Delia and Warren were only on the first floor, the views were amazing already.

"Clarissa thinks we should have the ceremony here tomorrow," Delia said as they looked out at the forest. "What do *you* think?"

"Makes sense. If you want that."

"I believe I do. It's really lovely, if a trifle warm." She took off her bonnet. "I suppose that's to be expected with the sun beating down on all these windows. Perhaps we could have them open tomorrow. Would that be all right with you?"

"Anything you want is fine. I don't care about the wedding preparations." Warren turned toward her, looking suddenly serious. "There's something more important we need to discuss."

"Oh?"

"During my time in London dealing with your harridan of an aunt, certain information came to light. About your brother. And Camden Hall."

Her heart began to pound. "What sort of information?"

"Well, your aunt had already told me that Camden Hall is heavily mortgaged because of his gambling losses. I'd assumed that they'd happened over time, that he was the usual young and reckless buck gambling his life away. But in the course of our negotiating terms for my helping keep the manor running until it could recoup, I learned more details about that. In short, I found out that your brother lost the funds in one night, apparently while playing in a gaming hell."

She sighed. The truth had been bound to come out eventually. And she was relieved it had. Because if she and Warren were to marry, she needed him to know that she intended to continue her search. More discreetly, of course.

It galled her that the card cheat who'd brought her and Brilliana—and her brother—to this pass should get off scot-free. "Yes, that's what happened."

"I take it that the gaming hell was Dickson's?"

She nodded.

"And the tattooed lord you've been seeking was the one to trounce him."

Facing him, she said, "Not trounce him. Cheat him."

Warren gazed steadily into her face. "How do you know your brother was cheated?"

"He told me so shortly before he . . ."

"Drowned."

She swallowed hard. "My aunt revealed that, too, did she?"

"Actually, I'd already heard that at St. George's. I also heard he was drunk at the time."

"There's some question of that," she prevaricated.

But that was all she said. Her soon-to-be husband didn't need to know that Reynold had thrown himself into the river purposely. Because if Warren realized he was about to marry the sister of a man who'd committed suicide, he surely wouldn't want to risk being tainted by such a scandal. He might even refuse to marry her.

And she needed Warren to marry her. If she were honest with herself, she *wanted* him to marry her. How strange that it became more natural by the hour to think of him as her future husband.

He now watched her with that curious intensity that always both thrilled and worried her. "And you're certain your brother was cheated out of the money."

"Utterly. Didn't you hear my aunt the day we had luncheon together? Reynold and I have always excelled at piquet. So while I could understand his losing a small amount if faced with a truly superior player, I can't believe he would lose enough to require mortgaging the estate. Why would he risk so much? Until that visit to London, he'd sworn off gambling completely."

"Or so he said. And if he really had been cheated, why didn't he confront the man there and then? Demand that the man give him his money back?"

"First of all, he couldn't see exactly how the man was doing it, which would have made it difficult to confront him. Second, Reynold was afraid to risk the wrath of a man far beyond him in station. Reynold was sure no one would believe him, and then *we'd* all be ruined. That's why he wouldn't tell me the fellow's name, either."

She wrapped her arms about her waist. "Reynold said he was thinking of me, of my future in society. Of his son's future. He didn't want me to make a fuss about it and bring trouble down upon all of us."

"No, far better to leave his family without the funds to survive."

She'd thought the same thing, many a time. Some of Reynold's actions made no sense to her.

Frustration lit his features. "So finding the tattooed man has been about what? Revenge for the death of your brother and the possible loss of your estate?"

Chewing on her lower lip, she debated whether to reveal everything. But since she fully intended to keep up her search, it made no sense to hide it from him any longer.

"Actually," she said, "I was hoping to entice the card cheat to play *me* at piquet. I knew I could beat him, and that losing might prompt him to try cheating again. Then, once I caught him at it, I would have threatened to expose his actions to the world unless he returned the money he stole."

The color drained from his face. "Because he's a lord. And you figured that revealing his cheating—the way your brother had not—would ruin him in society."

She bobbed her head.

Eyes glittering, he snapped, "You were going to blackmail a man you don't know, a man who might be of such consequence that he could ruin you or even hurt you physically. How the hell did you think to manage that? If you called him out for cheating, it would have been over. He would have been ruined, and thus have no reason to pay you. Or worse yet, he would have denied it, and—as your brother feared—people would choose to believe him over you."

"Owen and I had a plan. Once I caught the man cheating, I was going to signal Owen, who would ask the fellow if they could speak privately. Then Owen would have told him I was a cousin of Brilliana's bent on retrieving the money her husband was cheated out of. *Owen* would have been the one to make the threat, not me, and he would have acted as a second witness. He could have handled the fellow. You see? My plan would have worked."

"A plan that assumed this lord wouldn't try to shoot you or Owen, or have you thrown out of the club bodily. Or just bluster his way through it." He snorted. "Why not just ask around about the fellow?"

"We did. No one knew who the man was. And we couldn't be too bold in our questions or we'd risk scaring off our quarry. If he's a card cheat, he must be used to avoiding angry players who want his blood."

"If he's a successful card cheat, no one's caught him at it." He gazed coldly at her. "I'm not entirely sure *you* would have done so."

She tipped up her chin. "If Reynold could tell, I certainly could. Which is one reason I had to be the one to do the gambling. During my first months in London, when Owen was merely asking around, he couldn't learn anything. If Owen had been able to play cards as well as I, he would have been taking the risks for me there, too, but he can't. So I was forced to go into the hells myself. This devil is clearly very sly."

"Or, as that fellow said at Dickson's, he's simply a naval officer, which means he might have returned to sea recently. Did you consider that?"

"I'm considering it *now*, but when I started gambling at Dickson's I didn't know about the sun tattoo being common to sailors."

"Yes, you clearly made a number of problematic assumptions when you embarked on your scheme." He stared her down. "*You*, my dear, were utterly mad if you thought such a hole-ridden plan would work."

"Not mad. Desperate."

That seemed to give him pause. "I can see that," he said, a hint of sympathy in his voice. Then his eyes hardened on her. "But there's no need to despair anymore, now that I'm involved. So this nonsense of searching for the card cheat at Dickson's must end. At once."

Sixteen

Warren gazed at the woman he meant to marry, the woman who'd gone strangely silent and wary. But he wouldn't take back his words. The very thought of Delia trying to blackmail some card cheat made his blood run cold. If he'd had any idea she was plotting such a mad thing, he'd have fought harder to stop her earlier.

"Are you forbidding me to continue looking for the card cheat?" she asked with deceptive calm.

Uh-oh. "I'm saying that since the situation with Camden Hall will be handled by me and my attorneys, there's no longer any reason for you to search for this fellow and risk your very life to get money from him."

"I still can't let him get away with what he did. Surely you see that."

A vise tightened around his gut. "So it *is* revenge that you seek. Not just money."

Hanging her bonnet from the latch on the

window, she headed for the spiral staircase. "Can you blame me? My brother died because he was so distraught over what he'd done that he stumbled off a bridge. If not for that blasted lord—"

"I realize that." Warren was missing something here. Why did she so directly connect her brother's death with his losing all the family funds? Men got drunk and stumbled into rivers and lakes all the time. The drowning could have been just a tragic accident.

Not that he would be able to convince *her* of that. She was clearly consumed by the idea of avenging her brother's death. "Nonetheless, revenge is another of those dangerous games that rarely turn out the way you plan."

"How would you know?" she clipped out.

"Trust me, I do." He'd seen what had happened when Niall had taken his just vengeance on Clarissa's attacker. "I understand how you feel, probably better than you can imagine. So if you're determined to exact revenge, I can take care of that, too."

She halted to regard him warily. "What do you mean?"

"God, I know I'm going to regret what I'm about to say," he mumbled. "But if you really want me to, I'll root out your card cheat on my own and get him to admit to what he did."

"How?"

"By asking questions of the right people. It should be easier for me than it was for you or Owen. A lord showing a casual interest in another lord won't be considered suspect."

She sighed. "But as the new brother-in-law of the late Mr. Trevor, you'll be more suspect. So if *you* start asking questions, everyone will know why. And no one will admit the truth."

"I can be discreet. One of the hallmarks of the St. George's Club is discretion. Among our members are the former investigator Lord Rathmoor, and Lord Fulkham, undersecretary of state for war and the colonies. Either of them might know something. And the club exists to look into troublesome matters for the women in members' lives."

She lifted an eyebrow. "Really? Aunt Agatha says your club exists so men can get together and gossip."

He bit back a smile. "That, too. We do drink and play cards and the like there. It *is* still a gentlemen's club, after all."

Hope lit her face. "And you would seriously pursue my card cheat for me?"

"Do you think I'm lying about it?" he asked quietly.

"No! I mean . . . it's just that—"

"—you've already been lied to a great deal by the men in your life. I'm right, aren't I?"

With a terse nod, she turned away to climb the first flight of the staircase. He ascended behind her in silence, wondering if she would reveal anything else.

When she reached the next floor, she released a shuddering breath. "My father often made empty promises to us. 'This is the place we'll settle, my darling,' he'd say to Mama. Or he'd tell me, 'Here we'll stay for good, my girl.' "

She hardened her voice. "But then, it was always, 'Next time, dear. We have to leave town now—things have grown sticky with that club owner.' Or 'I heard that there's lots of money to be made these days in Nice.' He dragged us across half of Europe, following rumors about pigeons ripe for the plucking. If he hadn't won Camden Hall in that card game, I daresay he'd still be at it."

Coming up beside her, Warren placed his hands on her waist. "As I recall, your brother also promised to stop gambling, then headed off to London to lose all his money."

"Exactly. He railed against the life of a serious gambler. Wouldn't even go to the city. He was always saying he couldn't afford to leave the estate because of one thing or another."

"I remember your aunt saying he wouldn't even take the time to give you a proper debut."

"Yes." She gazed off past him to the window that showed the forest beyond. "But I suspect it was more a matter of money than time. The estate was already in a bad way when Papa won it. It took a lot of work *and* ready blunt. Plus, Reynold said he wanted to bring it up to snuff not by seeking an infusion of capital from gambling but by managing the place properly—investing in better crops, helping his tenants improve their farming practices."

She looked distant, contemplative. "He must have felt very desperate for funds to have changed his mind about that. To have resorted to gambling in London." She gazed up at Warren. "I didn't resent his doing that, you know. Papa had always settled financial matters that way, too. It's just that, well . . . Reynold never did. If he'd told me what he planned, I would have understood. I wouldn't have approved, but . . ."

Her voice caught, and Warren tugged her close, wanting to comfort her somehow.

With a shaky breath, she accepted his embrace. "It's just that Reynold *lied* about it, to me and to Brilliana. He waltzed off to London for a couple of weeks and threw everything away on a card game without a word to us about his plans. In the end, he turned out to be as irresponsible, feckless, and utterly unconcerned about how his actions affected us as Papa."

"In light of all that, I see how you find it hard to trust men—especially given that you've routinely seen the worst side of them in the stews." Warren gazed down into her eyes. "But I'm not just any gentleman. Have I ever lied to you, ever told you anything but the God's honest truth?"

A frown creasing her brow, she ducked her head. "Not that I know of."

The faintly distrustful words pierced him. "I've behaved honorably toward you, Delia Trevor, or you wouldn't be marrying me now. Your instincts are telling you I can be trusted. You should listen to them."

"Very well." With a hard swallow, she drew away from him. "As long as we're talking about trust, I have something to ask you, and I need you to answer me honestly. Your answer won't change my decision to marry you. It will merely help me know what to expect."

Bloody hell. He dearly hoped she wasn't going to ask about the nightmares again. Because what would he say? That he periodically turned into a sniveling coward in the dark? That the man standing here offering to solve all her problems couldn't even stop his own night terrors?

But if he wanted her to trust him . . . "Ask whatever you wish."

She released a nervous sigh. "Do you . . . intend to be faithful to me after we marry?"

For a moment, he could only gape at her. *That* was what she wanted to know?

Good God, what an idiot he was. Of *course* she was concerned about that, given his reputation and the hastiness of this marriage.

"I mean," she went on quickly, as if fearing to hear his answer, "before you were forced to change your plans, you often said you had no intention of settling down with one woman anytime soon. And I've heard that men of your rank tend to have, well, fashionable marriages. Where the husband and wife do as they please."

He tamped down the sudden irrational anger that seized him. "Is that what you want?"

"No! I would prefer something more . . ."

"Unfashionable."

She brightened. "Exactly." Then her face fell again. "But if that's not what *you* want . . . if you intend to go on as you have been, I will . . . attempt to look the other way. As long as you're honest about it, I will attempt to be a dutiful wife."

The word *dutiful* scraped him raw. "You really think you could do that." Sarcasm crept into his voice. "You could just blithely go on about your daily activities while I screw anything in skirts."

The blunt words made her blink. "I suppose I could . . . *try*—"

"Don't you dare!" He strode up to her, his temper flaring even higher. "I don't want a 'dutiful wife,' whatever the hell that is. I want *you*, the intrepid and impudent Delia Trevor. And I can tell you right now that I bloody well won't 'look the other way' if *you* go hunting for some other man in your bed. So you can put that thought right out of your mind."

God, had he spoken those jealous and possessive words aloud? Apparently, he had.

And given the sudden softening in her features, she was taking them exactly the way they sounded. Damn it all. He'd better repair the damage. "That does not, however, mean I'll stay home every night dancing attendance on you. I'll continue to go to my club and—"

"The stews?" She fixed him with eyes gone as still as lake waters.

"No." He'd simply have to find another way to make it through the dark hours. Despite her brief sojourn gambling all night at Dickson's, she wouldn't want to stay awake until dawn for the rest of her life, especially in the country. "I think I can safely promise never again to spend my nights in the stews."

"Don't make promises you can't keep," she whispered.

As she turned to climb the next flight of stairs, he followed her, anger boiling in his belly. "Do you still trust me so little? You said you'd be a 'dutiful wife' if I continued my bachelor ways. So why would I lie and claim that I won't, when you've already given me carte blanche to do as I please?"

"I'm not saying you're lying. You may truly believe now that you can promise it. But once you and I . . . Once you realize that I know so little of how to . . . to please a man—"

"Is that what this is about?" Relief banished his anger. "You're worried about your ability in bed?"

She halted ahead of him on the stairs. "In truth, I'm terrified about our wedding night."

The word *terrified* reminded him painfully of

what Clarissa had gone through before her marriage. Perhaps he'd better clarify what she meant. "Of sharing a bed with me? Or of not doing it well?"

"Not so much the former." She climbed the rest of the way to the top, with him dogging her heels. "I mean, I trust you to make it as easy for me as you can, given my inexperience. But after all the seductive women you've bedded—"

"That was a different thing entirely, and not nearly as exciting as you apparently imagine." As soon as they emerged onto the rooftop, with its lovely views and large wooden table at the center for picnics, he tugged her into his arms. "In the brothels, it was an even exchange of money for services, and neither I nor the women ever forgot that."

She wouldn't look at him. "What about all those fine married ladies and widows you . . . you had affairs with?"

"Damn Clarissa for telling you so much about my habits," he muttered, annoyed that all his pigeons were coming home to roost. Literally.

Her gaze shot to him. "I didn't find out all of it from her. I read the gossip rags the same as anyone else."

"Well, don't believe everything you read," he said irritably. "Yes, I did indulge myself a few times with . . . certain ladies of the *ton*, but that hardly bears mention. We coupled merely to assuage our mutual loneliness."

Good God, that was true. He'd never thought about it that way before, but his illicit affairs had always included more than a hint of desperation. For him as well as the bored wives.

"It won't be that way with us." At least he prayed it wouldn't. "You and I are trying to build a life together."

"That doesn't mean I know what I'm doing in the bedchamber," she said in a small voice.

"I wouldn't expect you to. What matters most to a man is not a woman's expertise but her enthusiasm." He bent to whisper in her ear, "Luckily for me, you've always had ample amounts of the latter."

"Still, when it comes to the point, I may disappoint you."

"I doubt that." He caught her by the chin. "Will it help if I tell you that I, too, am terrified?"

Her eyes flashed with scorn. "Don't be ridiculous. You've been with so many women—"

"Yes, but I've never deflowered one. So I'm just as worried about disappointing you as you are about disappointing me. After all, introducing a woman to the pleasures of the marital bed is tricky. I might cause you to hate it."

"I highly doubt that," she said dryly.

He smiled. She was always so bloody honest about her feelings, one of the many reasons he felt comfortable with her. "Aren't you the least bit worried about your own enjoyment?"

Her cheeks turned a bright pink. "You've

always made our intimate encounters . . . very pleasurable. So I can't see how doing . . . the deed itself . . . would be otherwise." Her tone turned glum. "Unless I mess it up somehow."

"Trust me, it's not *that* tricky." He smoothed back a lock of her hair. "How long have you been fretting over this?"

She darted a nervous glance at him. "Since you left for London."

"So I daresay by the time we consummate our marriage, you'll be in a fever pitch of worry over it. I won't have that." Cupping her head in his hands, he kissed her until she softened against him and returned the kiss with equal eagerness.

"What are you doing?" she whispered against his mouth.

He tossed his top hat onto a bench at the nearby table, then scattered openmouthed kisses down her jawline to her neck. "Having the wedding night before the wedding."

Her pulse quickened against his lips. "Here? Now?"

"Why not?" Shrugging off his coat, he threw it onto the table, then backed her toward it even as he continued caressing her throat with his mouth. "We have a penchant for being intimate in the most inappropriate places. Might as well go on as we have."

"But . . . but . . ."

He lifted her to set her atop his coat on the

table. "Tell me, dearling. Do you like it up here on the rooftop?"

She gazed about, her eyes brightening as she drank in the beautiful views. "Of course, but . . ."

"Then it's here I mean to take you."

Here, she might regain her usual reckless self and feel less compelled to behave as his "dutiful wife." That would go a longer way toward easing her fears than all his reassurances.

So he took her mouth again with all the pent-up lust he'd felt since that night he'd fondled her so boldly. And to his delight, she rose to the kiss.

"We really shouldn't be doing this, you know," she murmured after a moment. "It's scandalous."

"Says the woman who generally thumbs her nose at scandal." He dragged her skirts up above her garters, then skimmed his hands along the silky skin of her bared thighs with a feverish need to touch and caress and *have*. "I want you. You want me. So let's take what we want. Because I bloody well can't wait until tomorrow to have you."

She stared up at him with such longing that it made his heart miss a beat. "Y-you really mean that?"

Grabbing her hand, he pressed it against his erection, which strained against his trousers. "It's not as if I could lie about it, given *this*."

Her eyes darkened to the blue of storm clouds as she caressed him through the fabric. "My . . . well . . . that *is* very . . . interesting."

"This shows how much I ache to be inside you, dearling," he said hoarsely as he slipped his hand between her legs to rub and arouse her. "To take you and make you mine. In this place. At this moment. And I realize you deserve a proper bedding, in a soft bed with sheets. You deserve better than a quick tumble on a table on a rooftop."

He thrust his growing cock against her hand. "Yet even knowing that, knowing it's mad and unwise, I want it. I want *you*. But only if you're willing."

"It's not as if I could lie about it," she rasped, echoing his words as she undulated against his hand, her damp warmth driving him utterly insane. "Lord help me, but I do want you . . . as much as you want me. I just don't know . . . what to do."

"I'll show you." He'd show her that marital relations could be intoxicating. That even a marriage based on lust could be pleasurable. And that, in her case, he felt something more than—

God, no, it was only lust. Surely it was.

But as he slid his hand inside her wrapped gown to fondle one of her sweet breasts, he knew he was lying to himself. This was obsession. And for a man who'd never been obsessed before, it felt dangerous.

He didn't care. Caught up in his need, he pulled her bodice apart enough to jerk down her shift and corset cup so he could seize her lovely naked breast in his mouth.

"Oh my, yes . . ." she breathed as he frantically undid his trousers and drawers. "But you must show *me* what to do, how to . . . to touch you. I want . . . to be a real wife to you."

A *real* wife? He wasn't even sure what that was, or that he could be a real husband to her. But he couldn't think about that just now. Because he would die if he couldn't be inside her, with her, part of her.

And none of the rest mattered.

Seventeen

Delia couldn't believe she was sitting half-naked in the sun and wind while Warren put his hands all over her. She ought to be embarrassed.

Instead she felt wild and daring and giddily happy. Warren had sought her out as soon as he'd arrived from town. He'd done his best to reassure her about their future, despite now knowing more about her family and their troubles.

And he'd promised to be faithful to her. Sort of.

I can safely promise never again to spend my nights in the stews.

She would hold him to that. But first . . . "Show me how to please you. I want to touch you, too."

With a growl, he grabbed her hand and curved it around his now bared arousal. His eyes slid shut as a look of pure bliss swept his features. "God, yes, dearling. I *love* having you caress my cock. You have no idea . . ."

She'd heard the men speak of their cocks at Dickson's, not knowing that they meant this strange rod of flesh.

Fascinated by the length and rigidity of it, she stroked it with great delicacy. "Like this? Am I doing it right?" She didn't want to hurt him.

"It's fine," he breathed, "but it would be better if you held it . . . more firmly. Show me . . . you're not afraid of me."

"I'm not." Well, that wasn't entirely true. He was much larger than she'd expected. And that . . . that cock was supposed to go inside her? Lord.

But she did as he asked and gripped him more tightly. With a taut groan, he thrust into her hand. "Like that, yes. Oh, God, you're perfect."

Then he blotted out whatever she might have answered with a soul-consuming kiss. His hands grew bolder, one of them darting a finger inside her below while the other pinched her nipple lightly and made her gasp with surprise, then pleasure.

"I've thought of nothing but this since the day I met you," he said against her mouth. "Even then, I wanted you."

"I wanted you, too," she admitted. "But I knew it was mad."

He nipped her lower lip. "Why? Because of my reputation?"

"Yes. And the fact that you can . . . have anyone you want."

"Not anyone." He freed her other breast. "I gained *you* only by default."

As he bent to lave her with his tongue, she threaded her fingers through his luscious hair. "That's not true. If you'd offered for me at any point—"

"You would have accepted? Never." He tugged gently at her nipple with his teeth, shooting lusciously wanton sensations throughout her body. "You're too stubborn . . . to go easily."

"Yet I'm here now." She clutched him against her breast. "With you."

"Thank God. I don't think I could have borne another day without making you mine." He delved deeper inside her with his finger while his thumb fondled her at a different spot, making her squirm at the delicious thrills coursing through her. "You're so hot and wet for me, dearling. I need to be inside you."

"Yes," she murmured. His finger in her wasn't enough, though she wasn't sure why. "Make me your wife."

With a growl, he shifted their bodies so he could ease his rigid cock inside her.

My oh my. That was . . . different. It fit better than she'd expected. She was plenty aware of its size and girth, of the strange feeling of having something foreign thrust up inside her. But that warred with the satisfaction at having him joined to her at last.

There was a quick piercing discomfort, so

fleeting she hardly noticed. And then Warren was filling her to the brim, giving her all of himself.

"Heavens," she gasped, swept up in the acute pain-pleasure of having him buried inside her. She wished he'd withdraw, then wished he wouldn't.

He stopped moving entirely. "Are you all right?"

She didn't know how to answer. *All right* wasn't exactly how she'd describe how it felt. Invasive. Fascinating. *Intimate.* "I—I think so."

"It will get better, I swear."

Better?

Next thing she knew, he was drawing out, then coming in again with slow, steady strokes that made her pulse beat a rapid tattoo. At first she felt dragged upon a journey she didn't understand. She told herself it was enough to be here with him beneath the azure sky dotted with clouds. To know he would be her husband. Forever.

Then he pulled her a bit more forward on the table and caught her behind her knees to urge her legs around his waist. "Tuck your heels behind my thighs, dearling," he urged her.

She did so, giving a little gasp of delight when that sensitive spot between her legs bumped squarely against him.

That's when everything changed. This time when he drove inside her, it sent a frisson of pleasure echoing through her. He did it again and again, changing the journey into a thundering rush into the unknown, where he was driving her forward with thrust after thrust against the part of her that craved his touch.

"Ohhh . . ." That's what he'd meant by *better*. "That is . . ."

"Incredible?" he breathed. "Because that's how . . . you feel to me."

"Yes. Oh yes." Incredible and astonishing and beyond anything she'd ever known.

She fisted her hands in his shirt to hold him close as her body rose to meet his. The more he pounded into her, the more the world shrank until the only thing in it was her and Warren barreling forward. Together. Inextricably joined.

Soon all she knew was the rasp of his whiskers, his rapid breaths against her cheek . . . the ache in her heart to have the whole of him. It was mad and rash and she wanted it to go on and on . . .

"My lovely . . . amazing . . . wife. You belong to *me* now," he growled against her throat.

His possessive words delighted her. But they weren't enough. She needed him to be *hers* as well.

She'd make him hers if she had to seduce him every hour of every day for a month. "You belong to me, too," she hissed against his ear. "Promise me."

He choked out a laugh. "Yes, wife. Whatever you want."

His caresses grew rougher, sweeter, until a

roaring filled her ears and her body surged up and on, and she felt as if she were almost at the end . . . of her journey.

His jaw tightened. "God . . . bloody hell . . . that's it . . . Come for me, dearling. Please, my sweet, sweet . . . Delia . . ."

Then he drove into her hard one last time, and with a cry, she vaulted over into paradise.

~~~

Warren wasn't certain how long he'd stood there after he'd exploded inside his soon-to-be wife. Long enough for him to soften inside her, yet not long enough that he wanted to let go of her.

God, had he really just taken her like some tart on a table on a rooftop? That wasn't the way to endear a respectable woman to him.

Yet she hadn't seemed to mind. Judging from the way she'd clenched on his cock as she'd come, she'd found pleasure in it, too.

As she let out a long sigh of what he hoped was satisfaction, he buried a kiss in her lovely neck, fragrant with her lemony scent. "So. Are you still worried about . . . not pleasing me?"

"*Did* I please you?" she asked, a hint of coyness in her voice.

"As if you need to ask."

He lifted her off the table so she was wrapped around him, and she squealed. Strutting around with her clinging to him, he said, "I can demonstrate again exactly how *much* you pleased me, if you want."

She laughed down at him, his wanton wife-to-be. "Perhaps we should save *something* for the wedding night."

He cast her a mock frown. "Oh, very well. If you insist." And in truth, she was probably sore, anyway.

Letting her slip down his body inch by intoxicating inch, he took her mouth for a long, hot kiss that had her straining against him. Only then did he pull free.

She made a moue of protest, and he laughed. "That, brat, is so you'll be just as eager for me tomorrow night as I'm going to be for you."

"I don't think you need to worry about that," she said with a secretive little smile that had his body rousing again.

But before he could do anything about it, she strolled over to the table. He followed, fastening up his drawers and trousers as he went.

She laid her hand on his coat. "It appears I've given your valet more cause for complaint."

He looked over her shoulder to see a spot of blood staining the inside of his coat. It sobered him. "I didn't hurt you *too* badly, did I?"

"No. I'm told that a little bit of blood is normal."

"Told by whom? Your sister-in-law, who informed you that a woman must 'endure' marital relations? I don't know if I'd trust her."

"The deflowering part wasn't that bad, truly." She faced him, her eyes gleaming with mischief. "And what came after was quite . . . nice."

"Nice?" He dragged her against him. "*Nice?* I'll show you nice, you teasing wench."

As she gave a giddy laugh, he bent to kiss her.

Suddenly a noise sounded from far below them. "Warren? Delia? Are you there?"

Damn. Clarissa.

"Shh," he breathed against Delia's lips. "If we stay very quiet, perhaps she'll go away."

Two floors below them, the door to the folly opened and closed.

"Where are you?" A voice came wafting up the spiral staircase.

"That's Brilliana." Delia broke free of him. "And she will *not* go away. Besides, they're sure to see my bonnet hanging on the window latch."

Bloody hell, she was right.

As she hurried to restore her clothing to rights, he picked up his hat, then went to examine his coat. The blood hadn't gone through to the other side, thank God, though the coat was pretty much ruined now.

Even realizing that some of the blood might stain his shirt, he put the coat back on. He was happy to lose a shirt and coat in the process of reassuring his wife-to-be about their . . . suitability for each other in the bedchamber.

Hell, he was happy to lose them just for the chance of bedding her.

They heard steps on the stairs, and Delia hastened over to call down, "We're up here, admiring the views!"

Moments later, the two women emerged onto the roof.

Mrs. Trevor eyed him with suspicion. "Didn't you hear us come in?"

Delia cast him a warning glance even as her lips twitched in a clear struggle not to laugh. "It's very windy up here," she said blithely. "You can hardly hear a thing."

Clarissa accepted that explanation. "So what do you think? Shall we have the ceremony here at the folly?"

"Yes," he said, eager for mischief. "We could do it right here on the roof."

Now Delia's lips were *really* twitching. "We could *not*. First of all, the table is in the way. Second, someone is sure to back up and fall over one of those parapets. We'll do it downstairs. With the windows open, since it's a bit warm inside."

"That does sound marvelous," Mrs. Trevor said with one last wary glance at him. "Let's go down and figure out where we wish to put things. We need to get the servants over here soon to start decorating, too."

And with that, Mrs. Trevor and Clarissa trooped down the stairs, chattering about roses and doilies and something called a pom-pom.

Delia paused only long enough to chide him. "Have the wedding up here, indeed. You just want to revel in watching a holy father stand on the spot where we indulged in a bit of—"

"Ecstasy?" he said with a smug smile.

"Wickedness, more like. You love to surround yourself with it."

"I do indeed. Let this be your warning, my dear. You can remove the man from the wickedness, but you can't remove the wickedness from the man." And for emphasis, he swatted her lovely plump bottom with his hat.

"Stop that!" she said, and hurried to the staircase. But he caught a ghost of a smile crossing her lips as she disappeared down the stairs.

With a chuckle, he followed her more slowly, reminded that he hadn't seen her bottom in the flesh yet. Or her hair tumbling down around that bottom. He hadn't even really had a good look at her breasts or her dewy quim.

Well, as she'd said, they should save something for the wedding night. He meant to do a better job of making love to her then, when he had all the time and space in the world for it. She wouldn't refer to his efforts as merely *nice* next time, to be sure.

For the next hour, he tried to endure the prattle of the women as they tramped about the folly, measuring and plotting. By the time they headed back toward the house, the sun had begun to sink.

Clarissa glanced over to where he strolled arm in arm with Delia. "Where are you two going after the wedding tomorrow? Lindenwood Castle is rather far from here. And doesn't Parliament open soon?"

"It does, indeed. Which is why I mean to spend at least our wedding night at my town house." Warren slanted a look at Delia. "Assuming it's all right with my future wife."

"You mean I get a choice?" she teased.

He arched an eyebrow at her. "Pray do not cast me in the role of overbearing ogre, brat. It doesn't suit me."

"I don't know." She smirked at him. "Sometimes I think it suits you quite well, Lord High-and-Mighty Knightford."

Clarissa laughed. "Like my husband. These two have a tendency to announce their plans with an air of fait accompli. 'Command first, ask afterward' seems to be their motto."

Warren scowled. "In my case, it's only because I'm not used to taking a wife into account."

"You'd better *get* used to it," Delia said saucily. "You're stuck with me now."

"You mean, you're stuck with *him*," Clarissa teased.

Warren shot his cousin a hard look. "Don't pretend you're not pleased as punch about it, dear girl. You've been trying to marry me off since you were sixteen."

"And it only took me nine years to be success-ful." Clarissa's smile faded. "Though I do wish I'd started planning the actual *wedding* nine years ago. We still have so much left to do tonight. However will we get it all finished?"

"You could borrow some of Niall's servants," Warren said. "I'm sure he wouldn't mind." Someone hailed them from the path ahead, and he added, "Speak of the devil, here he comes now. You can ask him yourself."

Mrs. Trevor, who'd been walking ahead of Warren and Delia on the path, stopped short so quickly that they nearly mowed her down.

Even as Warren was wondering about that, Niall reached them. "There you are, sister," he said jovially to Clarissa. "I hear there's to be a wed—"

He halted mid-sentence as he caught sight of Mrs. Trevor. "Brilliana!"

Brilliana? Niall *knew* Delia's sister-in-law? And by her Christian name, no less?

Having noted that herself, Delia glanced up at Warren in bewilderment, and he shrugged. He'd had no idea.

Mrs. Trevor dropped into a curtsy. "Lord Oliver. How good to see you again."

Hastily, Warren corrected her. "Pardon me, Mrs. Trevor, but it's Lord Margrave now that he's inherited the title."

"Oh, right, of course," the woman said, her cheeks now a peculiar shade of red.

Niall said nothing, just stood there gaping at

Mrs. Trevor as if someone had brained him with a mallet. Having never seen his cousin at a loss for words before, Warren was tempted to torment the man about it.

But some instinct kept him silent.

"I . . . had heard you were living in Spain, my lord," Mrs. Trevor ventured.

That snapped Niall out of his trancelike state. "I was. Well, Portugal, more recently. Until a couple of weeks ago when I returned to England." He drew himself up stiffly. "*I'd* heard that you were married." He glanced beyond them. "Is your . . . husband around here somewhere?"

"I'm widowed."

Niall's gaze shot to her, and something flickered in his eyes that Warren well recognized. Hunger.

Hmm. How very interesting.

Clarissa narrowed her eyes on her brother. "You two *know* each other?"

Niall started, then forced a smile. "We do. We did. A short while. Before I left England."

Mrs. Trevor seemed to have regained her composure, too, for now she looked her usual serene self. "His lordship and I met in Bath several years ago, when my father took the family there one summer."

"And Mother had gone there for the waters," Niall said. "You were still not out as I recall, Clarissa, so you stayed at Margrave Manor with your governess."

"Oh," Clarissa said. Warren could almost see the wheels turning in her head. "I think I remember that." She shifted her gaze to Mrs. Trevor. "I can't believe you didn't tell me you knew my brother."

"It was only a brief acquaintance," Mrs. Trevor said. "And I knew him as Lord Oliver, not Lord Margrave. I'm afraid I didn't put together your being his sister and . . . I just didn't connect you."

Clarissa snorted. Clearly she found that explanation as spurious as Warren did. "Well, I wish to hear more about this 'brief acquaintance' later, but we still have a wedding to finish planning, and very little time to do it in."

"I almost forgot," Niall said, "that's why I was sent out here to look for you lot. We gentlemen wish to take Warren to the tavern in town for his last night of bachelorhood."

Thank God. If he drank with the fellows, he wouldn't have to endure the long night alone. "Sounds like an excellent plan," Warren said jovially.

Too jovially, apparently, for Delia frowned at him. "Now see here, I hope you don't mean to show up foxed at our wedding in the morning."

"I'm not making any promises," he drawled.

"Warren!"

He bent to kiss her forehead. "I'm joking, dearling. I'll be sober as a judge."

Niall was now sizing up Delia. "I take it that

this lady is the poor woman cursed to be your bride, old boy?"

"Ah, yes, you haven't met, have you?" Swiftly Warren provided the introductions, noting how Mrs. Trevor seemed to watch Niall furtively whenever the fellow wasn't looking.

Normally that wouldn't surprise him, since Niall was a fine-looking chap, with a strong jaw, a good head of sun-bronzed hair, and a lean but muscular build. Women generally liked his looks.

But Mrs. Trevor clearly liked more than his looks.

"Sorry to tear your fiancé away," Niall told Delia, "but it *is* bad luck for the groom to see the bride once night falls."

She smiled at him. "Thank heaven *someone* in your family appreciates the old traditions. My fiancé is oblivious to all of it."

"Yes, well, Warren has never been much for following rules," Niall said with a chuckle.

"Don't let her fool you," Warren put in. "She's not much of a rule-follower herself. Now come on, coz, let's go drinking."

"You don't have to ask me twice." Niall tipped his hat to the ladies. "I promise to bring him home in plenty of time to sober up for the wedding."

"You'd better," Clarissa said. As Warren and Niall headed for the stables, she called out, "Or I'll sic Edwin's dogs on you!"

"She probably would, too," Warren grumbled under his breath.

Niall cast him a rueful glance. "My sister has changed quite a bit since I went abroad."

"Yes. For the better, I think. Edwin has done her a great deal of good."

"And she has done the same for him."

Now that they were well away from the ladies, Warren asked what he'd been dying to know since Niall had joined them. "What's the truth about Mrs. Trevor and you?"

Niall stiffened. "I don't know what you mean."

"The hell you don't."

"Didn't you hear her?" Niall's tone turned acid. "Ours was only a 'brief acquaintance.' "

"Right. So brief that the two of you recognized each other instantly after seven years apart. That you called her by her Christian name. That she blushed so deeply at the sight of you that I thought her cheeks might catch fire."

"Did she?" Niall stared grimly ahead. "I hadn't noticed."

Right. "How is it that I'd never heard of your connection to her before today?"

"Because there wasn't one," he clipped out.

"Now that, coz, is a blatant lie if ever I heard one."

Niall rounded on him, fists clenching. "For God's sake, will you shut up about it?"

"Not until you explain yourself. The woman is going to be my sister-in-law, after all."

"Hardly. She's the sister-in-law of your wife-to-be, which makes you nothing to her."

"I won't debate that with you. The point is, I intend to keep an eye out for her and her son."

Shock darkened Niall's hazel eyes. "She has a son?"

Warren nodded. "Her bloody arse of a husband lost all their money at the card tables and then stumbled off a bridge drunk, leaving her with a newborn and an estate heavily in debt."

Niall stood there rigid, as if each revelation were a blow to his chest.

"A lot can happen in seven years," Warren added softly.

Drawing himself up with a shuddering breath, Niall continued his march to the stables. "Yes, it can."

"Niall—"

"I'm not going to talk about it," Niall said firmly. "You can ask and wheedle and taunt all you want, but the subject is closed. Understood?"

Warren took in the carved features of the man he'd grown up with and considered to be as much his brother as Hart or Stephen or any of them.

Clarissa wasn't the only one who'd changed. Niall's forced exile after killing her attacker in a duel had changed *him*, too. Gone was the lighthearted youth who'd always taken life as it came, and in his place was a hard man who'd learned that life could be tremendously unfair, even for an earl with a fine estate.

"Very well," Warren said.

But he suspected that if Niall wouldn't talk, Mrs. Trevor would, at least to Delia. So he would learn the truth that way.

Apparently having a wife included advantages he hadn't considered. It never hurt to have a gossipy female in one's pocket, after all.

Eighteen

Several hours after the ladies had parted from the gentlemen, Delia wasn't terribly surprised to have a servant inform her that Brilliana had retired with a headache. She had begun to realize that her sister-in-law had been avoiding being alone with her and Clarissa ever since they'd met up with Lord Margrave.

At first, Delia had thought it merely the result of their frenzy to finish plans for the wedding. As soon as Warren and his lordship had left, the servants had approached to help them with choosing flowers from the garden, and from then on, she and Clarissa and Brilliana had constantly been surrounded by others. Clarissa's sister-in-law Yvette Keane had joined them, as had Aunt Agatha, and it had been one task after another in trying to get things ready for the ceremony.

Yet when Delia had finally found a moment to be alone with her sister-in-law and had attempted to ask about Brilliana's peculiar response to Lord Margrave, the woman had changed the subject and plunged into another task that would land them in the midst of a group of people.

Now she'd gone to bed, which Delia found highly suspicious. Brilliana never retired without saying good night to her.

"I'll be right back," Delia told Clarissa, then hurried up to her sister-in-law's room. Something was wrong, having to do with Lord Margrave, and Delia meant to find out exactly what.

But when she knocked at Brilliana's door, there was no answer. And after knocking harder, then trying the door and discovering it latched, Delia realized there would be no response tonight. Apparently Brilliana was determined not to talk about this afternoon's peculiar meeting.

She would let Brilliana play the coward for now, but her sister-in-law couldn't avoid her forever.

Clarissa came up next to Delia, having obviously followed her upstairs. "Is Mrs. Trevor all right?"

"I don't think so." Delia raised her voice. "But I can't be sure since she's pretending not to hear me!"

Even that got no response from inside the room.

"Perhaps she really does have a headache," Clarissa whispered.

"I doubt it. Brilliana doesn't get headaches."

"Well, I came to find out if you want a few rosettes sewn on that veil of your aunt's, to make it look less plain."

With a sigh, Delia headed down the hall with Clarissa. "At this point, I'm so tired I don't even care."

"Of course you are." Clarissa halted outside the door to Delia's bedchamber. "We're fairly ready; you should go to bed." A sly smile crossed her lips. "You'll need plenty of sleep tonight to make up for your lack of it tomorrow night."

Delia bit back a smile of her own. She certainly hoped she would. Because her one experience of conjugal relations with Warren hadn't been nearly enough. Why, she had yet to see him naked. That alone had her eager for her wedding night.

Clarissa left her to the tender care of a maid, and by the time Delia was in her nightdress she was practically dead on her feet. Despite her desire to play her lovely time with Warren over and over in her head, she fell asleep as soon as she climbed between the sheets.

It seemed like only a moment later that she was awakened by a commotion on the lawn. Singing? What in heaven's name? Was someone actually singing on the lawn in the dead of night?

No, it was more like a caterwauling, punctuated by loud laughter. Dragging herself from her bed, she headed to the window and opened it to look out.

The lawn below was ablaze with torches held by stumbling gentlemen. And in the midst stood Warren, weaving along between Lord Margrave and Lord Blakeborough, who seemed to be holding him up. Well, sort of holding each other up, since all three were staggering, obviously in their cups. Mr. Keane was little better, though he was managing to smoke a cigar as he walked unsteadily behind them.

His companions were singing, "With women and wine I defy every care / For life without these is a bubble of air."

Good Lord.

"Would you gentlemen please be quiet?" cried an imperative voice from another window nearby. Aunt Agatha's, of course. "Some of us are trying to sleep."

Warren glanced up, caught sight of Delia in *her* window, and broke into a grin. "Behold, what light through yon window breaks," he said, slurring every other word. "It is the west . . ."

"No, *east*!" Lord Blakeborough interrupted, in what he apparently thought was a whisper but was actually quite thunderous. "It is the *east*, damn you."

"Right," Warren said. "The east. And Delia is the sun." Pleased with himself for that comparison, which he obviously considered terribly original of him, he flicked his hand vaguely in her direction. "Arise, fair sun, and . . . and . . . something about the moon . . ."

"Kill the moon?" Mr. Keane offered. "Can't remember exactly."

"And you aren't to look at the *bride*," Lord Margrave hissed loudly. "It's bad lush."

"Bad *luck*," Lord Blakeborough corrected him. "And it's 'kill the enemy moon.' *Enemy*, you sots."

"It's 'envious moon,'" Aunt Agatha called from her window, "and if you gentlemen don't stop murdering Shakespeare, I shall empty my chamber pot on your heads!"

That finally got them to shut up. For about half a minute.

"Very well," Warren said. "Then we'll sing."

"Lord help us all," Aunt Agatha muttered before she banged her window shut.

Delia knew she ought to be horrified by their inebriated state—or at the very least, annoyed—but having watched men in their cups many a time at Dickson's, she merely found it amusing. "I thought you said you weren't going to be foxed for the wedding!" she called down to her hapless fiancé.

"I'm not foxed!" he protested, then made a liar out of himself by stumbling into a stone bench and nearly bringing his companions down.

After a few harrowing moments, they recovered their balance.

He held up his arms. "You see? Not foxed a'tall!"

Before Delia could do more than laugh at him, Clarissa was rushing out onto the lawn in her nightdress and wrapper, accompanied by an army of servants who each grabbed a gentleman and tugged him into the house. The last Delia saw of her groom-to-be was his gray top hat disappearing through the French doors downstairs.

With a sigh, she glanced at the clock. Five a.m. And the wedding was to take place at ten. She ought to return to bed, but how could she? In only a few hours, she'd be *marrying* a man who, at least in his drunken state, compared her to Shakespeare's Juliet.

A smile tugged at her lips. There were worse things, to be sure. At least she wasn't marrying a gambler.

But other fears crowded in, making it impossible for her to sleep. Instead, she found a pack of cards and sat down to play Patience. She was still doing so an hour later when the maid came to wake her.

"Is my sister-in-law up yet?" Delia asked the girl.

"I believe so, miss. Shall I ask her to join you?"

"No. I'll go, thank you."

Delia slid out past the maid and hurried stealthily down the hall, then scratched at Brilliana's door the way servants generally did.

"Enter!" Brilliana called.

With a triumphant smile, Delia did. She'd cornered her sister-in-law at last.

Brilliana looked up and started. "Delia! You're up?"

"How could I not be, after that caterwauling earlier?" She strolled to the bed and sat down. "Didn't you hear them?"

"I tried not to, but it was no use. It sounded as if some of them were drunk."

"Every last one of them was drunk. Including your old friend, Lord Margrave."

Brilliana colored. "Not *my* old friend. I barely know him."

"Don't lie to me, dearest," Delia said. "The two of you clearly had more than a brief acquaintance years ago."

"If we did, it is well in the past," Brilliana said firmly. "Notwithstanding that he's the brother of your friend, he is not to be trusted."

"I don't see why not. If you mean to marry for the sake of Camden Hall, you couldn't ask for a husband better suited to handle Silas's inheritance and help improve it."

The woman snorted. "Have you not heard why Lord Margrave ended up abroad in the first place?"

Delia sifted through her store of gossip. "Because he dueled with a man over some woman?"

"Over some *soiled dove*. A mistress the two men shared, apparently."

"Or so the gossips say."

"In this case, the gossips are right."

"You know that for a certainty?"

Brilliana rose to go throw open the curtains. "I know enough. And having endured the results of Reynold's ruling vice, I shan't marry a man whose vice is even worse. Because the kind of men who become enamored of such women—"

When she stopped short, Delia sighed. "You're thinking that *my* husband is that kind of man."

To her shock, Brilliana rushed over to seize her hands. "Then don't marry him. To the devil with the scandal. We'll get through it all somehow."

Delia tugged her hands free. "He's not like that now. And he says he'll be faithful to me."

Brilliana's expression grew troubled. "Reynold said he wouldn't gamble, yet he did."

"I *want* to marry Lord Knightford. Mad as it seems, he makes me happy."

"Do you love him?"

The pointed question startled her. She hadn't thought about it, too caught up in worrying over how much he knew of her circumstances and what he'd do about them. "I don't know," she said truthfully. "I enjoy his company and—" *He excites me physically.*

No, she could hardly admit that to her sister-in-law.

"Does he love *you*?" Brilliana asked.

That was an even harder question. Somehow she couldn't see Warren being the sort of man to fall head over heels for anyone.

And I can tell you right now that I bloody well won't 'look the other way' if you go hunting for some other man in your bed.

Then again, did men say such lovely possessive things if they *didn't* have some affection for a woman? "I don't know that, either. It's not as if we've been acquainted with each other very long."

"That's what worries me."

"Please don't fret over it." Delia rose. "He's a good man at heart, I believe. Aunt Agatha said he gave me a most generous settlement, and he's even promised to help with Camden Hall until arrangements can be made to keep it from being foreclosed upon."

Brilliana blinked at her. "He has?"

"Oh, right. I haven't had a chance to tell you about that yet."

But even as she started laying out what of Warren's conversation yesterday she could reveal, her mind kept circling that one question of Brilliana's.

Does he love you?

How she wished she knew the answer.

❦

By the time Warren stood at the head of the rows of chairs in the folly, waiting for his bride to come down the spiral staircase from the floor above, he was entirely clearheaded.

Nothing like attending one's own wedding to sober a man right up.

And the gallons of coffee Clarissa and her servants had poured into them early this morning had certainly helped. So had delaying the wedding until noon to give the men a chance to sleep it off.

He felt bad about that. All he remembered of last evening's festivities was drinking himself senseless to hold back the dark, and then serenading Delia from the lawn.

It *had* been Delia he'd serenaded, hadn't it? Her aunt kept getting mixed up in that image, which was rather disturbing.

Bloody hell, if he'd serenaded Lady Pensworth, how would he ever live *that* down?

Mrs. Trevor stepped forward and began to play a violin, jerking his attention back to his wedding. The woman really was quite good. How surprising.

A sound on the stairs caught his attention, and he looked over to see a cloud of blue silk descending.

Delia. His bride. He had a *bride*, for God's sake.

She came fully into view, and his heart stopped. She was so lovely. Her cheeks shone rosy, and her lips curved in a hesitant smile that made his blood run hot. She wore some frothy thing that spilled down the steps as she walked. The bodice accentuated her small but pert breasts, which he'd ravaged less than a day ago.

And wanted to ravage now. Wouldn't that shock the parish priest?

She carried a bouquet in her lace-gloved hands. The bride's bouquet, with hydrangeas and roses and God knew what else wrapped in more lace and ribbons, brought home the fact that he was really getting married. To Delia.

That hit him with all the weight of an anvil. He would be responsible for her happiness. Somehow he would have to reconcile her needs with his strange way of life—the mornings and days spent sleeping short hours so he could do the work of an heir.

They were marrying. They would be linked forever, would have children together.

Children? God, he'd forgotten all about that. They hadn't even discussed it. What if she didn't want children? He must have an heir. Surely she would understand that.

But how could he have children when he couldn't bear the night? Would he wake them with his screaming? Would they know him only as the man who roamed the city to keep his fear at bay while they slept?

This was happening too fast. He was marrying. Had he lost his bloody mind?

Then Delia reached the bottom of the stairs, and her eyes locked with his—so blue that they seared a path right to his soul—and he saw in them the same uncertainty he felt.

Oddly, that calmed him. They would get through this together, somehow.

She walked down the aisle, an ethereal creature in lace and silk, and he concentrated on their wedding night to come. The rest would fall into place. It had to. Because he couldn't back out now.

When she joined him before the priest, a surge of something that felt oddly like possessiveness seized him. How mad was that? This was an unplanned consequence of his nightmares, nothing more. Yet the sound of her voice, repeating the vows after he had done the same, made his blood roar through his veins with an avaricious satisfaction he couldn't deny.

Still, he couldn't ignore the twitching of her lips when the priest said, "Wilt thou obey him, and serve him," et cetera, et cetera.

"I will," she said, deliberately not meeting Warren's eyes.

So when Warren was asked to take the ring, to speak the words, "With this ring I thee wed, with my body I thee worship, and with all my worldly goods I thee endow," he made sure to catch her gaze.

And the blush that suffused her face told him that they might do very well together. As long as he could keep his weakness secret from her.

Then came the part of the ceremony where a kiss was expected. And he damned well gave

her a kiss to remember. Because if they were
to start a life together, then she might as well
know one truth.

He would start this marriage as he meant to
go on. He would thoroughly enjoy the part of
marriage that allowed him to bed his wife.

And God help them both if that wasn't
enough.

Nineteen

Delia was so exhausted, she scarcely made it through the wedding breakfast. In addition to having had little sleep last night, the tension of today's events had sapped her energy. By the time she and Warren climbed into his carriage shortly before nightfall and headed for London, she could barely keep her eyes open.

She tried, though. She really did.

"What did you think of the service?" he asked as he settled back against the squabs across from her.

"It was lovely. Didn't you think so?"

"It was a wedding. What else is there to say?" When she glanced out the window, trying to hide how that answer disappointed her, he added, "But you made a beautiful bride in all that lace and silk."

The words, huskily spoken, set her more at ease. "You didn't look too bad yourself, my lord."

In a coat of royal-blue superfine with black silk lapels and black breeches, he'd looked every inch the marquess he was. It was a little unsettling to realize that the magnificent fellow with the gold buttons and sapphire stickpin in his silk cravat belonged to her. She hardly knew what to do with such extravagance.

He acknowledged the compliment with a nod. "You must tell my valet as much. He was in a dither of worry about making sure I looked the part."

Of course. "I still haven't met this illustrious fellow. I begin to think he's a ghost." His valet had gone on ahead to the town house to unpack his lordship's belongings and probably have a maid unpack hers as well.

"You'll meet him tomorrow. I gave him tonight off. I don't think I'll need him for our wedding night."

The hungry look in his eyes sent a delicious excitement down her spine. "Does that mean you'll play lady's maid for me?"

"I wouldn't miss that for the world," he said in that rough rasp that never failed to heighten her pulse. "I can't wait to see what lies beneath that frothy gown."

"But you've already seen what lies beneath my gowns."

"Not enough of it, trust me. You have no idea how often I've imagined you in the altogether."

Altogether? Did he mean *naked*? Somehow it

hadn't occurred to her that he might wish that. What if he didn't like what he saw? Her breasts were awfully small and her derriere far too large. "Even my maid never saw me . . . without anything on. Are you sure that's what you want?"

He eyed her as if she were mad. "Of course. You know perfectly well I desire you in every way. What I've seen so far has only fired my determination to see more."

Now that she thought about it, his Roman costume hadn't shown her near enough of his lean form, either. Perhaps seeing each other naked could work both ways.

"You'll let me see you in the altogether, too, won't you?" she asked.

His gaze smoldered. "To be sure. I can't wait to feel your hands all over my naked body."

That sounded perfectly marvelous, though she wasn't sure she should admit it. "Oh." She was sure her cheeks were quite rosy now.

"But if we keep talking like this, I'm going to take you right here and now, and to hell with waiting."

"Why wait?" she blurted out.

Raw need flared in his face, and he shifted on the seat as if suddenly quite uncomfortable. "Because, dearling, this time I mean to do it right."

"Did we do it wrong before?"

He gave a rueful laugh. "No. But the wedding night at least should be in a bed."

"How very conventional of you," she teased.

"Watch it, brat, or I *will* strip you naked right here in the carriage—and then we'll have a devil of a time getting you properly dressed again. Is that the condition you want to be in when you meet my servants?"

"I suppose not," she said, sobering at the idea of facing his staff. "How much do they know about me, anyway?"

"They know you're a respectable lady and my wife," he said firmly, "which is all they need to know."

Hmm. She wasn't so sure about that. Servants could be a tricky lot.

"I should have asked before now," he added, "but do you have a lady's maid of your own back in Cheshire, whom you wish to have me bring to London?"

"Brilliana and I used to share a maid, but we've had to play lady's maid to each other ever since . . ." She swallowed. "We had to let most of our staff go. Only Owen and our cook remained."

"Ah. Well, then, instead of going on to Lindenwood Castle, perhaps we should stay in London so you can hire a lady's maid and any other additional servants you think you might require. I have to be in town for Parliament soon, anyway."

"And I'll need to pack up all my things at Aunt Agatha's and have them brought over to your town house."

"Already done. Your aunt's servants and mine

took care of that while she and I were at the lawyers."

"You were that sure of me?" she said, raising
an eyebrow.

"Your aunt was that sure of *me*. She had me
over a barrel, and she knew it."

She couldn't help laughing. "Sorry. I ought to
feel guilty about that, but I can't say I do just
now."

"I should hope not. I'm considered quite a
catch, you know."

"Are you?" she said lightly. "I suppose that
means you have gobs of money and more than
one property and loads of servants." All of which
she would be expected to help him manage. The
prospect sounded rather daunting. "Oh, dear,
how many servants *do* you have, anyway?"

He launched into a description of the staff at
his myriad properties, which proved to be diz-
zyingly varied. After a while, she could scarcely
keep up with it all, especially since her lack of
sleep had begun to take its toll. Before long, she
found herself yawning.

"Please forgive me." She covered her mouth.
"It's all very fascinating, but I am just rather . . ."

"Tired?" In an instant, regret shadowed his features. "I can't imagine why, since your oaf of a
husband woke you in the middle of the night by
yowling outside your window."

"True," she said tartly, then yawned again.

"Come here," he ordered, holding out his hand.

When she took it, he tugged her over next to him, then settled her comfortably up against him. "Sleep," he murmured. "I daresay you need it after the past few days."

When he put his arm around her, she snuggled up against him with a sigh. In moments, the steady rocking of the carriage and the warmth of his body lulled her into a dreamless slumber.

The next thing she knew, she was being carried out of the coach and up some steps. By Warren, judging from the scent of his cologne. She burrowed deeper into his arms, and he chuckled.

"Are we at your town house already?" she whispered.

"It's been over an hour since we left Stoke Towers, Sleeping Beauty. But yes, we're in town. And I think we'll wait until morning for you to meet the staff."

"Mmm, all right." She dozed again . . . until the sensation of being laid upon a bed and having her shoes removed woke her once more.

She gazed up into an enormous velvet canopy with gold tassels and blinked. As Warren turned away, she sat up. "Wait, where are you going?"

He paused to look at her. "You're clearly too tired for a wedding night, dearling."

"I've had a good nap. I'm ready for anything."

"I'm not so sure about that."

Rather than argue with him, she threw her legs over the side and glanced about the room. Aside from being the largest bedchamber she'd ever seen in a London town house, it was curiously feminine, with rose motifs on everything and curtains of rose brocade. Not to mention huge gilded mirrors and a marquetry dressing table fit for a queen.

"Is this our bedchamber?"

"*Your* bedchamber." He gestured to a door. "Mine is through there."

She stared at him. "But . . . but why wouldn't we share a bed?"

"We shall, I promise." He grinned at her. "Indeed, I greatly anticipate it. When we sleep, however, we'll retire to our own rooms."

"My parents always shared a bedchamber."

His grin faded. "Mine did not." He added hastily, "I realize the décor is probably too old-fashioned for you, since this was my mother's room before she embraced the Methodist faith and began sleeping in a smaller, more sober one, and I'm fine with your altering it to suit your own tastes. Indeed, you may wish to make other changes to—"

"Warren," she said, to halt his flow of words. "Just because your parents slept separately doesn't mean *we* have to."

He stiffened. "No, but I prefer to do so." When he saw the hurt look on her face, he softened his tone. "I promise, you won't actually *want* to sleep in the same bed with me. I don't . . . rest well most nights, which is why I wander."

"You mean because of the nightmares."

His jaw tightened. "Partly. And I talk in my sleep. Among other things."

"So does Brilliana, and I've shared a bed with her in inns without a problem. Trust me, it won't bother me in the—"

"It will bother *me*," he said in a voice that brooked no refusal. "So I shall sleep alone, as I always do."

Another lordly pronouncement she was supposed to simply accept without question. Fine. She didn't wish to get into an argument with him on their wedding night.

Still, that didn't mean she would forget about it. Having witnessed one of his disturbing nightmares and hearing that he'd had others, she wondered how much his wandering had to do with them. One way or the other, she intended to get to the bottom of that—and figure out how she could help him sleep more easily.

But not tonight.

"Whatever you wish." It was easy to speak the lie. To choose to wait until he trusted her more with his heart.

His heart? Lord, she was in trouble if she thought she could ever capture it.

"Whatever I wish, eh?" His mood lightened as he approached. "And what if I wish to see you naked?" With eyes gleaming, he drew her up off the bed and into his arms. "Will you permit me to play lady's maid now? Or are you too tired, still?"

"I assure you I'm quite thoroughly awake." She looped her arms about his neck and gave him a quick kiss, which he turned into a longer, hotter one.

Then he began to undress her . . . slowly, achingly, punctuating every motion with kisses and caresses. Her heart hammered harder with every piece of clothing he whisked away. There was something very unnerving about having him bare her completely. Especially when he was fully dressed.

So she halted him after he'd removed all but her shift and her drawers. "I want to see you, too," she whispered. "Let me play valet for you."

He sucked in a harsh breath. "Your wish is my command, wife."

She had a cursory knowledge of how all the pieces of clothing went together, but after removing his coat and waistcoat, she had some trouble undoing his cravat, which seemed to be tied in an unnecessarily complicated knot.

"Want some help?" he asked in a throaty murmur.

She gave a tight nod. When he laughed and obliged her by removing the pesky strip of cloth, she muttered, "Now I see why you have a valet. No one could ever do so extravagant a knot on their own."

He gestured to her elaborate coiffure. "I could say the same about your hair. Take it down, dearling. I'm sure I'd snarl it in the attempt."

As she let it fall and turned to place her hairpins on the dressing table, he came up behind her to fill his hands with her curls. "Ah, how lovely it is." He caught a lock of it up to his lips and kissed it. "I knew it would be as luscious as the rest of you."

She caught her breath at the compliment. "It's very hard to . . . manage."

"Rather like its owner. And I enjoy all that glorious unmanageability." Sweeping the mass aside so he could kiss her neck, he murmured, "Time to remove the rest of your clothes, dearling."

She faced him. "You first."

He arched an eyebrow. "For a woman reckless enough to gamble in the stews, you certainly are shy."

"Not shy," she lied, reluctant to admit her real fear. That once he saw her naked, he'd regret marrying her. She tugged at his shirt collar. "I'm just eager to see what I bartered my freedom to gain."

"So that's it, is it?" His gaze boring into her, he stripped off his shirt.

At her first glimpse of his fully bared chest, she could hardly breathe. Spreading her hands over it, she whispered, "For a man who spends all his time in the stews, you are quite. . . muscular."

His throat moved convulsively. "I do ride, you know. And fence. And—" That ended in a groan when she ran her thumbs over his nipples.

"You were saying?" she teased. She rather liked

having him at *her* mercy for a change. Sliding her fingers down his taut belly, she unfastened his breeches and reveled in the way the bulge beneath them thickened at her touch.

But before she could go any further, he brushed her hands aside so he could undo the rest and shuck breeches, drawers, and stockings in one fell swoop.

Leaving him naked at last.

She drank her fill. My oh my. So *this* was what a man looked like beneath his clothes. Much hairier than she would have expected, not to mention more . . . sculpted. And his . . . cock . . . was sticking right out, the impudent thing.

When it bobbed under her gaze, she grew a bit embarrassed to be caught staring at it and dropped her gaze lower. That's when she caught sight of a scar that ran about six inches down one of his well-wrought calves to his foot.

With her heart in her throat, she bent to trace the deep groove. "What's this?"

He tensed. "Nothing."

"Clearly not nothing." She stared at it. "It looks awful. It must have hurt terribly."

His breath grew heavy as he pulled her up from the floor. "I stepped on an oil lamp while in the cellar as a boy, and the glass shattered, slicing my leg."

"Good Lord! How deeply?"

"Deep enough."

"What were you doing in a cellar?"

He shrugged. "You know how boys are—always getting into trouble and going places they shouldn't."

Something about the sudden darkness in his eyes told her there was more to it than that, but before she could ask for details, he reached up to unbutton her shift.

"Enough stalling, wife," he said hoarsely. "Now it's *my* turn to see what I bartered *my* freedom for."

Twenty

Warren had only a moment to congratulate himself on avoiding the subject of his scar before Delia slipped off her shift and drawers, and his every sense went on high alert.

Damn. She was even more beautiful than he'd imagined—skin as smooth and silky as cream, breasts like two custards topped with juicy cherries, and a jet-black thatch of hair covering what he knew from touch to be a delectable quim.

But best of all were the loveliest full hips he'd ever seen in his life. God help him. She was a work of art.

As she flushed under his gaze, he circled her so he could get a look at the rest of her plump arse, and the minute he saw it, he knew he was in deep, deep trouble. With her hair spilling sweetly down to frame it in raven curls, it was absolutely exquisite.

"Bloody, bloody hell."

She went rigid. "What's wrong?"

"Not a damned thing." He gave in to the temptation to fill his hands with those two perfect globes of flesh and took his time squeezing and molding them. "You, my dear, have the bottom of an angel."

The tension ebbed from her. "Do you make a practice of looking at angel bottoms, sir?"

He was tempted to say that her arse exceeded the best of any woman he'd ever seen, but no point in reminding her of his less-than-stellar reputation. "It's a figure of speech. And one you amply deserve."

"'Ample' being the operative word," she said dryly.

"I like ample." Rubbing up against her, he let her feel the length of his hardening cock against that pretty bottom. "As perhaps you can tell."

"You like everything," she murmured.

"On you, I do." He reached around to fill his hands with her bosom next. "I like these." Continuing to knead one pert little breast, he slid his other hand down to fondle her shamelessly between the legs. "And this. You're a feast of pleasures, dearling."

As he slipped one, then two fingers inside her, she gasped. "And we both know you like feasting."

"I definitely enjoy feasting on *you*." He leaned over her shoulder to nip her ear. "One day, my sweet, I'm going to bend you over and take you from behind so I can view that lovely bottom of yours the entire time I plunge into your sweet quim."

She got wetter at the words, which told him that he wasn't alone in finding the idea exciting. "No time . . . like the present."

That made his cock leap. "Don't tempt me. I promised you a more conventional bedding," he reminded her. "But I confess I can hardly breathe for wanting to take you that way."

"Then do it," she said.

That was all the encouragement he needed to walk her over to the dressing table and bend her over it, where she braced herself against the top with her hands. Then he drew back to survey how lovely she looked: her lush behind so perfectly displayed for him, her fine back so nicely arched, and her wild hair spilling over her shoulders onto the dressing table.

"Spread your legs, dearling," he said hoarsely, and she did. Now he could see the furrow between her thighs that he wished to plunder thoroughly. "God, you're so damned beautiful."

He glanced up to meet her eyes in the mirror, that steady blue that always arrowed right to his chest. The blush was fading from her cheeks, replaced by an expression of rampant curiosity.

How had he been so fortunate as to find a wife who seemed as interested in bed sport as he?

"You make me randy as hell." Sliding his hand between her legs, he caressed the pouting nether lips drenched with her arousal. "And I'm not the only one enjoying this, am I?"

"No." A coy smile crossed her face. Then she echoed his words, "As perhaps you can tell."

His cock certainly could, for it got hard enough to pound nails. "I begin to think you and I are more evenly matched than I originally believed, brat."

He needed to be inside her, damn it. But he was determined that she find pleasure in this, too. So he concentrated on caressing her sweet spot until he had her panting and shimmying against his hand. At the same time he bent over to reach beneath her so he could rub one of her breasts while he continued to fondle her quim from behind.

When her eyes slid shut and she moaned, a heady satisfaction coursed through him. She was so damned responsive. It made him want her even more.

Unable to bear the intensity of his arousal any longer, he eased himself inside her. She made an odd sound, a cross between a gasp and a moan.

"Are you all right?" he rasped.

Because God knew *he* wasn't. He was already half-mad for his wife, who would take over his life if he allowed her the chance.

"No," she replied. "I'm out of my mind with wanting you."

Her answer spiked his need higher. "Then you shall have me. Hold on, my sweet. This may be a rough ride."

Then he was plunging into her, drinking up her soft cries and moans, losing himself in the hot, wet silk of her that milked his cock with every thrust. All the while he fingered her, determined not to lose control of his own arousal before she came.

"Warren . . ." She gripped his forearm. "Oh . . . yes, my darling. Yes, yes . . . my husband!"

The possessive words sent him beyond control. With one last hard thrust, he spilled his seed and collapsed atop her. Half a moment later she convulsed around him and cried out her own release.

As he stood there inside her, with his body plastered against her sweet bottom, it dawned on him that until tonight he'd never lost control with a woman. Never been so obsessed with a woman that even after bedding her, he couldn't keep his hands off her.

Even now, as his cock softened, he couldn't get enough of her. He wanted to kiss every inch of her sweetly bowed back, to wrap himself in her hair . . . to make her come again in as many ways as possible.

Fighting the panic that such an impulse made him feel, he slipped out of her, then pulled her around into his arms so he could crush her to his chest and forget that he'd just taken her like a whore. His *wife*. Whom he wanted again.

And again and again and—

She kissed his cheek, and he groaned.

God, what if he disappointed her? Because in the long run, he was bound to, the way he'd disappointed his mother, his father, his tutors, and every woman who'd come before Delia.

Don't be a sniveling coward, boy. Lords aren't afraid of the dark. Buck up and be a man.

He shivered at the thought of such words—or something like them—coming from his wife.

That mustn't happen. So he must take care to set the terms of this marriage very clearly. And do his damned best to abide by them. Better to give her a little bit of disappointment now than let her see the rank fear that lay at the center of his soul.

~⁓~

Delia felt him withdraw from her as palpably as she'd felt him inside her. And not just physically. As he pulled away, she saw a mask come down over his face.

She couldn't muster a mask if her life depended on it. She couldn't stop trembling, couldn't stop the repeated clenching of her "quim," as he'd called it. It had just been so . . . astonishing. She'd watched him in the mirror taking her, thrilling to the rapt expression on his face. Feeling the power of him behind her, inside her . . . conquering her.

Conquering her? No man did that. This had just been conjugal relations.

She stifled her snort. Right. The most amazing conjugal relations she could ever have imagined. With her husband, of all things.

Hers. He was *hers*! And she would hold on to what was hers for dear life, no matter what it took.

Even if he *was* staring at her now as if he regretted what they'd done. "I'd meant to have our wedding night go differently," he said, raking his hand through his hair. "To linger over you and make soft, sweet love to you, like a husband should."

"I liked it," she said gently, not willing to let him spoil things when she was still quivering from their joint pleasure. "I don't have any clue what a husband *should* do, but I loved knowing that I could make you . . . insane with desire."

His gaze shot to her, careful, diffident. "Of course you did. You've been making me insane in every other way for the past week—I can't imagine why you wouldn't continue the entertaining practice."

"Me?" she said with a lift of one brow. "You're the one who's been making *me* insane from the beginning by keeping me from my purpose. Who kept showing up at Dickson's to torment me with fear that you'd expose me."

He bent close. "Let me tell you a little secret. I never had any intention of exposing you."

She'd already guessed as much, though she'd never let on. "You could have said something."

He glanced away, his mask in place once more. "That would have taken all the fun out of it."

"Is that all it was for you? Entertainment?" She poked a finger at his naked and quite impressive chest. "Well, that came back to slap you in the face, didn't it, Lord High-and-Mighty? I daresay you wouldn't have been so cavalier if you'd known you would end up forced into marrying me."

Having made her point, she tried to slip from between him and the dresser, but he caught her and kept her prisoner with his hands braced on either side of her.

"Let's settle something once and for all, my sweet." His dark eyes bored into her. "I was *not* forced into marriage. After your aunt and I left for London, she gave me the choice—attempt to squelch the rumors, or marry you. I *chose* the latter. Because I knew it would be best for both of us."

That stunned her. Aunt Agatha had offered him an escape, and he hadn't taken it? Truly?

Just as that began to soften her, the full impact of his words hit her. "Funny how you 'knew' what would be best for me, without consulting me."

"Your aunt didn't give me the choice of consulting you." He caught her chin in his hand. "Tell the truth—do you regret the marriage?"

She stared into his eyes. "No." *Not yet, anyway.*

Satisfaction lit his features before he masked it. "Then what's done is done." His gaze hardened on her. "So don't ever let me hear you say again that I had no choice. You may feel as if *you* had none, but I damned well had a choice. And I chose you."

Those firm words melted some of her worry about the future. Until he added, as he released her, "This may not be a love match, but it's a good one all the same."

And that was that. For him, this was nothing more than a wise union between two respectable people who needed to be married.

As he turned away, she fought to hide the bleeding of her heart. He was only speaking a truth she would have said herself a day or so ago. But now that she'd fallen in love with him . . .

She stifled a groan. She couldn't have been so foolish as to fall in love with him, could she?

But the truth hit her with staggering force. Lord. She had.

Curse him to hell. He made her feel things, want things . . .

It wasn't fair! Especially since his matter-of-fact statement about this being no love match made it clear he didn't feel the same.

So she must keep her secret safe. The only thing worse than falling in love with a man who didn't love you was letting him see you wear your heart on your sleeve. That made a woman look pathetic.

As if his words had reminded *him*, too, that theirs was nothing more than a convenient arrangement, his mood grew even more distant. He picked up his clothes and began to dress. "I suppose it's time I let you get some sleep."

The coolly spoken words sliced deeply into her, but she forced herself to ignore it. "That would be lovely, thank you," she managed to say. "But you need sleep, too." *Stay with me. Be with me. It's our wedding night!* "You didn't get much more rest than I did last night."

"Ah, but I'm used to that." Without meeting her gaze, he gestured to a chest of drawers. "You'll find your nightclothes in there, I believe."

She choked down the howling of her heart and concentrated on searching the chest for her nightdress and wrapper.

As she donned them, he pulled his shirt on, then gathered up the rest of his clothes and headed for the door of the adjoining bedchamber.

All her pride fled. "Warren!" she called as he reached it. "Won't you stay with me a while longer?"

A hint of regret crossed his face before he shuttered it. "I don't think that's wise. You need sleep, and I . . . have business matters to attend to. It's not as late as it probably seems to you."

"Oh. Of course." It was probably only about eight or so. "I didn't think of that."

With a nod, he opened the door, and a ball of white fur flashed into the room and headed right for her.

"Flossie!" she cried, picking up the cat, who instantly began to purr.

"I forgot. They put her in my bedchamber. I meant to surprise you with her."

"And you did."

She nuzzled her darling pet, fighting not to let him see her tears. Not only had he kept his promise, but he'd had Flossie brought here for her arrival, which meant he cared a little, didn't it?

Or perhaps it just meant he was every bit the gentleman he kept insisting he was. Either way, it was lovely. "I'm so glad you're here, dearest," she murmured to Flossie. "I missed you so much!"

"You see?" he said softly. "You don't need me. You have her."

She glanced up just in time to see what looked like yearning on his face. But it flashed past so quickly that she must have mistaken it.

Clutching Flossie to her breast, she stared at her husband. "You'll come back later, right?" Lord, she sounded pathetic.

But she couldn't help it. It was one thing for him to leave her bed once she had fallen off to sleep, but to have him share such an incredibly erotic experience with her and do such a kind thing for her, then go off as if he was done with her . . .

He flinched, apparently realizing how she was taking his abandoning her on their wedding night. Then he turned away. "We'll see," he said, in that awful, noncommittal voice of his. He gestured to the bed. "Get some rest. I'll see you at breakfast, if not before."

At *breakfast*. Surely he couldn't mean that. Yet he went through into his bedchamber and closed the door as if it were the most natural thing in the world.

Despair seized her. She would never have guessed he would be so formal in his relations with her. Did he truly mean *never* to stay with her at night? To depart as soon as he'd bedded her?

The thought of that was rather lowering, especially after their bedding had been so exciting.

"I don't understand him," she told Flossie as she headed for the washbasin. "One moment, I think he's enamored of me, and the next I fear he's only tolerating this marriage."

Flossie licked her face. At least the puss understood Delia's worries.

Sadly, neither of them could do a thing about it. So after Delia performed her ablutions, she went to bed. What other choice did she have?

As she pulled back the coverlet and lay down, his earlier words drifted into her mind. *This was my mother's room before she embraced the Methodist faith and began sleeping in a smaller, more sober one.*

His mother had converted. And he had obviously rebelled against his mother's beliefs, or he wouldn't be spending his evenings in the stews.

What had happened between him and his mother to make him go so entirely in the opposite direction?

Normally a question like that would have kept her awake, but she was so very tired, especially after her enthusiastic lovemaking with Warren. So only moments after she slid between the covers, she fell asleep with Flossie in her arms.

When next she woke, she was briefly disoriented, not sure where she was. A ticking clock entered her consciousness and she sought it out by the light of the fire still burning in the hearth.

Three a.m.

That made sense, considering how early she'd retired. Leaving the bed, she headed for Warren's bedchamber, but a knock at the door got no response. The handle was unlocked, and when she opened the door she was surprised to find the bedchamber empty.

Utterly empty. The bed hadn't even been slept in.

That meant he was out *wandering*, as he'd put it. But where? In his study? Somewhere outside the town house? In the stews?

He'd promised not to do *that*, yet the possibility nagged at her. Putting on her wrapper, she headed downstairs in hopes that she might encounter him. Instead, she startled the night footman awake.

"Milady!" He jumped to his feet and rubbed

a hand over his features. "I . . . didn't expect . . . that is, his lordship didn't expect—"

"It's all right," she said. "I couldn't sleep."

She glanced about the foyer and down the hallway, neither of which she'd seen earlier. Even from here, there appeared to be a great many rooms; this must be quite a spacious town house. "I'm looking for my husband."

The footman turned crimson. "Of course. Well . . . that is . . . his lordship isn't at home just now."

She swallowed the jealous retort that came instantly to her lips. "Do you know where he is?"

"I don't . . . actually. I came on duty after he'd already left."

Her throat tightened. "I see."

With a look of pity, he added, "But I daresay he's gone to his club. St. George's. You know. In Piccadilly."

She nodded absently. "I daresay he has."

It wasn't as if he hadn't warned her that he might spend his evenings at his club. But . . . on his *wedding night*? After bedding his bride?

With her heart sinking, she slowly ascended the stairs and headed back to her bedchamber. *Hers*. Not theirs.

Did he mean this to be one of those fashionable marriages after all?

She clenched her fists. To hell with it if he did, because he wouldn't get one from her. A fashionable marriage required *two* people, and she refused to have any part of that. But chiding him over it wouldn't accomplish much. He didn't seem to take well to being told how he should behave.

Instead, she would show him that she could be more than just a bed partner—that she could be a good wife to him, an enjoyable companion, and yes, even a friend who could endure his nightmares and whatever else plagued him.

Because becoming important to him for more than just lovemaking might be the only way to secure his heart. And she wanted very much to do just that.

Twenty-One

Warren sat hunched over a cup of coffee in his breakfast room at the ridiculous hour of 11:00 a.m. Normally, he wouldn't have risen until noon at least, having stumbled into bed at dawn.

But he'd awakened early, unable to sleep for thoughts of his lovely wife lying all alone in the adjoining room. Pining for him. In her flimsy nightdress. With no drawers on.

Damn. Best not to dwell on that just now. Judging from his behavior thus far, she must think him the most randy fellow in all of England. He meant to show her otherwise, now that the night was past.

As if he'd conjured her up, she appeared in the doorway. She was fully dressed, damn it all to hell, in a very respectable blue-striped day gown that covered up far too much of her beautiful body.

Still, it brought out the brilliance of her eyes

and rather complemented her figure. All of which he'd thoroughly enjoyed examining last night.

As his cock twitched in his trousers, he stifled a groan. "Ah, you're awake."

"Oh, I've been awake for *hours*," she said cheerily as she entered. "Ever since I heard you fall into bed around six, as a matter of fact."

Damn, she'd *heard* him come in? He'd tried to be quiet.

When she said nothing more, he realized she was waiting for an explanation. But he'd be damned if he'd give her one.

With a slight shadowing of her gaze, she walked over next to him to pour herself a cup of coffee, leaning close enough that he could smell her lemony scent. "Anyway, I figured that since you were abed and couldn't officially present me to your staff, I would make the introductions myself." Straightening, she sipped some coffee. "I hope you don't mind."

"Would it make a difference if I did?" he asked.

"Of *course*. But I didn't think you would. And I didn't want to wake you too early after you'd gone to bed so late."

Another pause for an explanation. He ignored it.

She tipped up her chin. "So I've now met your cook and your butler and a number of your adorable footmen."

For some reason, that last one annoyed him. "I don't have 'adorable' footmen."

"Really? They seemed quite lovely to me." She cocked her head. "Are you sure you know your staff?"

"I know my staff perfectly well," he growled.

She sniffed. "My, my, no need to become agitated over it."

"I am *not*—" He caught himself. "Never mind me. I'm rather out of sorts at the moment."

Instead of making some tart remark about how that happened when one got no sleep, she patted his arm in sympathy. "I'm so sorry to hear that. Because it's truly a lovely morning. I've already been for a walk in your garden with Flossie."

He eyed her warily. She wasn't going to demand to know exactly where he'd been and what he'd been doing? And was she really so cheery simply because of the 'lovely morning' and her walk with Flossie?

Last night, she'd seemed very disappointed when he'd laid down the rules for spending their nights apart. Yet this morning she acted as if she barely cared that he'd abandoned her.

That didn't sit well. Which was ridiculous. He should be happy that she was content to go her own way. "I'm just not usually up this early."

"So I hear." She eyed him closely. "And you're obviously not a person who likes mornings."

"I like mornings just fine," he snapped. "As long as I can spend them sleeping."

"Ah. Perhaps, then, you should have something

more than coffee in your belly." She wandered over to the buffet, which held his usual preferences for breakfast—cold meats, cheeses, and some bread—and began to pile food on a plate. "I looked for you at three a.m., the first time I rose. But you weren't home."

The forced casualness with which she dropped *that* bombshell brought a fierce satisfaction to him. She'd noticed that he'd left. She *did* care. "Yes, as I told you, I tend to wander."

At last would come the typical jealous-wife response, the one that had kept him from marrying all this time.

Instead, she faced him with a smile. "Yes, I remember. And I greatly appreciated your being so considerate last night as to allow me the chance to rest. Alone."

That flummoxed him. Was she being sarcastic? "I was at St. George's," he said, though he wasn't sure why he felt the need to explain.

She waved a hand dismissively. "Oh, I assumed as much, since the footman said you might be."

He eyed her warily. "You weren't . . . worried?"

"Why should I worry? From what you said last night, I gather you've been going out and about late at night for years."

"Well, yes, but . . ."

She lifted an eyebrow. "But?"

"No need to harangue me," he said testily. "I did tell you I would look into the situation with your brother's card cheat. So I spent most of the evening at St. George's asking discreet questions about that tattooed lord of yours."

"How kind. And I wasn't haranguing you. I can't imagine why you'd think I was."

Because that was a wife's duty, damn it. To harangue her husband about his whereabouts.

Then again, Delia was anything but a typical wife. Indeed, she returned to the table with a plate overladen with buttered toast, cheddar slices, and roast beef, then set it down in front of him. Even his servants wouldn't be so presumptuous.

Yet somehow she'd managed to choose all the things he liked.

"Were you able to discover anything about the tattooed fellow?" she asked as she took a seat across from him.

"Not much," he grumbled as he began to pick at the food. God, he was behaving like a churlish schoolboy, complaining about everything and nothing. He forced himself not to sound so surly. "I spoke to Rathmoor, who used to move in certain unsavory circles, and he'd never seen a lord with a tattoo of any kind. Unfortunately, Fulkham wasn't there last night, since he had some matters to attend to for the cabinet, but I hope to talk to him tonight."

"That sounds like an excellent plan." She sipped her coffee. "I take it that neither of these gentlemen are married, which is why they can spend all night at St. George's?"

The barely detectable strain in her voice told him she wasn't as sanguine about this arrangement as she appeared. That stabbed guilt through him. She really was trying hard. And he was being unreasonable in his expectations.

The least he could do was acknowledge it. "Actually, I spoke to Rathmoor early in the evening, after I left you sleeping. But yes, he's married, and no doubt returned home at a reasonable hour. Fulkham, on the other hand, is not married. Clarissa has been working on finding him a wife, poor man."

"She's very good at that," Delia said. "She and my aunt ought to band together to start a matchmaking club. They could hold us up as an example of their success."

He didn't know what to say to that. So he changed the subject. "I thought I would place an advertisement for a lady's maid in the paper this morning, and then we could go pay calls. That's generally expected of newly married couples."

"Probably. But you're a marquess, so I'm sure you can make your own rules on that score."

"You'd be surprised." He settled back to stare at her. "Perhaps I could take you shopping after that. You do *like* shopping, right?" He dared not take anything for granted with Delia. His wife could be an odd bird.

"It depends on what we're shopping for." She uttered a long-suffering sigh. "Though I suppose I should acquire more fashionable clothes. *That* would definitely be expected of a newly married marchioness."

Her dejection made him laugh. "Most women would jump at the chance to spend their new husbands into debt plumping up their wardrobes."

"Most women have female friends to help them choose clothes. My friends and relations are all still at the house party."

"Ah. So would you rather wait until they return to town to go shopping?"

She brightened. "Oh, *could* we? I would much prefer it." Her face fell. "Unless you're embarrassed to be seen about town with me dressed so shabbily."

"First of all, you aren't dressed shabbily. Secondly, I'd never be embarrassed to be seen about town with you for any reason."

A smile blazed across her face. "Why, Lord Knightford, I do believe you gave me a compliment."

"Of course I did." He cast her a mock frown. "I'm not completely devoid of husbandly virtues."

She patted his hand. "I know."

He caught her hand and held it as something oddly like affection swirled in his chest. "I tell you what. After I introduce you *officially* to the staff and give you the grand tour of the town house, we'll pay our calls and go riding in Hyde Park to be seen as a proper married couple." He kissed the back of her hand. "Then tonight we can go to the very *improper* Vauxhall Gardens to dine and view the new exhibit."

"The Grand Moving Hydropyric Panorama?" Her eyes lit up. "Oh yes, I've longed to see that ever since it opened! But Aunt Agatha thought Vauxhall too scandalous a place for a young unmarried woman."

"And so it is." He bent forward to whisper, "Fortunately, you're married now."

"How nice of you to notice."

He ignored her arch tone. "Besides, it's no more scandalous than a gaming hell in Covent Garden. Although the parts *we* plan to see of it may skirt the edges of propriety."

She clapped a hand to her breast dramatically. "Why, Lord Knightford, don't tell me you intend to show me the dark walks and try to assail my honor."

"*Try*, my dear? I should hope I have a better chance of success than that."

"You are very presumptuous, sir." She rose to cast him a saucy smile. "Not to mention cocky."

As she turned away, he rose to catch her about the waist and pull her back against the bulge in his trousers. "Cocky is exactly what I am," he whispered in her ear. "And I'd like nothing more than to start the day with a bit more cockiness."

So much for showing her that he *wasn't* the most randy fellow in all of England. He sighed.

"Unfortunately, I really should introduce you to my staff before we do anything else."

She surprised him by rubbing up against him. "I've already met your 'staff,' remember?" she teased. "But, yes, I do think you should introduce me to the rest of the servants."

A laugh sputtered out of him. "Very amusing."

"Besides," quipped the little minx as she darted off ahead of him, "you should leave *something* for us to do tonight at the dark walks."

Perhaps. But either way, for at least part of tonight he'd have Delia to help him keep the dark at bay. He rather liked that.

Then perhaps when he fled the house in the wee hours of the morning in search of light and noise and people, she wouldn't mind too terribly much.

❧

Vauxhall was as delightful as Delia had anticipated. First there was the musical presentation in the rotunda, a wonderful comic ballet that had both her and Warren laughing. Then the fireworks burst into the sky from amid colored fountains and gushing waterfalls in a truly spectacular interplay of light and water that wrung gasp after gasp from the crowd.

Much later, after the excitement died down, her decidedly "cocky" husband was true to his word and, with almost no difficulty at all, seduced her in one of the dark walks. It was surprisingly enjoyable to do such a thing in a public place. She wouldn't have thought it.

Granted, there had been a few bad moments in the evening—like when a widow who either hadn't heard of Warren's marriage or didn't care what that meant attempted to coax him into her box. Alone.

Or now, when a couple of what could only be described as light-skirts stood watching and whispering as she and Warren strolled past.

"Do you know them?" she asked.

"Who?"

She could tell from his blank expression that he genuinely hadn't noticed the light-skirts. She supposed that was a good thing. But it was still a rather uncomfortable reminder of his past experiences with women.

"Nobody." She threaded her arm through his. "I'm getting tired. Let's go home, shall we?"

"If that's what you wish."

What I wish is for my husband to sleep with me tonight.

But she couldn't say that. Her tactics to win him over as a wife were going well. No point in ruining everything by becoming peevish.

They spent the carriage ride back comparing opinions on the ballet performance. As they disembarked at the entrance to his town house—

their town house—she wondered if he would attempt to seduce her again, or if he would just pack her off to bed to sleep alone with her cat.

Then the butler met them at the door. "My lord, your brother is here."

Warren started. "Which one?"

Delia had already learned that he had five, one of whom was married and off in America. So, obviously it wasn't that one.

"Captain Lord Hartley, sir."

"Warren!" cried a voice from down the hall. "You're back!"

Striding toward them was a burly fellow who looked nothing like his brother. Green-eyed, sporting a thick brown beard, and wearing a Hussar uniform, he was every inch the cavalry officer.

And judging from the exuberant hug he gave his brother, none of that made one bit of difference between them.

"*I'm* back?" Warren said as they pulled apart. "I've been here all along. You're the one who keeps dashing off to parts unknown. How long has it been? Two years? Three?"

"Only a bit more than one, old chap. Can't believe you don't remember." He paused. "Oh, wait, you were in Bath with Clarissa and our aunt last time I was in London. And my visit was too short for me to go down there to see you."

"Obviously, since I didn't even know you were in England."

"That's why I came straight from the transport ship this time. I didn't want to miss you. I arrived in town only three hours ago." Lord Hartley turned to Delia with a gleam in his eye. "And this must be your new wife. Can't believe I had to hear of your wedding from the servants."

Warren scowled at him. "We've been married all of a day and a half, and I wrote to inform you of it. But the letter is on its way to James Island. Clearly, you weren't there to receive it." Possessively, he laid his hand in the curve of Delia's back. "So may I present my wife, Delia? Delia, this is Captain Lord Hartley Corry of the 10th Royal Hussars. The oldest of my younger brothers."

"Pleased to meet you, madam," Lord Hartley said with a bow and a grin. "And do call me Hart. We're family now, it seems." Then he raked her with an assessing look that reminded her very much of her husband. "I must say that my brother is a lucky man, indeed."

"What fustian. But I thank you, sir." She smiled as she held out her hand, which he pressed for a shade longer than was proper. "And *I* must say that you're more like him than I at first realized."

"Don't let his uniform fool you," Warren said dryly. "He's a scapegrace masquerading as a soldier."

Hart struck his chest dramatically with his fist. "You wound me to the heart. That's like a wolf calling a fox a beast of prey. Compared to you, I'm merely a junior scapegrace."

"Oh, trust me," Delia put in, with a sly glance at Warren, "I have no doubt my husband can out-scapegrace any man in society."

Hart grinned at her. "I see that your wife is not only beautiful but clever."

"She is indeed. Not to mention prone to making up words." Warren tightened his proprietary hold on her. "So have you eaten?"

"I have. Your servants took good care of me."

"And I assume you're staying here while you're in town?" Warren asked.

Hart flashed Delia a quick glance. "I don't know. You two *are* newly married. I wouldn't wish to intrude."

"Nonsense, you must stay," she said hastily. If ever there was a way to show her husband her wifely abilities, it would be by playing hostess to his brother. "You're family, and we're happy to have you. It's no intrusion at all."

She knew she'd made the right decision when Hart let out a relieved breath. "Thank you, madam, that is very kind of you. I am delighted to accept."

Warren nodded to their butler. "Pull out my best bottle of brandy from the cellar and bring it to the drawing room. And have some wine brought for my wife."

"And some bread and cheese and fruit for all of us," Delia put in. "I fear that Vauxhall doesn't offer much in the way of food these days, and I daresay my husband will soon want some sort of supper."

"Very good, madam," the butler said, and headed off.

"A gracious hostess as well," Hart said. "You landed in clover this time, brother." Offering Delia his arm, he added, "Come, my lady. Tell me all about why you were mad enough to take such an unrepentant scoundrel as this fellow for a husband. And how very much you regret it now that you've met his far more superior brother."

With a laugh, she let him tug her down the hall toward the drawing room as Warren followed behind. Clearly, these Corry brothers were all cut of the same cloth—self-assured, arrogant, and far too charming for any woman's sanity.

"Watch it, Hart," Warren drawled. "I daresay I can still out-box you, even if I can't outshoot or outride you."

"I doubt that. I've been practicing." He bent to say to her in a conspiratorial voice, "Do let me know when you want to throw over my less accomplished brother. I'm sure I could sneak you into the barracks without being caught."

"Why would she want to sleep in a bloody barracks," Warren said testily, "when she can sleep in comfort here?"

"We wouldn't be sleeping, you dolt," his brother said as the three of them entered the drawing room. "Wait, don't tell me you've merely been sleeping with your wife. Do I have to explain to you how marriage works, old chap?"

"Oh, Lord," Delia said before her husband got

even more surly with his brother. "Are all the Corry brothers such rascals as you two?"

"Not Stephen," they said in unison.

Then they both laughed.

Curious to learn anything she could about her husband's family, she took a seat on the settee and asked, "Why not Lord Stephen? He's the one who married Mr. Keane's sister and moved to America, right?"

"That's the one," Warren said.

"Our youngest brother takes after our mother," Hart explained as he sat down across from her. "Whereas Warren and I take after . . . I don't know. Not Father, to be sure."

Warren snorted. "I imagine it's some ne'er-do-well far back in the family line."

"Either that or it has nothing to do with blood," Hart pointed out. "Father merely spoiled us for stuffy pillars of virtue so much that we went the other way out of spite."

"Could be." Warren poured himself a glass of brandy from the decanter kept on the side table, then lifted the glass with a glance at his brother. "Want some?"

"I'll wait for your butler to bring the good brandy," Hart said with a grin.

"You know damned well I have nothing *but* good brandy." Warren took a sip.

"Ah, but the 'best' is the best, which means nothing else will do."

Before they started sparring again, she wanted

to hear more of their family. "So, how exactly does Stephen take after your mother? Is he Methodist, too?"

"God, no," Hart said. "But he's reform-minded like her. Always intent upon feeding the poor, healing the sick, providing clothes for little mill-worker children."

"That's a good thing, isn't it?" she said.

"It is when Stephen does it," Warren said genially. "He doesn't offer his charity with a strong dose of religion, the way our mother did."

"Yes, I can see why that wouldn't sit well with you," she teased. "Given your choice of enjoyments."

"All of which I've given up, now that I've married."

"Surely not *all*," his brother put in. "You're still drinking fine brandy, I see."

"And going to his club for half the night," Delia added.

Hart eyed his brother. "That's only because Warren hates the darkness. He needs lots of light and activity around him."

"Enough, Hart," Warren said with a warning glance.

"What? Have you not told her about Mr. Pickering and the cellar?"

She ignored Warren's muttered oath. "Who is Mr. Pickering?"

"Who *was* Mr. Pickering," Hart said. "I heard he's dead now, the bastard. When we were boys

he was our Methodist tutor, stricter even than
Mother. 'Spare the rod and spoil the child,' and
all that rot."

"No worse than what we got at Eton," Warren
said. "Remember old Chilton?"

"The cellar," Delia prompted, determined not
to let Warren change the subject. "What happened
there?"

"Can't believe he hasn't told you this." Hart
settled back against his chair. "One time, when
Warren was nine and the rest of us were at our
grandmother's while Mother was away in London,
Pickering locked Warren up in an old unused cellar to try to, as he liked to put it, 'purge the wickedness from him.' "

"It didn't work," Warren clipped out. "And this
is a wholly inappropriate subject."

"I don't see why," Delia said hotly. "I'm your
wife."

"And if anyone should hear such things," Hart
said, "it's one's wife, don't you think, brother?"

Warren's glare spoke volumes.

Delia turned to Hart. "How long was he in the
cellar?"

When Hart hesitated, Warren took a long swig
of brandy, then said tersely, "Five days."

He wouldn't look at her. Which was just as
well, or he might have seen the abject shock on
her face. Delia could hardly breathe for thinking of the nine-year-old boy locked in a cellar for
days. Alone. In the dark.

Oh, Lord, the nightmares! Of course. It all made sense now.

"What about your father?" she asked. "Didn't *he* put a stop to it?"

"He was in London with Mother," Hart said. "Though I doubt he would have even known if he'd been there, much less done anything. He wasn't what you'd call the coddling type."

"So he was Methodist, too?"

"No," Warren said, his face carved in stone. "Just a cold fish in general."

"Then what about the servants?" she asked. "Why didn't *they* protest it?"

Warren poured himself more brandy. "Pickering told them I'd changed my mind and wanted to go with my brothers to my grandmother's, and that he'd walked me over to the village and sent me off by coach to her house. They took him at his word."

"Of course they did!" Delia said. "Methodists aren't supposed to lie."

"None of us are supposed to lie," Hart put in, "but we all do."

"Ah, but I have a Wesleyan servant," Delia said, "and he takes that stricture about not lying very seriously. The fact that this man lied to cover up such horrible behavior shows that he knew what he was doing was wrong."

Hart nodded. "Pickering was an arse, always disapproving whenever we boys got away with mischief. Since he knew he'd have Warren to himself a whole week, he decided it was his chance to set my rebellious brother straight once and for all. Pickering stuffed Warren in the cellar and brought him food and drink, but that was about it. Only left him enough oil for the Argand lamp to last a couple of hours each day, and after that . . ."

"Total darkness," she whispered, pity swelling up in her for her poor husband.

"I think he meant to keep him there the whole week," Hart went on, "but Warren stepped on the Argand lamp in the dark and broke it, gashing his leg in the process."

Ah, yes, his scar. Oh, Lord, how awful. "How did you step on a lamp?" she asked her husband.

Warren downed some brandy. "I was trying to stomp on the rats."

"Rats! The devil you say!" Her heart could scarcely bear the thought.

"I never knew that," Hart said. "I always wondered how you managed to break that lamp by stepping on it." He turned back to her. "Anyway, that put an end to the cellar treatment. Pickering had to let him out."

"So my leg could be treated," Warren said dully.

Hart shot his brother a look of sympathy. "Pickering was the sort of fellow more focused on the hatred of wickedness and less on the good works taught by the Methodists. Mother was badly mistaken in his character."

"Was she?" Warren snapped. "Or did she just

not care, as long as her minion succeeded in getting the *heir* to toe the line?"

"Your mother sanctioned the punishment?" Delia asked.

"Of course not," Hart said. "She was appalled when she learned of it. Dismissed Pickering straightaway."

Turning to face the fireplace, Warren took a large gulp of brandy but said nothing in response. Apparently he blamed his mother still. Not that Delia was surprised, given how the woman's neglect had doomed him to a lifetime of nightmares.

Just then, a footman came in bearing the brandy Warren had asked for, along with food and a bottle of wine.

The three of them fell silent while the servant set everything out. But as soon as the man had gone, Hart went to pour himself some of the "good" brandy. "Anyway, Warren used to have awful nightmares about his time in the cellar. Fortunately, he grew out of those as he got older."

Her husband froze with his back to her.

"Did he?" Somehow she managed to speak past the tears clogging her throat. "That's good, at least."

Warren jerked his head around to meet her gaze, a flush rising up his cheeks as his eyes bore into hers.

"They were horrible," Hart said. "He used to

keep everyone in the nursery up at night with his thrashing about and his screams."

She couldn't take her eyes from her husband. "Then I'm glad to hear he got over them. I'd hate to think of him suffering so for all his life."

Was that gratitude she saw flash in Warren's eyes?

It broke her heart. Could he really think she would betray his secret? Because clearly he'd been hiding his ongoing nightmares from his family.

He probably would have hidden them from *her*, too, if she hadn't accidentally witnessed one. God forbid that he let anyone see anything he would regard as a weakness. Even his wife.

"Anyway," Warren said with clearly feigned nonchalance, "that is all far in the past, and frankly, rather boring." He set down his glass. "So, Hart, what do you say? Shall we go paint the town red as we used to in the old days?"

Hart glanced from Warren to her and seemed belatedly to recognize the undercurrents between her and his brother. "That was before you were married, old chap. Now that you are, I wouldn't dream of keeping you from your beautiful bride. Especially a mere day and a half after the wedding."

With a faint smile for her, Hart picked up the brandy bottle. "Besides, I just got off a transport ship after weeks at sea, and I'm exhausted. I never sleep well on those things. So I shall take myself and your fine brandy off to my usual room and my usual comfy bed and let you get on with your evening." He bowed to her. "Lovely to meet you, Lady Knightford."

"Lovely to meet you, too, Captain Lord Hartley. I'm so glad to get to know one of Warren's brothers." And to get to the bottom of the issue with the nightmares.

"I'll see you in the morning," he said, and winked.

Then he sauntered out, leaving her alone with her husband.

Twenty-Two

Warren couldn't look at his wife, couldn't bear to see the pity on her face. Or worse, contempt.

Damn Hart for coming here *now*. For telling her his most shameful secret. For letting her know what a bloody madman he was.

At least she'd kept the truth from his brother—that the nightmares were still plaguing him. And that had to mean she was on his side. That she would defend him even when he hadn't trusted her with his secrets.

He heard the settee creak as she rose. And still he wouldn't look at her, *couldn't* look at her.

"Why didn't you tell me?" she asked softly.

"It's not something I'm proud of," he clipped out.

"What? Misbehaving as a boy? Being locked in a cellar?"

The incredulity in her voice gave him pause.

He drained his brandy, relishing the hard burn. "Having nightmares over it at this advanced age."

"You can't possibly blame yourself for that."

The sweet sympathy in her voice both warmed and terrified him. "Can't I? Lords aren't supposed to be afraid of the dark."

"And young ladies aren't supposed to go gambling in hells dressed as men, either. Yet I did."

"It's not the same."

She came to stand between him and the fireplace, forcing him to look at her. "You mean, because I was merely a miss and you're a marquess."

"No. It's not the same because you acted as you did to help your family. Whereas I have nightmares simply because I'm afraid of the dark. And the quiet. And of being alone in the dark and the quiet."

There, he'd spelled it out for her. Let her make of it what she would.

Yet she didn't even flinch. "I'm not surprised. Five days is a long time for a child to be trapped in a cellar. And at the age you were, children are very impressionable, very fearful. I'd think it odd if you *hadn't* been profoundly affected by the experience."

"But I'm not a child anymore, damn it! I should be able to conquer this!"

"Some things are harder to conquer than others. I still haven't conquered my fear that I'll lose my home and everything I hold dear. That *any-thing*, even risking my reputation in society, is better than being forced to move yet again to a new town, a new country . . . a new house."

The thread of pain in her voice hit him like a cold pail of water. It hadn't occurred to him that a fear of loss might be behind her recklessness. It made him admire her all the more.

"But you *have* conquered your fear, don't you see?" he said. "Thanks to me and my nightmares, you were wrenched from your cozy life in the country and set down here to live with a mad-man, yet—"

"Not a madman," she interrupted. "And you were never the cause of my being 'wrenched' from my 'cozy life.' That happened long before you came along, because of Reynold and his gambling. If not for you, Brilliana and Silas and I would soon be living in some cottage, trying to make ends meet."

"My point is, one way or the other, you've made the best of your change of circumstances, despite what it took from you. Whereas I am—"

"Fighting your fears." She stepped closer. "Or trying to manage them, anyway. I gather that your nights out in town are your way of avoiding the bad dreams."

He gave a jerky nod. She saw too much. Yet too little.

"Tell me about them."

A chill swept him. "The nightmares?"

"Yes. How often do you have them? Does anything in particular make them occur? How have you tried to prevent them, other than by flitting about town all hours?"

He dragged one hand through his hair. Leave it to his stalwart wife to attempt to solve the problem in a practical way, to seek to dissect it and thus understand it. But he'd done that a thousand times and never found answers that gave him any relief.

A footman knocked at the open door, and they both started.

"Is there anything else you need, milord?" the man asked. "Shall I bring more wine or food?"

Delia glanced at Warren, then said in a lowered voice, "I think we should continue this discussion in more private surroundings, don't you?"

"Probably." And once he had her alone in one of their bedchambers, he might be able to distract her from probing further by seducing her.

She turned to the footman with a smile. "No need for anything else, Thomas. Neither of us is very hungry, after all. I believe we'll be retiring now."

"Retiring?" Thomas squeaked, having never seen his master go to bed before dawn. Then he seemed to realize that his master had also never before had a pretty wife, and turned beet-red.

"Yes, retiring," Warren said dryly. "At least for the moment. So that will be all this evening, Thomas. And you may tell my valet—and the

maid who's been helping her ladyship dress—
that we won't require their services any further
tonight, either."

"Very good, milord," the footman mumbled as
he hurried to remove the tray and flee the scene
of his embarrassment.

Warren and Delia climbed the stairs in silence,
both painfully aware of the fact that the walls had
ears. Especially *his* walls. The lone servant who'd
witnessed one of his hellish dreams had quit
the next day, but Warren assumed that rumors
swirled among the staff about why he avoided
sleeping at home except during daylight hours.

Upstairs he opened the door to her bedchamber and ushered her inside, then shut it and took
her in his arms before she could jump back into
discussing his nightmares.

To his relief, she met his kiss with her usual
enthusiasm. But that relief rapidly vanished when
she pushed free of his arms and went over to the
bed to pick up Flossie, who was dozing there.

"You're not going to kiss me out of this, Warren," she said, clutching the cat to her chest like
a breastplate. "I want to know all about your
dreams."

"And if I don't want to talk about them?"

She tipped up her chin. "Then I suppose I'll
have to glean what I can from quizzing your
brother about what he remembers."

Bloody persistent female. "Blackmail doesn't
become you, Delia," he snapped.

"Evasion doesn't become *you*, my darling."

The endearment caught him off guard. Made him realize that somewhere down deep, he *wanted* to tell her. To unburden himself to someone who might not recoil.

Though if she did, he wasn't sure how he'd bear it.

"Fine." He released a harsh breath. "But if I'd realized you were going to insist upon continuing this discussion, I wouldn't have left the brandy behind."

She gazed at him steadily. "Shall I call for some?"

A smile tugged at his lips, despite everything. "You're supposed to be chiding me for drinking it, luv. Not offering to fetch me more."

"You don't play by the rules, either, so there's no need for you to play the stoic lord in this. Not with me, anyway." She settled herself on the bed, with Flossie in her arms. "So tell me about the nightmares. I take it that despite what your brother thinks, you've still been having them all these years?"

"Only when I go to bed in the evening, like a normal person." He began to pace.

"When did they start?"

"The night after I was taken from the cellar. After I'd had two or three a week for months, Mother decided the best thing was to pack me off to school instead of having me tutored at home. She figured it would teach me to . . . buck up and be a man."

"She just packed you off for someone else to take care of?" Delia said incredulously.

"Essentially, yes." He'd never thought of it like that before, but he supposed that was one way of looking at it. "Actually, her solution turned out better than you'd think. At Eton, students generally sleep in a long chamber with dozens of others, unless one's parents pay for one to have a private room and special privileges in some house in the village. Given my rank, I wouldn't normally have been put in the long chamber."

He gave a rueful shake of his head. "But thanks to Mother's determination to teach us that we were like all our fellow creatures—godless heathens in need of redemption—I wasn't afforded any special privileges or private rooms. And that worked to my advantage."

"Because you weren't alone at night."

"Not only that, but I was surrounded by lads who rarely slept or who snored or who were always getting up to some trouble. Between the whispers and the pranks and the usual boyish nonsense, there was generally enough activity about me to keep the nightmares at bay. That was true at university, too."

He glanced away. "It was only after I graduated that I had to find other ways of . . . dealing with the night. For some reason, I don't seem to have the nightmares when I sleep during the day."

"So it's darkness that sets them off? Can't you just keep a lantern burning throughout the night?"

"Believe me, I've tried that. But it's actually the quiet as much as the darkness that causes me trouble. I used to try to sleep at home at night, to be normal."

He faced her, determined to drive home what she was dealing with. "But I stopped attempting that after I punched a footman when the man tried to wake me from the throes of a bad dream. He quit the next morning, and I realized I had to do whatever I could to keep the night at bay."

"But even with your attempts, you still have the nightmares. I mean . . ." She colored. "You had one at the house party."

"Yes. That's why I avoid house parties: The country is too quiet, too . . . utterly dark. Everyone retires earlier, and I'm left alone to try to keep from sleeping. As long as I'm in town and I'm busy, I'm better. But in the country . . ."

He couldn't suppress a shudder.

"So what do you do when you have to go to your estate?" she asked.

"I only go there rarely. I hire an excellent staff, so I need only visit my properties once a month to deal with necessary affairs."

"So, no hunting, no leisurely country visits."

"Occasionally my bachelor friends and I go to the hunting box in Shropshire, but none of us is actually much interested in hunting. So we mostly drink and play cards and—"

"Enjoy the local light-skirts?" she said tartly.

"Something like that. But I never have such

parties at Lindenwood Castle. There, it's all business. I leave early in the morning as soon as I come back from the stews, sleep in the carriage on the way to the estate, and meet with my estate manager as soon as I arrive."

He walked over to stoke up the fire. "We spend the late afternoon discussing matters. Then I dine with the local magistrate, and I go to the tavern for the rest of the night. Early the next morning, I climb into my carriage, I sleep all the way back to town, and once I arrive, I head off for the stews or my club or some social engagement."

"That is an awful way to live," she said.

The words startled him. He'd never thought much about it, but she was right. It was. "But it's the way *I* live." He stared into the hearth. "Now you know why I haven't married before. It's no life for a wife."

"No, it's not." As the words cut into him, she added, "It's no life for you, either."

"Ah, but I'm used to it."

She left the bed and Flossie jumped to the floor. "Are you? It seems to me that this patchwork way of dealing with your fear isn't very successful. You still have nightmares sometimes, don't you?"

He debated whether to tell her the truth. But there was no longer any point in prevaricating. If she knew everything, she would be able to make her own adjustments.

"Actually, ever since I took the trip to Portugal to find my cousin Niall last year, the nightmares have grown worse. I assume it was because I was cooped up in a cabin at sea for weeks, with no real means of entertainment and a very tight space to contend with."

"That makes sense. Ship cabins are damp, cold, and small, with no windows. Like cellars."

He managed a thin smile. Only she, who'd traveled so much in her life, could understand that. "Exactly. I think it dredged everything up. Now I have the dreams even when I'm in the stews, if I happen to fall asleep there. And as I'm getting older, it's becoming harder to stay awake all night."

"Which is precisely why you can't go on the way you have." She put her hand on his arm. "You've got to find some way to end them."

"Why didn't *I* think of that?" he said sarcastically.

"Sorry." Hot color filled her cheeks. "I know I'm being presumptuous, acting as if you can snuff them out like a candle, when clearly you cannot or you would have done so before now. But there must be a way to make nights more tolerable for you." She glanced away. "I mean, surely it helps some for you to have bed companions."

"Not unless they're dancing on my head," he quipped. "And whores do a lot of things, but not that."

She eyed him askance.

"Right. Not funny." He let out a breath. "In the early days, it helped." His gut clenched. "Until the night I woke up screaming with my hands around some poor girl's throat. Apparently she'd tried to wake me, and in my nightmare I'd thought that it was Pickering come to let me out. Thankfully, I didn't hurt her—just frightened her. But I couldn't go back to *that* brothel for a long while."

"So you don't sleep at the brothels."

"Not if I can avoid it. Too afraid of what might happen." His throat tightened. "And now you know: Your husband is a sniveling coward at heart."

"Don't call yourself that!"

"Why not?" he snapped. "It's what my mother called me."

She gaped at him. "Surely not."

"She put up with the dreams right after it happened, but as the weeks went on and nothing halted them, she grew impatient." The sense of betrayal swamped him, as it always had. "'Don't be a sniveling coward, boy,' she said. 'Lords aren't afraid of the dark. Buck up and be a man,' she said."

"Sounds like guilt to me."

That took him entirely by surprise. "What do you mean?"

"Your mother felt guilty that she'd left you alone with that wretched tutor. And then, when she was helpless to stop the nightmares that resulted, that must have tortured her. So she lashed out at *you*. Blamed *you*. Otherwise she would have had to blame herself, and that is a great burden for a mother to bear."

He just stared at Delia. "Not once in all these years has that ever occurred to me. Hell, I thought she *died* ashamed of me. Because I couldn't get over the nightmares . . . because I flouted her moral strictures and lived wildly in London."

"Is that why none of your family knows you still have them? Because you were hiding them from *her*?"

"From all of them." Shame clogged his throat. "She was right, you know. I *am* a sniveling coward. I can't endure the dreams, so I drink and I whore and—"

"You're merely handling it the only way you know how. That doesn't make you a coward. A coward wouldn't try to keep everyone else safe from his nightmares."

Her loyalty cut through all the cruelty of his mother's words. He cast her a rueful smile. "You can be so fierce in your defense of me sometimes. Why is that?"

"Because I see the strong man of character beneath the rakehell. I know you can get past this. You just need help."

He snorted. "And how do you propose to help me?"

"I think you should spend your nights sleeping with *me*."

The air whooshed out of him, and his heart seized up. "No."

"Hear me out—"

"I don't have to." He stalked away, visions of her lying bruised and battered beneath him clogging his throat with fear. "Because there's not a bloody chance in hell of that *ever* happening."

Twenty-Three

Panic gripped Delia as Warren headed for the adjoining door, and she raced to block his exit. "You are *not* leaving! We aren't finished."

He scowled at her. "Didn't you hear a word I said about nearly throttling a woman to death in my sleep? And you want me to risk that with *you*? You're out of your mind."

She grabbed him by the arms. "You didn't attempt to throttle me the time I witnessed you having a nightmare. Besides, I'm not some light-skirt you've taken to bed for the night. Nor am I a servant. I'm your *wife*."

"Which is precisely why I don't want to hurt you," he growled.

"You can't be sure that you would. Or that you'd even have a dream in my presence. For all you know, sleeping with someone you . . . care about might change things."

"And if it didn't? I don't relish murdering my wife."

"You would never do that to me."

A muscle worked in his jaw. "For God's sake, you don't *know* that."

"Not for certain, no. But I'm willing to risk it."

"I'm *not*. If I did something to you, I could never forgive myself."

That touched her beyond words. She cupped his head in her hands. "Listen to me, my darling." *My love.* "I'll do whatever it takes to make this possible—keep a truncheon by the bed to bash you if you hurt me, or keep the room lit with candles for as many nights as it takes."

"Delia—" he began.

"Give me a chance. When you had that nightmare at the house party, my being there helped you. Admit it."

"Yes, it helped so much that I ruined you," he said acidly.

"But you didn't *hurt* me. You clung to me, you held me close, you . . . fondled me—you didn't strike me. It's worth a try, don't you think?"

A skeptical expression crossed his face. "I still had a horrific dream that night."

"Yes, but perhaps if I were there from the beginning . . ."

He pulled free of her. "God, I don't know."

"I don't want to spend the rest of my life enslaved to your fear. And I daresay neither do you."

The faintest hint of hope shone in his face.

"You really think that your being there would make a difference."

"I have no idea. But I'm willing to try." She held out her hand. "I'm bone-tired, my darling, and I suspect you are, too. So come to bed. And we'll see where we stand in the morning."

He stared at her, clearly torn between hope and fear. At last he said, "All right. But you must promise me: if I harm you tonight in any way, you will never try this again."

She shook her head. "I won't promise that. Sometimes it takes more than one try to get something to work."

"Delia—"

"No! This may take a while, and I'm willing to attempt it as often as necessary. What about you?"

His hollow gaze bore into her. "I don't want to risk . . . driving you away from me."

The words sounded wrenched from him, and her heart flipped over in her chest. It was the closest he'd ever come to admitting that he cared for her. "You won't drive me away. I can assure you of that." She thrust her hand out at him again. "So? Will you come to bed with your wife?"

He released a shuddering breath. "All right. But I still fear you'll regret it."

"You know that I'll be honest with you if I do."

"True. You're the most forthright female I've ever met."

When he took her hand, she exulted. Somehow she would get him past this. She didn't know how, but this seemed like an excellent start.

This time when he took her in his arms and kissed her, she didn't protest it. Whatever made it easier for him was fine.

He undressed her, and she undressed him. She wasn't surprised when he tumbled her down on the bed to have his way with her. He tended to forget his troubles when he was inside a woman, and she certainly didn't mind that, given how good it felt *having* him inside her.

After he made love to her with his usual skill, they lay naked and entwined on her bed. Her happiness knew no bounds. They were growing closer. He was *trying*.

"At last, we've had an ordinary bedding," he murmured against her cheek. "I feel vindicated as a husband."

She laughed. "I've enjoyed every single time you've made love to me, whether it was 'ordinary' or not."

"I'm happy to hear it." He nuzzled her neck. "Do let me know if I ever disappoint."

"I hope you'll do the same for me."

He chuckled. "I can't imagine your ever disappointing me."

The sincerity in his voice touched her, and she cuddled close to him. "Likewise." After a few moments, she said, "Tell me about Pickering."

He stiffened. "What do you wish to know?"

"Well, for one thing, why on earth did your mother hire him?"

"He was a member of her congregation. And he'd previously been a schoolmaster."

She scowled. "That doesn't make it right; she should have learned something more about his character beforehand."

"True," he said, relaxing. "But he's dead now, so there's no point in dwelling on it."

"When did he die?"

"Last spring."

Turning over to look at him, she said, "Before or after you went to Portugal?"

"Shortly before. What does it matter?"

"Because perhaps it wasn't the trip itself that upset you. Perhaps it was the fact that you could never avenge yourself against him for what he did to you. And the thought of that so disturbed you that it stirred the nightmares up."

He eyed her closely. "I suppose that's possible. But there's no way of being sure, is there?"

"I suppose not."

They lay there awhile, quite content. Then he moved, as if to leave the bed.

She caught his arm. "Please. Not tonight. Stay with me."

"I am. But I need to make preparations."

She watched as he went over to the washbasin, then brought back a large porcelain pitcher and set it on the table next to her side of the bed.

He fixed her with an earnest look. "Promise me you'll brain me with this if I hurt you."

"Of course."

"*Promise* me."

"I promise." But she doubted she'd have to make good on that. At least she hoped she wouldn't. Because she wasn't sure she could hit him.

"I suspect we're both going to regret this," he grumbled as he crawled into the bed and drew her into his arms. "And I just want you to know that if I prove to be right, I'll never let you live it down."

"No doubt." She burrowed into his arms, so warm and cozy.

"I mean it."

"Hmmm."

"You're not listening to me, are you?" he asked.

"Uh-huh." It had been a long day, coming on the heels of several *other* long days. Her eyes had already slid shut of their own accord, and she didn't want to move.

He gave a soft chuckle. "Doesn't matter. Sleep, dearling. One of us ought to."

So she did.

~⚬~

She wasn't certain when she first became aware of it, but sometime in the night, she felt him thrashing beside her. He was moaning and begging as he'd done that last time, and now that she knew why, it broke her heart.

She laid her hand against his cheek. "It's all right, my love," she whispered. "You're safe now."

With a hoarse cry, he rolled her under him and lay atop her, shaking violently. "Let me out of here! Damn it, someone please let me out . . . please . . . I'll be good . . . I swear!"

His weight kept her from moving, and she had a moment's panic when she couldn't budge him. But knowing that the pitcher was right there and that he didn't *mean* to hurt her helped her remain calm.

She gripped his head in her hands. "Wake up, my darling," she said firmly. "It's a dream. Wake up. It's just a dream."

As she kept chanting it and brushing kisses over his cheeks, he seemed to grow a bit calmer, though his eyes remained closed and he still shuddered some. "Delia?"

"Yes, it's me. I'm right here with you."

"Delia . . . let me out, dearling. Please . . ."

"You're not in the cellar anymore," she whispered. "You're with me. With *me*, Warren."

With his eyes still closed, he smothered her mouth in a kiss, not shaking anymore. Then, to her surprise, she felt him hardening against her.

"Delia . . ." he said hoarsely, and parted her legs with his knee. Since they were both still naked it was easy for him to enter her, and she gladly accepted him inside her, praying that somehow it would help. He began to thrust into her, hard and quick, and she gave herself up to it with a moan.

She wasn't sure exactly when he awoke from his mindless state, but at some point he froze above her. He stared down at her, his cock buried deep and his eyes glittering in the semidarkness. "Do you want me . . . inside you?"

"Yes," she said, and brushed a kiss to his lips. "Yes, my love, yes."

The word *love* made him moan, but she had no time to dwell on it before he was ravishing her mouth and driving into her in slower strokes that roused her thoroughly.

He lingered over her a long time, as if to make up for how he'd awakened her. He kissed her shoulder, kneaded her breast, caressed her where they were joined, until she thought she might go mad with wanting him.

"Please . . ." she begged. "Please . . . I love you . . ."

"You . . . shouldn't . . ."

"Can't help it . . . please . . . my love . . . please . . . I want you . . . now."

"Whatever my lady wishes," he rasped.

He increased his strokes until she felt her release rising . . . just . . . *there* and she went over into oblivion with a scream of pleasure. He gave a hoarse cry of his own as he spilled his seed inside her.

She clutched him close, her body convulsing around him and her heart in her throat. "I love you, Warren," she whispered.

He nuzzled her cheek. "Shh, dearling, sleep now. I promise not to . . . wake you again."

With that, he rolled off her and lay panting in the bed.

She probably shouldn't have said those words, for she was clearly alone in how she felt. And when he left the bed and she saw him go drag on his drawers and shirt, she realized in despair that he wasn't going to stay with her anymore tonight.

Perhaps no more nights at all.

No, she refused to accept that. Surely she could eventually convince him to take a chance on her. Because the alternative, living with a man who didn't love her, who couldn't even bear to sleep in the same bed as her because of his fear, seemed too awful to contemplate.

~ ❧ ~

Warren went to his room and pulled his dressing gown on over his drawers and shirt, his heart pounding.

I love you.

He really *was* a coward, because those words had sent him fleeing.

His wife loved him. And that alarmed him even more than his nightmares. Loving him meant she would expect things of him. Expect him to try to be a good husband to her. To stay with her at night and attempt to change his way of life.

How could he? He'd never been so terrified as when he'd awakened to find himself *inside* his wife and entirely unaware of how he'd ended up there. What if he'd forced her?

It hadn't occurred to him that he might react to her presence in his dreams by attempting to take her against her will. He'd *never* done that, had been appalled when he'd learned of the arse who'd forced Clarissa. So the thought of his doing so, even in his sleep . . .

His throat closed up. She'd said she was beneath him by choice, but he knew bloody well that he could be aggressive in his dreams. And she might just be putting a good face on it because she wanted so badly for him to get past his fears.

He wanted that, too, but not at any cost. Not if there was a chance of losing her in the process.

I love you.

Damn, but those words enticed him. Which perversely made them all the more terrifying.

He glanced at the clock. Nearly 5:00 a.m. Normally he would be going to bed about now, but there was no point in trying to sleep anymore. So he headed down the hall to his study. Might as well get some work done, since he'd fallen behind on estate affairs of late.

Besides, it would keep his mind off his lovely wife and what to say to her when she arose. He had to say *something*. He couldn't let her go on thinking she could change his dreams by the sheer force of her will.

Two hours later, he was startled by a noise in the doorway. He looked up to see Hart, wearing just a pair of drawers and a dressing gown, eyeing him with a bemused look.

"You're awake," Hart said inanely as he entered the study.

Warren leaned back in his chair. "I have been for a while. What are you doing up so early?"

"I came looking for you. I was about to knock on your bedroom door when I heard you in here." Hart wandered the study like a caged tiger. "I see nothing much has changed since the last time I was in London."

"Other than the wife, no."

Hart chuckled. "I like her."

"I could tell," Warren bit out.

"Oh, come now, you know perfectly well my flirtations were merely meant to annoy you."

He lifted an eyebrow. "Doesn't make them any less irritating."

Hart grinned at him. "I've never seen you jealous before. It's rather entertaining."

"I'm not jealous," Warren said sullenly.

"All right, then. Besotted."

No point in disputing it. "Now, *that* I very well may be."

Sobering, Hart sat down in the chair before his desk. "Can't say I blame you for that. She's quite a character, your new bride. Seems different from most women in society."

"She is. *Very* different." To say the least.

"That's why you're besotted with her, isn't it?"

"For that, and so many other reasons."

"Yet you never told her about the cellar." Hart glanced at him, an earnest frown on his face. "I suppose I shouldn't have said anything. I just figured she must have seen the scar, so she had to know *something* about it. You don't mind that I revealed all that to her, do you?"

"No." He really didn't. Hiding the past indefinitely wouldn't have worked, anyway. Delia wasn't the sort to stand idly by while he kept such a massive secret. Eventually she would have wrested it out of him.

"Good. That's actually why I came to talk to you. Wanted to make sure you weren't furious with me over spilling your secrets. Now that I know you're not, I'm returning to bed." Hart reached up to rake his fingers through his hair, and his sleeve fell down to expose his forearm. And a tattoo just above the wrist.

Warren caught his breath. "Damn it all. It can't be."

Hart blinked. "What?"

Lunging over the desk, Warren caught his brother's arm and shoved the sleeve up to expose an inked image of a sun. "What the hell is this?"

A flush rose up Hart's neck. "It's . . . it's a tattoo. What of it?"

Warren lifted his gaze to Hart. "It's a *sun* tattoo."

Hart shrugged. "I crossed the equator a couple of years ago, and my chums in the navy dared me to get one like the sailors do. We were drunk and—"

"You were in London last year." Warren couldn't breathe, couldn't think. His own brother was the sharper Delia had been looking for.

No, Hart would never cheat anyone.

But he could. He knows how.

"Did you go to Dickson's while you were in town?" Warren demanded.

Hart turned instantly wary. "Why do you ask?"

A new voice came from the doorway—a wounded, bitter voice Warren knew only too well. "Because that's where a lord with a sun tattoo cheated my brother at cards."

Delia came into the room, already fully dressed and heartbreakingly beautiful in that yellow gown that made her look like a sunny day.

Except that no sun shone in her face this morning. She faced Hart down. "It was *you*, wasn't it? You were the one who ruined my brother."

Bloody, bloody hell.

Twenty-Four

Delia could tell from Warren's face that he was as shocked as she was. She *liked* Hart, for pity's sake! And he was the one who'd driven Reynold over the edge? Oh, Lord, how could he be the one? Her husband's *brother*, of all people!

"Delia," Warren said hoarsely, "I swear I didn't know."

That jerked her up short. "Of course you didn't. How could you?"

Even as relief spread over Warren's face, Hart snatched his arm free of his brother's grip. "What are you two blathering about? I've never cheated anyone in my life. Well, other than my cousins. And my brothers."

"You aren't helping, you damned arse," Warren bit out.

Hart glanced to Delia. "Who the devil is your brother, anyway?"

She stared him down. "Reynold Trevor." When

Hart paled, she knew for certain that he was the one. "You cheated him. You took everything from him!"

Hart jumped to his feet. "Yes, I won everything he wagered. But it was only to protect Niall."

That caught Delia by surprise. "Lord Margrave was there?"

"Of course not," Hart said. "That's the point. My cousin was still hiding out on the Continent, and your brother kept asking questions about where he was, how to find him . . . rot like that." He cast Warren a desperate look. "I figured that her brother wanted to hunt Niall down and bring him to justice because of that damned duel."

Delia just gaped at him. This was about Lord Margrave? Warren looked as mystified as she.

"I assumed Trevor was a relation of the man Niall killed," Hart continued, "so I couldn't let him go searching for Niall, damn it. I figured if I took enough of his money at cards, he wouldn't be able to afford a trip to the Continent to look for our cousin."

Muttering a curse, Warren stood. "You're saying that Reynold Trevor lost everything at the card tables because you were trying to keep him from hunting for our cousin."

"Exactly." Hart frowned. "Wait, what do you mean, lost everything? I only won three thousand pounds off him."

"Which he got by mortgaging our already debt-ridden estate to the hilt!" Delia cried. "My brother is dead because of you! Because of the money you cheated him out of."

The blood drained from Hart's face. "Your brother is *dead*?"

That caught her off guard. "You didn't know?"

"How could I? I've been on James Island off the coast of Africa for the past year. The last time I saw him was right before I left town, when he showed up with the money he owed me. I never dreamed—"

"That losing so much might drive him to suicide?" she said bitterly.

"Suicide?" Warren laid a hand on her arm. "You don't know for certain that Reynold killed himself."

"I do. Because Reynold left a note for me, telling me *why* he killed himself."

Shock suffused Warren's face. "You never told me that before."

"You may not believe this, but I worry about scandal, too, sometimes. Especially when it might taint my nephew's future. I didn't even tell Brilliana. I figured she'd suffered enough."

"Who the devil is Brilliana?" Hart asked.

"Reynold Trevor's wife," Warren said.

Hart dropped into a chair. "The man had a bloody *wife*, too? He didn't mention her."

"Now *that* I know is a lie," Delia said. "He always talked of her."

"Not to me, he didn't," Hart muttered.

"What did the note say?" Warren asked her.

Delia crossed her arms over her chest. "What do you think it said? 'I've lost everything, so there's no more reason to live. Take care of Brilliana and Silas for me. I can't bear it anymore. Forgive me.' If that's not proof of suicide, I don't know what is."

"It's proof, all right," Warren said in a hollow voice. "So you didn't know until then that he'd lost everything."

"Of course I knew. He told me the moment he returned from London. That's how I found out he was cheated by a man with a tattoo." She stabbed a finger toward Hart. "*Your brother.* Who claims that he took all my brother's money over some nonsense having to do with . . . with . . ."

And just like that, the truth hit her.

Lord Margrave. Brilliana. Oh, Lord.

All this time, she'd assumed that Reynold's reference to what he'd lost had been about the money, the estate. But what if he'd meant something else entirely?

Some*one* else entirely. His wife.

What if Reynold had decided that Brilliana couldn't love him because she loved someone else? Could that be why he'd come to London, demanding to know where Lord Margrave was? If Brilliana really had been . . . romantically involved with the earl in the past, and if somehow Reynold had found out about it . . .

"No, no, *no*! It isn't possible." To believe that, she'd have to take Hart's word over Reynold's. But how could she?

She whirled on her husband. "I have to go to Stoke Towers. I have to talk to Brilliana."

"Brilliana?" Warren exclaimed. "What can she possibly add to the discussion?" When Delia flushed under his scrutiny, his eyes narrowed. "Wait a minute. You think this has something to do with the odd way Niall and Brilliana behaved when they saw each other."

Blast him for always reading her mind. Now he would be even more determined to believe his brother guiltless of everything. "Don't be ridiculous. You heard the two of them—they were barely acquainted with each other."

Warren snorted. "Right. You and I both know that was a lot of rubbish. Perhaps it's time we sat them down and got the real truth. I agree—let's talk to Brilliana. We'll all go."

"The devil we will!" She gestured to Hart. "I'm not going anywhere with that . . . that *murderer*. Nor with you, either, if you mean to blindly defend him."

"Now see here," Hart put in, "I realize you're upset about your brother, but I had nothing to do with his suicide."

She glared at him. "Nothing? Really? My brother was a brilliant card player. The only way he would have lost is if you cheated."

Was that guilt she saw flash over his face? Or

did she just want so badly to believe it that she was grasping at straws?

"I'm a damned good card player myself," Hart said sullenly.

"It's true," Warren put in. "And Reynold was delving into matters he should have left alone."

"That's what your brother claims." She scowled at her husband. "But of course you would believe him over me."

"I'd damned well believe him over *your* brother." When she shot him a look of sheer betrayal, he cursed under his breath. "It's Hart's word against Reynold's, and we can hardly question your brother. That's all I meant to say."

"I know exactly what you meant to say—that somehow this was entirely Reynold's fault. Well, since he's dead and can no longer defend his actions, I have to defend them for him."

Warren's eyes glittered at her. "And what does that mean, exactly? That you'll brand Hart as a card cheat to one and all? Ruin his reputation solely because of your brother's angry rants after losing a lot of money at the gaming tables?"

Her heart sank into her stomach. "Of course not."

"That's what you said you'd do if you ever found Reynold's card cheat."

"That was before I knew that the card cheat was your *brother*, for pity's sake!"

"I'm not generally a card cheat," Hart grumbled.

"Shut up!" she and Warren cried in unison.

"Listen to me," Warren told her in that placating voice that rubbed her raw. "Let me go with you. Just me. We'll talk to Brilliana together and figure out what really happened."

"I *know* what really happened. Your brother cheated mine, and now he's trying to put a good face on things. And you mean to overlook that because he's family."

"*You're* family," Warren said hoarsely. "My family. My *wife*. I will always support you. That's why I want to be there."

"No, you want to be there because you're afraid I'll expose your brother's perfidy. You want to smooth everything over, give me no choice in the matter, protect your brother at all costs."

His jaw hardened. "Look, I know how you get when it comes to Reynold and his actions. You tend not to think rationally. I can't let you march in there demanding answers and making wild accusations, and to hell with the truth!"

"The truth? You may not have noticed, but your brother hasn't yet explicitly denied cheating mine."

Warren blinked, then whirled on his brother. "Did you cheat Reynold Trevor at cards?"

Hart blanched, his gaze darting between hers and Warren's. "I . . . um . . . kind of didn't have . . . a choice . . . exactly."

Judging from the flush rising over her husband's cheeks, Warren hadn't expected that answer. "What the bloody hell does that mean?"

His brother jumped up. "Well . . . the wager was that if I won, he'd give me three thousand pounds, but if *he* won, I'd . . . sort of . . . tell him where Niall was."

"Damn it all." Warren scrubbed a hand over his face. "And you *took* that wager? Knowing that if you lost . . ."

"I didn't expect to lose! And it *was* three thousand pounds, after all. But . . ." He cast a sheepish look at Delia. "As she said, he was really good at piquet. And when I realized he might win, I . . . got desperate." He crossed his arms over his chest. "By that point I honestly thought, after the way he was going on and on about Niall, that he wanted to hunt him down and kill him."

"Now you know why I want to speak to Brilliana," Delia said softly. "Three thousand pounds is an awful lot of money to wager to find out where a man is."

Visibly shaken, Warren nodded. "We'll go talk to Brilliana."

He started for the door, and Delia caught him by the arm. "No. I meant what I said: I want to go alone. You always insist on doing things your way. Mucking up my attempts to find Reynold's card cheat. Marrying me to squelch scandal." Her throat tightened, and with a furtive glance at Hart, she lowered her voice. "Handling certain . . . difficulties of yours the way you see fit, without considering other methods."

His gaze bore into hers. "I'm trying to protect you."

"I know! And your brother. And everyone in your whole blasted family." She softened her voice. "And I realize that's because no one was there to protect *you* when you most needed it. It's what has made you who you are. But you don't see that in trying to protect the ones you care about, you're telling them you don't trust them to handle things themselves."

She fought for the right words. "That you're telling them you can't trust them with your secrets. That you don't believe them when they say . . . things like 'I love you.' You want to protect them from finding their own way. Even when your ways of handling things aren't really working."

He stared at her, stark, unmoving, seemingly unemotional. Until she saw hurt flicker in his eyes.

"So I'm going to talk to Brilliana alone, without you and Hart there to badger her or frighten her or make her close up, as she always does. And you are just going to have to trust, for once, that I love you too much to harm you." She cast Hart a quick look. "Or your family."

With that, she strode for the door. "I'll be back before dark, if I can."

He did nothing more to stop her.

Thank heaven. She needed to be away from him right now, to decide how she felt about what Hart had revealed. She needed to learn the truth about Reynold without seeing it through the eyes of either Warren or Hart.

Because in her heart, she feared that her brother had lied to her about more than the gambling. That Brilliana had hidden the truth, too. That there was no one she could trust in the whole wide world except Warren, the man who couldn't even bring himself to love her.

And the thought of that was killing her.

<hr />

"You should go after her," Hart said.

Warren stared out the window as his wife rode off in his carriage without him. "She doesn't want me there."

"I know, but if she really means to accuse me of being a card cheat publicly, when neither of us is there to defend what I did—"

"*That's* what you're worried about?" Warren asked. "My wife is riding away with her heart breaking because I stood up for you, and that's all you can say?"

"You're the one who said it, not me," he said defensively. "She's *your* wife. You ought to know what she's capable of."

A direct hit. He *had* said those unfair words about what she might do. He couldn't blame Hart for taking them at face value.

Hart didn't know Delia. And yes, Warren ought

to. If he was truthful with himself, he already *did*. He certainly knew she wasn't capable of running off half-cocked to ruin his family.

She might be reckless of her own safety, but he'd never seen her expose her *family* to scandal, never seen her try deliberately to hurt *him*. Yet he had behaved as if she couldn't handle her own affairs.

Meanwhile, he'd done things to put *her* at risk— by showing up repeatedly at Dickson's, bullying her servant into not going . . . putting her in a situation where she had to marry him.

Well, that last, he hadn't done on purpose. But the result had been the same. The end of her freedom. So she was right about his methods not working any better than hers.

"So you don't think she'd expose me as a card cheat," Hart said.

He sighed. "No. Not under the circumstances. If anyone understands doing stupid things to protect family, it's my wife."

"I figured as much, but you never know. Some people surprise you."

"Yes." Like his brother, and his wife, who'd taken his nightmares in stride even as he pushed her away. The thought of it lodged a lump firmly in his throat.

"I'm going to pay back every penny of the money I won from Reynold Trevor."

"You certainly are." Warren glanced at his brother. "Do you even *have* it anymore?"

"Well . . . not all of it. But—"

"Then I'll pay it."

"You will not!" Hart glared at him. "She's right about you, you know. You're so busy 'protecting' us from everything, you forget we're perfectly able to handle our own lives. I'll get the money and repay every penny, even if I have to borrow it for now. You can be sure of that."

Warren choked down a hot retort. Time to learn from his mistakes. "Would you consider . . . accepting a loan from me, then?"

Hart looked embarrassed. "I might. I don't know. I think I can get the money together, but it would take time. How . . . um . . . bad is it with her family? Trevor's wife, I mean?"

"Bad. I've spoken to the bank about stopping the foreclosure on the estate, and I've offered to pay the mortgage until things can improve. But Reynold's son—"

"Oh, God, he had a *child*, too?" Hart dropped into a chair, looking like someone had just smacked him. "I really mucked things up, didn't I?"

"You couldn't have known. And to be fair, Reynold Trevor had no business making such a wager since he knew what was at stake."

"I wish *I'd* known what was really at stake. I would have refused to play him."

Warren threaded his fingers through his hair. "I don't know if it would have made a difference. He was clearly bent on . . . settling a score of some kind. He would have found someone else to take the wager."

"So her brother *wasn't* looking for Niall to get revenge on him because of the duel."

"I doubt it. But he might have had another equally disastrous reason. Delia and I recently learned that Niall and Reynold's widow knew each other before Reynold married her. And you know how men can be with rivals for their wives' affections."

"Oh, I do. Just look at how much my good-natured flirtations with your wife irritated you."

Warren shot him a sharp glance. "Don't flatter yourself. Delia wouldn't even consider you as a lover."

"Of course not. She's in love with *you*. Even if she hadn't said so, any dolt could see it. I would kill to have a woman look at me the way she looks at you."

"Which is how?" Warren asked hoarsely.

"As if you are the key to paradise."

Warren frowned. "Not today, she doesn't."

"No, but she will again. As long as you show her, *tell* her, that you're in love with her, too."

"But . . . what if I'm not?"

Hart snorted. "Don't be an idiot. Of course you're in love with her. I can see how you look at *her*, too. As if you need her. Want her. Are desperate to be with her. If that isn't love, I don't know what you'd call it."

"You don't understand," Warren choked out. "Loving her means I could hurt her. Worse than you can possibly imagine."

"And not loving her means you might lose her. Which would you prefer?"

Warren gritted his teeth. He didn't want to lose her, that was certain.

"Besides, from what I understand, loving someone isn't really a choice. You either do or you don't. And you do. Don't you?"

"Yes."

It was true. What had Delia said last night after he'd told her she shouldn't love him? *Can't help it.*

Neither could he. He didn't *want* to be in love with a woman who drove him mad. Who made him do things he feared, risk things he shouldn't, desire things he'd never desired before. But he did. It was a simple, undeniable fact.

Perhaps it was time he accepted it. And that meant he had to show her that he *did* trust her, that he *could* be the husband she needed. That he was at least willing to try.

But how?

"Tell me what to do," Warren rasped.

"You're asking *my* advice?"

"You're my brother. It goes both ways."

"About damned time you realized that," Hart muttered.

"I don't want her suffering alone through whatever truths she finds out about Reynold and Brilliana. I need to be there, but she doesn't want me there."

"She *does* want you there, but as the husband

who loves her—not as the Marquess of Knight-ford who wants to fix everything for her. So only go if you can stand beside her, not in front of her. Can you do that?"

"Yes. I think so."

He had to. So he could tell her that he loved her before she gave up on him. Because if she did that, life would simply not be worth living any-more.

Twenty-Five

Delia arrived at Stoke Towers just as most of the guests were rising. As she entered the breakfast room, Clarissa waylaid her. "My dear, what are you doing here? Is something wrong?"

Forcing a smile to her lips, Delia said, "Not in the least. But I need to speak to my sister-in-law."

"She's still in her room, I believe." Clarissa eyed her closely. "Is Warren with you?"

"No, he stayed in town. Business matters, you know."

"Oh, of course." Clarissa searched her face. "Shall I have a servant fetch Brilliana?"

"No. This is a conversation best held in private." She started for the stairs, then paused. "Tell me something. Has your brother been here . . . much since we left?"

"Not at all, actually," Clarissa said. "After your wedding, he went back to Margrave Manor and stayed there. I had thought that perhaps he and

Brilliana were . . . well . . . interested in each other, but it appears I was mistaken."

Not as mistaken as she thought. "I see," Delia said tightly. "Thank you."

Delia headed up the stairs, feeling as if her heart was being knocked about in a whirlwind. A part of her felt horrible about how she'd left things with Warren. Another part of her said she'd had every reason to be upset. His brother had cheated hers!

But with good reason, or so Hart claimed. Meanwhile, her own brother had abandoned his family. Reynold had lied about his reasons for going to London. Reynold had . . .

No, she wouldn't think about it. Not until she knew everything.

She found Brilliana in her bedchamber, just as Clarissa had said. And her sister-in-law, who was standing before the mirror putting the finishing touches to her hair, looked shocked to see her.

"My dear!" Brilliana exclaimed as Delia entered. "What are you doing here?"

No point in mincing words. "I'm trying to learn the truth." She sat down on the bed. "I found the man who cheated Reynold."

Brilliana gaped at her. "You did? Was it anyone we know?"

"Sort of." Delia steadied her nerves. "It was Warren's brother Hart. It turns out that Reynold traveled to London because he was in search of

Lord Margrave. That's how he came to be playing cards with Hart. And how he came to lose so much money to him. Because he wagered three thousand pounds in exchange for information about Lord Margrave's whereabouts."

Brilliana went utterly white. "Oh, Lord."

"So now I need to hear the truth from you. What exactly was the nature of your friendship with Lord Margrave? And did Reynold know?"

Her sister-in-law crumpled onto the bed beside her. "I'd hoped that he didn't. Lord knows I tried hard to keep it from him all these years. But . . ."

"But?"

"I wondered if Reynold might have found out something before he rushed off to London."

Feeling as if her blood might erupt from her veins, Delia gazed at her sister-in-law. "Why would you think he'd found out, if you didn't tell him?"

Brilliana wouldn't look at her. "I found him one day . . . looking through a bunch of my old sketches I kept . . . rather hidden in my chest of drawers."

"And you had a sketch of Lord Margrave in it."

"More than one. Quite a few, actually."

"Enough to tell him that there was something between you."

Brilliana bobbed her head.

So Hart hadn't been lying about his reasons

for cheating. Not that Delia had really thought
he was. It would have been an odd coincidence
indeed for him to drum up a story about her
relations and his, without part of it being true.

Still, he'd cheated Reynold, destroyed their
lives. He ought to be held accountable for that.
Though she didn't see how he would, given her
husband's urgent need to protect everyone.

She couldn't think about that right now.
"What did you tell him was the nature of your
friendship with Lord Margrave?"

Brilliana shot her a sharp glance. "That's none
of your concern."

"It is if it helps me understand why Reynold
did what he did."

"And what is that?" Brilliana snapped. "That he
lost all our money? Stumbled off a bridge drunk
and drowned himself?"

It was Delia's turn to look away.

Her sister-in-law released a harsh breath. "He
didn't . . . It wasn't . . . Reynold didn't die by
accident, did he?"

It was time Brilliana knew. "No." When her
sister-in-law gave an anguished cry, Delia added
hastily, "His note said not to tell you, but—"

"He left a *note*?" Brilliana said. "And you kept it
from me?"

"You had so much to endure already! I didn't
want to heap more troubles upon you."

"It was my right to know!"

Delia's heart shivered in her chest. Brilliana

was right. Delia should have told her. Here she'd been accusing Warren of protecting people from dealing with things on their own, and she'd been guilty of exactly that.

She sighed. She and her husband were quite a pair.

Brilliana thrust out her chin. "Do you have the note with you? Can I see it?"

"I burned it. But I can tell you what it said."

After Delia recited the note, her sister-in-law moaned. "I should have realized . . . or perhaps I always did. I just didn't want to accept it. After Silas was born, Reynold got more desperate to have me love him. He always said he loved *me* to desperation. And I . . . wanted to love him. I tried. But I was—"

"In love with someone else. I know."

"Delia—"

"I don't need to hear the details. But admit it. At some point, you were in love with Lord Margrave. And Reynold found out and—I don't know—had to meet his rival? Get rid of his rival?"

She blinked. "Surely he never meant to do *that*!"

"People do a lot of foolish things for love. So perhaps that was why he was willing to go to great lengths to find out where Lord Margrave was."

Brilliana jumped up from the bed. "Yes, but I wasn't . . . I didn't . . . After Lord Margrave left

England, I cut him out of my life. From the time I married, I was entirely faithful to my husband. Reynold *knew* that, because he'd heard about the duel and Margrave's fleeing the country before I even met Reynold."

"It's one thing to cut someone out of your life. Cutting them out of your heart? That's quite a bit harder." She softened her voice. "And judging from the way you reacted when you saw Lord Margrave the other day, you never managed to do that."

Brilliana stiffened. "That's not true! I was just . . . startled to see him after all these years. But after what I went through with him . . . I just couldn't risk my heart again, don't you see . . . ?" She trailed off on a sob.

"And Reynold knew."

"I'm s-so sorry!" Brilliana stammered. "Your brother was a good man. He just . . . wanted something from me I couldn't give." She started weeping. "I-it was my fault he died, isn't it? He killed himself because of me!"

Delia leapt up to enfold her in a tight embrace. "It was *not* your fault. Don't take that burden upon yourself. He sealed his fate when he bought you as a wife."

She clutched Brilliana close, her own tears starting to flow. Her poor brother—thinking he could somehow coax Brilliana into loving him, even though their fathers had essentially arranged the marriage. And when coaxing hadn't worked, and trying to locate the man who'd once had his wife's heart didn't work, it must have made him a little mad.

No wonder he'd jumped. How desperate he must have been, to find himself not only lacking his wife's affections but also having lost everything else that might secure her respect.

Delia choked down her sorrow. Oh, how she wished he'd confided in her from the beginning. Perhaps all of this might have been avoided.

Then again, perhaps not. "Trying to force love to bloom has repercussions," she murmured to Brilliana. "Women are stubborn about their hearts. They love who they love. And there isn't a bloody thing the men—or the women—can do about it. It's just so awful that Reynold couldn't see that."

Brilliana drew back to gape at her. "You said *bloody*!"

Delia blinked at her. *That* was what she noticed? Helpless laughter rolled up out of her. "You have no idea how my vocabulary has changed in the last few weeks."

Her sister-in-law stared at her wide-eyed; then she, too, started to laugh. It was the laugh of a woman who couldn't alter her circumstances but realized the absurdity of them.

For a long while they clung to each other, laughing and crying and pouring out all their pain and frustration with the men in their lives, by doing what women always do: letting the emotions over-take them, giving their hearts free rein.

When the crying and laughing had run its course, and they'd both settled down on the bed, Brilliana smiled sadly at Delia. "At least we now know Reynold hadn't fallen into your papa's bad habits."

Delia swallowed past the lump in her throat. "True. And losing everything in an attempt to gain love . . . isn't the worst thing a man can do, I suppose."

Brilliana nodded, then nudged Delia with her knee. "Speaking of love, tell me how you're enjoying married life." An anxious frown crossed her face. "It's not like . . . Reynold and me, is it?"

"No." She ignored the tears welling anew in her throat. "I don't know. He's . . . hard to explain." Without betraying his secrets, which she refused to do.

"Do you love him?"

"Yes." That much was firm.

"Does he love *you*?"

"I don't know."

"So . . . in essence, you're in Reynold's situation."

"Not exactly," she said with a rueful smile. "My husband wasn't ever in love with anyone else. I'm just not sure—"

A knock came at the door, startling them both.

Brilliana went to open the door. "Yes?"

A footman glanced in and spotted Delia sitting on the bed. "Lord Knightford wanted me to inform his wife that he's here. If she needs him."

If she needs him? That didn't sound at all like Warren.

Her heart racing, she said, "Tell his lordship I'll be down shortly."

"Very good, milady," he said, then left.

"Lord Knightford didn't come here with you?" Brilliana asked.

"No. I wanted a chance to talk to you without his hovering about." She brushed tears from her eyes. "And apparently, he gave me one."

Though he had still come after her. She didn't know what to make of that.

"Brilliana—"

"Go, my dear." Brilliana pressed her hand. "Talk to your husband. It will all be fine, I promise."

Oh, Lord, she certainly hoped so.

She found Warren pacing the drawing room, looking as uncertain as she felt.

As soon as she came in, he faced her with a wary expression. "I didn't want you to . . . I was worried . . . Oh, God, I don't know what to say. Except that I couldn't bear the thought of your being here all alone."

There was something endearing about his uncertainty. Warren was never unsure of himself.

"All alone?" she tried to tease. "The house is teeming with people."

"You know what I mean. I didn't want you to go through this without someone in your corner. I feared that Brilliana would tell you things that upset you. And I thought perhaps you would need a shoulder to . . . lean on."

The sweetness of that touched her deeply. "So you came to be my shoulder?"

"If you wanted one, yes." He let out a heavy breath. "What did she say?"

"As I suspected, Reynold went to London to seek out your cousin because he was in love with Brilliana, and he couldn't bear knowing she had loved someone else and now couldn't love him."

"Niall."

"Yes." She cast him a wry smile. "At least at one time, from what I gather. She wouldn't give me details." She sobered. "So Hart was telling the truth about trying to protect your cousin. About why he cheated Reynold."

"I never doubted it." He drew himself up. "But it doesn't change what he did. Or excuse it."

That took her entirely by surprise. "Doesn't it?"

He stepped closer. "No. As I'm sure you realize."

Her shoulders slumped. "I don't know what I think about it anymore."

"Well, I do. What he did was wrong. He should never have taken the wager in the first place. He damned well never should have cheated your brother." His voice hardened. "And he knows it, too. In fact, he asked that I give you this."

Drawing a sheet of paper out of his coat pocket, he held it out to her.

Curious, she took it from him. It was an IOU for the three thousand pounds plus interest. Made payable to Brilliana Trevor.

"He fully intends to repay every penny," Warren said.

She arched an eyebrow. "Because you told him he must."

"No. He came up with that all by himself." He smiled faintly. "Apparently my brother has a will of his own. I had no idea."

Scarcely able to believe what Warren was saying, she glanced around nervously. "Where *is* your brother, anyway?"

"I didn't bring him. I knew you didn't want him here." A muscle flexed in his jaw. "I know you didn't want *me* here, either, but I couldn't . . . I didn't want to . . ." He fixed his gaze on her. "I thought you might need me for this. The way I need you for . . . everything."

That caught her so by surprise that she was hardly able to fathom it. "You need me?"

"More than you know." He released a ragged breath. "Last night when you said you loved me . . ."

She winced. "It's all right. I know you don't feel the same."

"No! I mean . . ." He cursed under his breath. "Damn it, I'm very bad at this."

"At what?" Hope sprouted in her heart.

With blatant yearning in his face, he neared her. "Saying I love you." He gazed at her tenderly. "Because I do, you know."

"Warren, you don't have to—"

"I mean it, Delia." A ragged breath escaped him. "I'm terrified that I'll disappoint you or hurt you or ruin things, but it doesn't change the fact that I love you. Helplessly. Hopelessly."

Her pulse danced as every fear she'd had was laid to rest. He was hers. Truly hers.

"Not hopelessly." She reached up to cup his cheek. "I meant it when I said I loved you. That's not going to change."

His eyes darkened. "Even when I thrash about in the bed at night or . . . do things in my sleep that I . . . don't know if you want—"

"I can't imagine your ever truly hurting me." Realizing that he was worried about how he'd started making love to her in his sleep, she brushed a kiss to lips. "No matter how bad the nightmares get, I know you'd never harm me. I'm utterly convinced of that."

He kissed her then, with a desperation that mirrored her own. Somehow they had found each other in the midst of her troubles, and no matter what happened from now on she refused to let him go. As long as he loved her, that was enough.

After he'd plundered her mouth long enough to weaken her knees and fire her blood, he drew back. "I brought you a present."

"Did you?" she said, surprised.

"Consider it my wedding gift to you, my love."

A thickness filled her throat. *My love.* She'd never tire of hearing that.

Releasing her, he reached inside his coat pocket again. This time, he withdrew a whole sheaf of papers covered in pencil sketches.

When he handed them to her, she couldn't at first figure out what they were. Clearly they were blueprints of some kind, but hastily drawn by someone who obviously had no architectural experience.

She looked at him quizzically.

"I did them in the carriage, so they're rather crude. But they're preliminary sketches for a renovation of your bedchamber."

Eyeing them more closely, she read the scribbled notations. "This one says 'Delia's boudoir.' Since when do I have a boudoir?"

"Since I decided to change your bedchamber into one. Assuming that you approve."

"There's no bed." Her heart began to hammer in her chest. "Where am I to sleep?"

"With me," he said earnestly. "But only if you want."

Breaking into a smile, she threw her arms about his neck. "I want, I want!" She kissed his lips, then added in a whisper, "I want very much to sleep with you, my lord."

He let out a relieved breath. "Then that's what we'll do." He gazed down at her, eyes gleaming.

"Although I think I should warn you: We won't only be sleeping."

"I should hope not," she said saucily. "Or I shall be very disappointed."

And as he took her into his arms and kissed her with all the love in his heart, she was not disappointed one bit.

Epilogue

Four months after their wedding, Warren woke to the sound of his wife snoring. He'd never heard her do that before; perhaps it was a result of their having been so vigorous in their love-making last night, after the private dinner she'd arranged in their bedchamber.

But the snoring didn't bother him. It seemed so natural, so normal. He rather liked it. He still preferred some noise to utter quiet at night. It was much more restful.

Still, who would ever have guessed he would become so conventional, sleeping at night like a normal person, with a wife who snored? Spending his days living his life instead of sleeping? It was the most spectacular gift she'd given him.

He couldn't resist kissing her awake.

She opened her eyes—those lovely starry eyes—with a soft smile. "Good morning, husband."

"Good morning, wife."

Eyeing him uncertainly, she propped herself up in bed. "You didn't have a bad dream, did you?"

"It's the middle of the morning, dearling. I don't have dreams then. Besides, it's been almost two weeks since I had a nightmare at all."

It had been rocky at first—Delia had resorted to pinching him awake once or twice when it was really bad. But these days she always seemed to appear in his dreams, soothing him, comforting him. The cellar rarely tormented him anymore.

She rubbed her eyes. "What time is it?"

"I believe it's around ten."

"So why are *you* awake? You tend to sleep later than that."

He chuckled. "You were snoring."

"Was I? How odd. I wonder if . . ."

As she trailed off, he could see her mind working. "What?"

A knock came at the door, startling them both. "Milady? You told me to wake you at ten. For the architect?"

Delia jumped up. "Oh, Lord, I hadn't meant to sleep this late." She called out to her maid, "Thank you, Rose! I'll call when I'm ready for you to help me dress."

"Very good, milady."

Warren watched as his wife hurried to do her ablutions. "Why is the architect coming? Is there something wrong with your new boudoir?"

She halted, a blush spreading over her cheeks. He hadn't seen one of those in a while. "No . . . actually . . . I wanted him to renovate— You see,

I was supposed to tell you something last night at our private dinner . . . but then we . . . you know . . . and I fell asleep and . . ." She steadied her shoulders. "It turns out there's a reason I'm snoring. And getting fatter."

"You are not getting—"

He halted. He'd noticed her middle being a trifle thicker, but he'd assumed that was because she was eating more, on account of having a lusty husband who wore her out most nights.

But that wasn't why.

His blood began to roar in his ears.

"I spoke to the physician yesterday," she went on, "and he's certain that I'm with child."

Bloody hell. "I'm . . . having a child?"

She eyed him askance. "Unless you've defied nature, no. *I'm* having a child. You're going to watch."

He left the bed in a daze. "But you're having *our* child."

"Of course *our* child," she said, looking insulted.

"No, no, I didn't mean . . . I'm just . . . We're having a *baby*?"

As if realizing he was flummoxed, she smiled. "You're adorable when you're flustered, did you know that?"

He drew himself up. "I'm a man, for God's sake. We're never adorable."

"To me you are." She came up to take his hands in hers, amusement shining in her face. "All that enthusiastic activity we've been engaging in does generally result in children, you know."

"Now you're mocking me," he grumbled. "I've only just become used to the idea of having a wife. And now I'm going—*you're* going—to have our child?"

With joy and terror rocketing through him equally, he started pacing the room. "God, I need to speak to my solicitor. And find the finest physician in London to attend you. And look into having the nursery—" When she burst into laughter, he said, "Oh. *That's* why you wanted the architect to come today."

"Exactly. The old nursery really needs work. And forgive me: I'd intended to tell you about the babe last night, but we were rather preoccupied—"

"Bloody hell! I took you like an animal last night!" With his heart pounding, he pressed his hand against her belly. "I could have hurt you or the baby!"

She rolled her eyes. "I can see you're going to be just as overprotective a father as you are a husband." She covered his hand with hers. "And do you really think I would jeopardize our child for even the most amazing intimate encounter with you?"

Now he could hear the faint tremor in her voice that said she was as nervous about this whole thing as he. "No, of course not." He forced himself to breathe, to calm the racing of his pulse.

It had taken him a while to learn this hard lesson—that his wife was a sensible woman who always had a reason for her behavior. That he didn't always have to protect her.

That sometimes she could be the one to protect him—from the dark and the quiet and the cellar. From thinking that his way was the only way.

From behaving like an arse when his wife told him he was soon to be a father. She deserved a husband who could reassure her.

He cupped her head in his hands. "If I could choose any woman in the entire world to bear my child, it would always be you. I can't imagine anyone who would be a finer mother."

To his horror, she burst into tears. When he looked alarmed, she said, "That has got . . . to be the sweetest thing . . . anyone has ever said to me."

Letting out a relieved breath, he drew her into his arms and held her tenderly while he rubbed her back and scattered kisses over her wild, unruly hair. "We're going to be parents," he whispered. "The very idea terrifies me. What if I'm awful at it?"

"Nonsense. You're a wonderful husband. Of course you'll be a wonderful father."

Letting the matter-of-fact words calm his fears, he kissed her long and deep, until his blood was stirring again in other places than just his heart.

He pressed his lips to her ear. "Was last night really the 'most amazing intimate encounter' you ever had with me?"

She drew back to eye him askance. "As if you even need to ask."

Lifting her in his arms, he carried her back toward the bed.

"We can't do this now," she protested. "The architect will be here soon!"

"He can wait." He laid her gently upon the bed. "Because I'm fairly certain I can improve upon my performance."

And as his wife burst into laughter, he did his best to do just that.

Will Niall Lindsey, the Earl of Margrave, and the widowed Brilliana Payne Trevor, the girl whose heart he broke seven years ago, be able to put their pasts behind them and work together to clear her father's name?

Keep reading for a sneak peek at the next sizzling installment in *New York Times* bestselling author Sabrina Jeffries's Sinful Suitors series!

The Pleasures of Passion

Coming Summer 2017 from Pocket Books!

Prologue

London
1823

Seventeen-year-old Brilliana Payne shoved the note from Lord Margrave's heir—Niall Lindsey—into her pocket. Then she slipped into her mother's bedchamber. "Mama," she whispered. "Are you awake?"

Her mother jerked her head up from amid the feather pillows and satin covers like a startled deer. Brilliana winced to see her mother's lips drawn with pain and her eyes dulled by laudanum, even in mid-afternoon.

"What do you need, love?" Mama asked in her usual gentle voice.

Oh, how she loathed deceiving Mama. But until her suitor spoke to his parents about their marrying, she had to keep the association secret.

"I'm going for my walk in Green Park." *Where Niall, my love, will join me.* "Do you need anything?"

Despite her pain, Mama smiled. "Not now,

my dear. You go enjoy yourself. And tell Gilly to make sure you don't stray near the woods."

"Of course."

What a lie. The woods were where she would meet Niall, where Gilly would keep watch to make sure no one saw him and Brilliana together. Thank heaven her maid was utterly loyal to her.

Brilliana started to leave, then paused. "Um. Papa said he won't be home until evening." Which meant he wouldn't be home until he'd lost all his money at whatever game he was playing tonight. "Are you *sure* you don't need me?"

She dearly hoped not. Niall's note had struck her with dread, partly because he rarely wrote to her. Usually he just met her at Green Park for her daily stroll when he could get away from friends or family. Something must be wrong.

Still, it shouldn't take more than an hour to find out what. And perhaps let him steal a kiss or two.

She blushed. Niall was very good at *that*.

Then again, he ought to be. He was rumored to be a rogue with the ladies, although Brilliana was convinced it was merely because of his wild cousin, Lord Knightford, with whom he spent far too much time. Or so she'd heard.

"I'll be fine," Mama said tightly. "I have my medicine right here."

Medicine, ha! It made Mama almost as ill as whatever mysterious disease had gripped her. The doctors still couldn't figure out what was wrong with Mama, but they continued to try everything—bleeding her, cupping her, giving her assorted potions. And every time a new treatment was attempted, Brilliana hoped it would work, would be worth Mama's pain.

Guilt swamped Brilliana. "If you're sure . . ."

"Go, dear girl! I'm just planning to sleep, anyway."

That was all the encouragement Brilliana needed to hurry out.

A short while later, she and Gilly were in Green Park, waiting at the big oak for Niall.

"Did he say why he wanted to meet, miss?" Gilly asked.

"No. Just that it was urgent. And it had to be today."

Gilly flashed her a knowing smile. "Perhaps he means to propose at last."

Her breath caught. "I doubt it. He would have approached Papa if that were the case."

"Not if he wanted your consent first." Gilly smoothed her skirts. "That's how all the gentlemen is doing things these days, I'm told. And just think what your mama will say when she hears you've snagged an heir to an earl!"

"I haven't snagged anyone yet." Besides, the word *snag* was too coarse for what she wanted from Niall—his mind, his heart, his soul. Since hers already belonged to him.

"There you are," said a masculine voice behind them. "Thank God you came."

Brilliana's heart leapt as she turned to see Niall striding up to them. At twenty-three, he was quite the handsomest man she'd ever known—lean-hipped and tall and possessed of the most gorgeous hazel eyes, which changed color from brown to green depending on the light. And his unruly mop of gold-streaked brown hair made her itch to set it to rights.

Though she didn't dare be so forward in front of Gilly. Not until she and Niall were formally betrothed. Assuming that ever happened.

Offering Brilliana his arm, he cast Gilly a pointed glance. "I'll need a few minutes alone with your mistress. Will you keep watch?"

Gilly curtsied deeply. "Of course, my lord."

Then, without any of his usual pleasantries, he led Brilliana into the woods to the little clearing where they usually talked.

Her feeling of dread increased. "You do realize how fortunate we are that Gilly is a romantic. Otherwise, she would never let us do these things."

"I know, Bree." Though he was the only one to call her that, she rather liked the nickname. It made her sound carefree, when she felt anything but.

He halted well out of earshot of Gilly. "And then I wouldn't get the chance to do *this*."

He drew her into his arms for a long, ardent kiss, and she melted. If he was kissing her, he obviously didn't mean to break with her. And as long as they had this between them . . .

But it was over far too soon. And when he drew back to stare at her with a haunted look, her dread returned.

"What's wrong?" she whispered.

Glancing away, he mumbled a decidedly ungentlemanly oath. "You are going to be furious with me."

She fought to ignore the alarm knotting her belly. "I could never be furious with you. What has happened? Just tell me."

"This morning I fought a duel."

"What?" Her heart dropped into her stomach. Good Lord. How could that be? "I-I don't understand." She must have heard him wrong. Surely the man she'd fallen in love with wasn't the violent sort.

"I killed a man, Bree. In a duel."

She hadn't misheard him, then. Still scarcely able to believe it, she roamed the little clearing, her blood like sludge in her veins. "What on earth would even make you do such a thing?"

"It doesn't matter." He threaded his fingers through his sun-kissed hair. "It's done, and now I risk being hanged."

Hanged? Why would he be—

Of course. Dueling was considered murder. Her heart stilled. Her love was a murderer. And now he could die, too!

"So I'm leaving England tonight," he went on. "For good."

The full ramifications of all he'd revealed hit

her. "You . . . you're leaving England," she echoed hollowly. *And me.*

His gaze met hers. "Yes. And I want you to go with me."

That arrested her. "Wh-what do you mean?"

"I'm asking you to marry me." He seized her hands. "Well, to elope with me. We'll go by ship to Spain, and we'll wed there. Then my friends in Valencia will help us settle in."

She gaped at him. He was *serious*. He actually meant for her to leave her family and home and run away with him now that he'd gone off and *killed* a man.

But in a duel. Might it not have been done with good reason?

"Do you *have* to go abroad?" she asked. "Sometimes the courts will acquit a gentleman of the charges, assuming the duel was a just one—"

"It was." His face clouded over. "But I can't risk defending myself in court."

"What do you mean? Why not?"

His expression grew shuttered. "I can't say. It's . . . complicated."

"It can't be more complicated than running away to the Continent, for pity's sake."

A muscle worked in his jaw. "Look, I've made a vow to keep the reasons for the duel quiet. And I have to keep that vow."

"Even from me?" She couldn't hide the hurt in her voice. "Why? Who demanded such a thing of you?"

"I can't say, damn it!" When she flinched, he said, "It's not important."

"It certainly is to *me*. You want me to run off with you, but you won't even explain why you fought or even with whom you dueled?"

Letting out an oath, he stared past her into the woods. "I suppose I can reveal the other party in the duel, since that will get around soon enough. The man's name is Joseph Whiting."

She didn't know any Joseph Whiting, so that bit of information wasn't terribly helpful.

"But that's all I can reveal." He fixed her with a hard look. "You're simply going to have to trust me on this. Go with me, and I will take care of you."

"What about passports? How can you even be sure that we can marry in Spain?"

"There's no reason we can't. And I have a passport—we'll arrange for yours once we arrive."

She didn't know anything about international travel, but his plan sounded awfully havey-cavey. "If you're wanted for murder here, surely no British consulate—"

"I promise you, it will all turn out well in the end."

"You can't promise that."

"Deuce take it, I *love* you," he said, desperation in his tone. "Isn't that enough?"

"No! You're asking me to risk my entire future to go with you. To leave my family and my home, possibly never to see either again. So, no, it is *not* enough, drat you!"

He squeezed her hands. "Are you saying you don't share my feelings?"

"You know I do." Her heart lurched in her chest. "I'd follow you to the ends of the earth if I could, but I can't right now." Certainly not without some assurance that he truly meant to marry her and not just . . . well . . . carry her off to have his way with her.

Oh, Lord, that was absurd. Just because he was heir to an earl and she the daughter of an impoverished knight didn't mean that Niall would stoop so low. Granted, she'd heard of women being fooled into thinking they were eloping when really they weren't, women who were discarded after they'd served their usefulness to some randy lord.

But Niall would never do such a thing. He was an honorable man.

Except for the fact that he fought a duel he won't tell me about.

She winced. It didn't matter. He would never hurt her that way. She couldn't believe it. And for a moment, the idea of being his forever, of traveling abroad and seeing the world without their families to make trouble—

Families. That brought reality crashing in. "You know I can't leave Mama." Regretfully, she tugged her hands from his. "She needs me."

"*I* need you." His lovely eyes were dark with entreaty. "Your mother has your father."

"The man who spends every waking moment

at his club or in the hells, gambling away my future and Mama's," she said bitterly. "She could die, and he wouldn't even notice."

All right, so that was an exaggeration, but not much of one. Papa had never met a card game he didn't like. Unfortunately, he'd never met one he could win at, either. But he certainly spent all his time and money trying to find one.

And consequently, Mama spent much of *her* time alone with Brilliana or servants. Brilliana had hoped that when—*if*—Niall proposed marriage, she could persuade him to let her take Mama to live with them. But that was impossible if he meant to carry her off to the Continent.

"What about *your* family?"

He tensed. "What about them?"

"Do your parents know that you mean to flee London? Have you spoken to your father about . . . well . . . *us*?"

"He knows I'm leaving England. But no, he doesn't know about us, because I wanted to speak to you first. In case you . . . refused to go."

His reluctance to tell his parents about their courtship before approaching *her* parents had been a bone of contention between them.

She'd understood—really, she had. She probably wasn't lofty enough to suit his family, and Niall had been waiting until she had her come-out and his parents could meet her in a natural setting. Then he could ease them into the idea of his wanting to wed her.

But now . . . "You could still speak to *my* parents, gain their blessing and agreement to the marriage. Then you . . . you could get a special license, and we could marry before we leave here."

Though that didn't solve the problem of Mama.

"There's no time for that! Besides, it takes at least two days to acquire any kind of license. And my ship leaves tonight." He drew her close. "For once in your life, sweeting, throw caution to the wind. You love me. I love you. We belong together. I don't know how I'll bear it if you don't flee with me."

His words tore at her. She wanted *desperately* to go.

And apparently he could read the hesitation in her face, for he took advantage, clasping her head in his hands so he could plunder her mouth with breathtaking thoroughness.

Oh, Lord, but the man could kiss. He made her heart soar, and her blood run fast and hot. Looping her arms about his neck, she gave herself up to the foretaste of what their lives could be like . . . if she would just give in.

But how could she? Reluctantly, she broke the kiss, even knowing it might be their last.

His eyes glittered with triumph, for he could always tell how easily he tempted her. "I know this isn't the ideal way for us to start out, Bree, but I'll make it up to you. Father will continue to send my allowance, and my friends will take care of us until we're settled. I might even find work in Spain."

She wavered. It sounded wonderful and exciting and oh, so tempting.

He cupped her cheek. "All we have to do is go. Tonight, with the tide. You and I, together for the rest of our lives. Trust me, you won't regret going."

Ah, but she would.

She could handle travel to a strange country and everything that such an upheaval entailed. She could live on a pittance. And yes, she would even risk ruin if it meant being with him.

But she couldn't leave Mama. Papa would never manage the doctors or sit wiping Mama's brow when she was feverish. Papa could hardly bear to be in the sickroom. He'd rather run off to his club. And with money short because of his gambling, they couldn't afford a servant to tend mother night and day. Besides, she could never entrust Mama's care to a servant.

She pushed away from him. "I can't," she said. "I'm sorry."

Discover your passion for the past with bestselling historical romance from Pocket Books!

Pick up or download your copies today!

XOXOAfterDark.com